THE

CRACKED

SPINE

ALSO BY PAIGE SHELTON

THE
CRACKED
SPINE

Paige Shelton

MINOTAUR BOOKS

New York

THE CRACKED SPINE. Copyright © 2016 by Paige Shelton-
Ferrell. All rights reserved. Printed in the United States of
America. For information, address St. Martin's Press,
175 Fifth Avenue, New York, N.Y. 10010.

www.minotaurbooks.com

Library of Congress Cataloging-in-Publication Data

Names: Shelton, Paige, author.
Title: The Cracked Spine / Paige Shelton.
Description: First Edition. | New York : Minotaur Books, 2016.
Identifiers: LCCN 2015043798| ISBN 9781250057488
   (hardback) | ISBN 9781466861213 (e-book)
Subjects: | BISAC: FICTION / Mystery & Detective / Women
   Sleuths. | GSAFD: Mystery fiction.
Classification: LCC PS3619.H45345 C73 2016 |
   DDC 813/.6—dc23
LC record available at http://lccn.loc.gov/2015043798

Our books may be purchased in bulk for promotional,
educational, or business use. Please contact your local
bookseller or the Macmillan Corporate and Premium Sales
Department at 1-800-221-7945, extension 5442, or by e-mail
at MacmillanSpecialMarkets@macmillan.com.

First Edition: March 2016

10 9 8 7 6 5 4 3 2 1

For my agent, Jessica Faust,
and my editor, Hannah Braaten.
Thanks for wanting to take
this journey with me.

ACKNOWLEDGMENTS

First of all, a giant thank-you to Lisa Shafer, a fellow writer who has spent a good amount of time in Scotland. I can't express how grateful I am to her for poring over maps with me, giving me insight into Edinburgh and all parts of Scotland, and answering all my crazy questions (she's still answering questions). From the bottom of my heart, thank you, Lisa, for your help and friendship.

The people of Scotland are just like I imagined them to be, even better actually. Thanks especially to: Alexandria Gibson and her mom, two lovely women who let me traipse through their cottage just so I could see its layout and the strange machine on the wall that supplies their electricity; the van drivers and the other passengers we met on the guided tours who were enormously patient as I asked questions and took notes. Thank you for putting up with me.

Because of some crazy circumstances we missed our first trip to Scotland and had to reschedule. When we finally arrived, our first stop was to The Cadies and Witchery Tours. Having heard about our previously cancelled trip, they had kept our names off to the side and didn't ask us to pay for another tour. I'm sure that they are that customer service–oriented all the time, but their attention to detail got our journey off to a perfect start and we loved their entertaining performances. Thank you.

There's a bookshop near the spot where I placed The

Cracked Spine. It's not The Cracked Spine, but I used some of the décor from inside. The proprietors were lovely and didn't hesitate to give me the okay to take pictures. The Wee Pub, the smallest pub in Scotland, is also in Grassmarket. I used the name and the location, but I made up almost everything else.

There are a bunch of bookshops in Edinburgh. We didn't make it to them all, but we visited many. Every single bookseller was just fine with me roaming around and taking pictures. Thank you for making my research so much easier.

Thanks to everyone at Minotaur who has worked so hard on this book. Allison Ziegler in marketing; Shailyn Tavella in publicity; Alan Bradshaw in production; my copy editor, Jane Liddle; the cover designer, David Rotstein; text designer, Nicola Ferguson; and my creative and attentive editor, Hannah Braaten. I'm stunned by how you all do what you do.

Some of my favorite authors agreed to an early read and offered a quote for the cover. Thanks to them for being so kind and for writing books that make me want to keep working to be a better writer myself. Jenn McKinlay, Susan Furlong, Daryl Wood Gerber, Ellery Adams, and Erika Chase.

My husband, Charlie, and my son, Tyler, are the best. They cheerfully took on the Scavenger Hunt papers I handed them as we boarded the plane to Scotland, and they helped me find almost everything on the four-page list. I adore them.

The Cracked Spine is a work of fiction, of course. I made up lots of stuff, but I also tried to weave in some real locations and details. It would be impossible for me to do Scotland justice. The country's beauty and the people's graciousness are beyond my words. Forgive any mistakes I made; they are totally on me.

THE
CRACKED
SPINE

PROLOGUE

Wanted: A bold adventurer who would love to travel the world from a comfortable and safe spot behind a desk that has seen the likes of kings and queens, paupers and princes. A humble book and rare manuscript shop seeks a keenly intelligent investigator to assist us in our search for things thought lost, and in our quest to return lost items to their rightful owners. This multitasked position will take you places you can't even imagine. Apply only if you're ready for everything to change. Please note: the position is located in Edinburgh, Scotland.

It was perhaps fortuitous. I'd never know exactly what had been set in motion for all the pieces to fall in place. But I knew this: when I was given my walking papers from the small museum in Wichita, Kansas, a place I'd worked since receiving my master's degrees in both literature and history from the University of Kansas, I knew I needed an adventure. I wasn't bold but I wanted to be, so when I happened upon the ad, I simply reacted and immediately sent an e-mail to the listed address. Only minutes later, I received a phone call.

I spent an hour and a half talking to the man who would become my new boss, Edwin MacAlister. Once I got semi-used to his light Scottish accent, the conversation flowed. Okay, maybe not flowed, but my ear became more accustomed to the words. "Aye" meant "yes," that I became sure of. He also said "yes" a few times too. There were words I didn't understand, but maybe I could chalk that up to the transatlantic nature of the call.

The time flew and before I knew it I'd told him about growing up on a farm in Kansas, a place that was so wide-open that as a teenager I'd wondered if I'd ever get used to being inside four walls. I told him that not only had I discovered that I did, indeed, like walls, I came to crave them; that when I went away from the farm, away from the unchallenging world of high school and farm duties that I'd never liked, and to college, I found that my moments indoors with my nose in a book or my attention upon a professor were *almost* the best moments of my life. I confessed to Mr. MacAlister that *the* best and most perfect moments had been spent in a hidden corner of the library with a stack of books and undisturbed hours to read them, or in the basement of the university's Natural History Museum, amid the many shelves of historical items, each of which, even the simplest arrowheads, was deeply fascinating to me. During those moments when I'd been surrounded by walls, I'd been comforted, held close. After my time in the library and basement, the Kansas farm became a contradictory source of claustrophobia, and I knew I had to be, to work, to exist some place full of items that fascinated me: books, historical things, things that spoke to me—Mr. MacAlister had liked hearing that; in fact, he almost crooned.

My previous job at the Wichita museum had extended to on-the-job-trained preservationist as well as archivist. I'd thrived there, grown in ways I never would have imagined in that small but interesting place. Always learning, always listening. My surprise dismissal due to budget cuts had been the worst shock of my life. My first real job had ended in an unceremonious layoff. *Sign this, here's a little severance pay, don't let the door hit you.*

I knew I'd eventually find another job, but I didn't want *just* another job. I wanted something I could throw myself into again, something that spoke to me. It was a lot to wish for, and not something I could afford to yearn for for very long.

I didn't even realize how much I was sharing with Mr. Mac-Alister on that phone call, how telling him about the walls, the books, the things, and my dreams seemed natural and easy. He loved hearing that I'd cared for a good number of rare books and manuscripts as well as meticulously preserved for archiving other things too: fossils, historical clothing, and other artifacts. Even a taxidermy buffalo. We laughed about that one and he was genuinely excited that I'd had such assignments.

I didn't tell him everything about me, of course. I hinted at that other thing that made me a little different, made it sometimes seem like I might have checked out for a second or two—even though that wasn't the case at all. But it wasn't easy to share that part of me with anyone over the phone, particularly a potential new boss and a stranger, even if he had seemed to transition from stranger to friend, and perhaps almost confidant, in the span of the call.

"Well, dear lass, you sound like a perfect delight," Mr. Mac-Alister had said, his *r*s rolling like I imagined the green hills of his country did. "I would be thrilled tae offer you the position and honored for you tae accept it."

The position was at his shop in Edinburgh. The Cracked Spine, a book and manuscript shop that specialized in rare offerings and was nestled (his word) into a charming block right in the thick of things, a part of Old Town Edinburgh called Grassmarket; an area that had once been a medieval marketplace and a site for public executions, though he assured me with a laugh that it was perfectly civilized now.

Despite my excitement, my immediate reaction had been a brief hesitation. As I thought back over our conversation, I realized that I'd told him lots about me, but I hadn't asked very many questions of him. My normal self was innately, almost compulsively, curious. It was rare that I wasn't asking questions or taking notes. Not asking for specific details about the circumstances and responsibilities of a job was unlike me. However, in that brief hesitation I realized that my answers to his questions had somehow told *me* what I needed to know too. Well, it was that or I was just afraid that if I dug too deeply I might find something, a tear in his Scottish tartan, that would make the job something less than the perfection it seemed. Maybe I didn't want to risk knowing.

"Thank you, Mr. MacAlister, I would love to accept the position," I said, swiftly becoming content and excited about the whole idea of uprooting every part of my life and moving to Edinburgh, Scotland, so that I could begin a whole new career and life. An adventure. A bold adventure.

"Excellent news! And, please, my dear, call me Edwin. Everyone does, except for those who take an ill will tae me."

"Thank you, Edwin," I said as a different voice also sounded in my mind.

If we do not find anything very pleasant, at least we shall find something new.

I silently thanked the character from Wilbur Smith's *The Seventh Scroll* for that sensible and timely piece of advice—he'd shared with me only. The words had been distinct in my head, understandable, though spoken with a heavy German accent. This was the part of me, the part my dad called my "bookish voices," that I wasn't quick to share with others, particularly strangers. I hurried to speak again, just so Edwin wouldn't think I'd drifted off. "I can't wait to begin."

I couldn't predict that in the mix of all that was to come, there'd be some wicked things too. But how could there not have been? It was Scotland, after all—the home of the likes of outlandish and murderous Shakespearean characters like Macduff and the true historical bloody battles fought in the name of independence and freedom; battles like Culloden and Bannockburn. The place where, in the 1800s, William Burke and William Hare went on a murderous spree and then sold the corpses to be used for anatomy lessons. Yes, adventure goes well with Scotland, but so does a little bit of wicked, and I was about to find out truly how much.

ONE

"Oh, um," I said, mostly involuntarily as I lost my balance. I reached up for a bar to grab, but there wasn't one there. It was on the side panel instead, next to the door that opened in what seemed like the wrong direction. I settled myself on the seat and tried to put my feet in better spots so as to save my body from being propelled out of the cab. There were no seat belts in the backseat to hold me in place. My safety would depend upon luck and my personal sense of balance.

"Sorry 'boot that. Hold tight, there's 'nother sharp curve ahead. We'el be there shortly. Directly in Grassmarket, correct?" the cabbie said. It took me a second to translate the words. His accent was thick and I wasn't used to it yet. So far with the few Scottish people I'd spoken to—people at the airport and the cabdriver and a man on the plane whose voice and physical build had reminded me of Shrek—I found the syllable dance delightful, though some accents were more difficult to understand than others. I'd only been in Scotland for approximately one hour and forty-seven minutes though. Not quite enough time to judge if I would be able to communicate without asking everyone to slow down and repeat.

I'd been clutching the piece of paper since the plane's wheels touched down at the Edinburgh airport. I glanced at it again and repeated the addresses of both the bookshop and the Grassmarket Hotel, my home until I could find one of my own.

"And the shop's called The Cracked Spine?"

"Yes."

"I've ne'r heard o' it, though I live a good distance away, a long stroll on a sunny day, or a quick coach ride. You wilna see many of those; sunny days, ye ken. Oh, *know*—not ken. I apologize. 'Ken' is know."

"Thank you." I smiled into the rearview mirror.

"Of course, I'm nae much of a reader myself. The missus is. She'll read a book a day, a book an evening when she's working hard on the guesthouses. We hae two of them, guesthouses that is. She also spends a few hours a week at the neighborhood primary school, helping there with some of the wee-uns' reading skills. Aye, she loves her books. I tried tae buy her one of those flat computer contraptions tae read them on but she told me that she wasnae interested, that if she'd been meant tae read from those sorts of things, she'd at least have figured out how tae have an e-mail by now." He laughed.

I'd understood him much better that time. I couldn't be sure if it was because he was working to make me understand better, or if I was already getting the hang of it. I'd originally thought I'd be encountering bits and pieces of Gaelic with the English, but my research told me it would be more about something called "Scots" and that Scots was neither Gaelic nor English. Nae way, nae hou.

According to the card tucked into the small plastic folder

around his neck, my cabdriver's name was Elias. In the picture on the card, he didn't wear a newsie cap, but today he wore one that was black and faded and matched the thin black sweater he also wore. He had very little hair, just gray puffs over his ears. I could see the puffs in both the picture and in person as they currently tufted out from under the sides of the cap. His face seemed swollen and his nose was too big, but neither unpleasantly so. I'd seen his blue eyes every now and then when he looked at me in the rearview mirror. They were clear, bright, and happy. I'd liked him immediately. I'd trusted those eyes enough to jump into his funny-looking cab that was more rounded and squat than the other cabs in the queue. I think I'd been searching for someone who seemed trustworthy, maybe someone who seemed a little familiar. The plane trip across half my own country and an enormous swath of ocean had given me time to become both excited and nervous. A big well of nervousness had built up, actually. Perhaps it had become bigger than that ocean. The cabbie had reminded me of my great-uncle Maury from Topeka, and he was a welcome sight.

I knew I should be tired, probably exhausted considering the distance and the time change, but along with the nervousness I was running on anxious anticipation. I hoped I wouldn't crash too hard when the most likely unavoidable crash came.

The cab was similar to a PT Cruiser, but stretched a little both sideways and upward, and slightly more snub-nosed than the sedan or vanlike cabs I'd seen. Both the black vehicle's front and back bumpers were dented. Magnetic signs had been crookedly stuck to the two front doors—the signs said: "McKenna Cab." There was no reason for me to feel confident about the McKenna Cab company except for the driver's friendly Great-Uncle-Maury-like eyes.

I was trying hard to be brave, be bold, not let anyone see that I was out of Kansas for the first time in my twenty-nine years of life. I was a grown-up and could handle anything. There are cities in Kansas. I'd lived in Wichita, for goodness' sake. There's traffic too. Perhaps there were no cities like Edinburgh and no traffic like what I was currently being swerved and jolted through—on the wrong side of the road, which was too confusing to contemplate at the moment—but I still wasn't going to let the differences make me reticent or timid; at least that was the plan.

The next jerky turn to the left gave me a perfect view of the castle on the hill. Of course, I'd done plenty of research about my new home, and Edinburgh Castle was at the top of my list of places to visit.

"There it is," I said to myself as I peered up and out of the windshield. Its backdrop was currently made up of light gray clouds, which I thought added the proper touch of menace to the otherwise majestic sight.

"Aye, that's oor castle. It's quite the place. Probably oor busiest spot for the tourists. Are ye planning on visiting it this trip?"

"Yes, but I'm not here on vacation. I'm here for a job. I have a work visa and everything."

"And ye say ye're from America?"

"Yes. I grew up on a farm outside of Kingman, Kansas, but I've been working in Wichita."

"Aye? Where's Kansas?"

"Oh. Smack-dab in the middle of the country. In fact, the contiguous geographic center of the country is close to Lebanon, Kansas."

"Well, it's verra exciting that ye're here. The missus and I will have you o'er for dinner. Ye'll be working at the bookshop?"

"Yes."

"Living close by? Surely not at the hotel?"

"I'll be searching for an apartment. Uh, a flat." Edwin had booked a room for me at the hotel, but I hoped to find a more permanent home soon. I wasn't supposed to report to work until tomorrow, but I couldn't wait that long. Edwin had said that the hotel and the bookshop were near each other. I decided I'd drop off my bags and go directly to the shop and wait until the weekend to tackle the task of finding a flat.

Elias scrunched up his nose and rubbed his finger under it. "Ye'll need some help, lass. When ye're ready I'll take ye around and show ye the good places tae live, and the places tae stay away from, if ye'd like."

"That would be great. Thank you," I said. I was sure it would take lots of people's help and advice to find the right place.

"It will be my pleasure." Elias glanced briefly in the mirror. "So, we're stopping at the hotel first?"

"Yes, please."

"Ah, such a fine American accent. The missus will be tickled tae meet ye. Ye ken, she used tae have the fiery red hair, just like yerself. Now, she's gray and beautiful, but her red hair was at one time as bright as yers."

"I look forward to meeting her too. I thought maybe I'd blend in a little more here in Scotland. There weren't many of us redheads in the area of Kansas I grew up in. Of course, in Wichita I wasn't quite so obvious, but my dad used to say he could always find the farm by looking for the flame of my hair along the horizon."

Elias smiled in the rearview mirror. "Och, lass, that's just one of those American things. There are nae more redheads here in Scotland than in, say, yer New York City. We dinnae make claim tae them all."

"Really?"

"Aye, really."

My nonsensical hopes of being mistaken for a redheaded Scottish princess of days gone by were suddenly dashed. I was surprised that even with all my research I'd missed that all redheads didn't somehow make claim to the Scottish landscape.

I'd been afflicted with the brightest tones: the fieriest red hair, the palest skin dotted with orange freckles, and light green eyes. I'd long ago become used to people's reactions when they first saw me back home in the small town close to my family's farm. There was usually a double take, sometimes a small gasp, and then a big forced smile to cover their shock at all my . . . glow. However in Wichita and Scotland, it seemed, no one had so much as given me a second glance.

I smiled to myself at my animated Hollywood ideas and then sat back and glanced out the side window up at the castle on the hill again. It had looked huge in the pictures I'd seen, but it was even more impressive in person, its brownish stone walls shaping a fortress on a high authoritative ledge, a "volcanic crag" that had been there for centuries. I imagined decked-out royalty riding regally outfitted horses up to the top, though from my current vantage point I couldn't tell the route they'd take. The castle looked impenetrable, perched at a spot that seemed impossible to reach. I thought back to the ad I'd answered. It had mentioned a desk that had seen the likes of kings, queens, paupers, and princes. I wondered if that was literal or just figurative. I couldn't wait to explore every single inch of Edinburgh, maybe the entirety of Scotland if I could swing it, but the castle was definitely at the top of my list.

There were many things I'd have to get used to though. There was so much traffic. It all moved quickly and it seemed that the drivers didn't require space in between their vehicles and the other ones. And there was that other-side-of-the-road problem. More than once, I'd felt a panicked swell in my chest as I thought Elias was headed for sure disaster, when all he was doing was turning into the proper lane—on the left side of the road. I wondered how long it would take to rewire my brain for that one.

The cars weren't the only things that were close together. The buildings were also side by side with little or no space in between them. Some had small alleyways in between, but mostly the passing landscape was one tall, interesting, beautiful old building after another. It was difficult to digest many specifics, but the architecture ranged from medieval to ultramodern. As I angled myself against some more g-forces from the cab's quick swerve, I briefly glimpsed a neon sign attached to an older building, noting to myself that the neon modern and the old stone walls somehow didn't seem out of place. Nothing seemed out of place. There was a lot to take in, but it all seemed to be right where it belonged.

Edinburgh certainly wasn't Wichita: four words that simplified the sense of curious displacement I felt, but still a pretty accurate description. Though the displacement was somewhat uncomfortable, it wasn't unexpected.

"We're at Grassmarket," Elias said as he cranked the steering wheel quickly to the left and pulled to the side of a narrow road, the left side. More g-forces, but I could handle them.

It was a square. Well, more a rectangle shape, but done with the idea of a town square, with small businesses on the bottom level of the older buildings around the perimeter, and a paved central gathering area surrounded by cobblestoned roads. The center made an ideal spot for benches and the farmers' market tents that were currently taking up much of the long space.

"Just up two doors on oor left is yer bookshop, and down along the row, at that far corner, is yer hotel. On the other side of the hotel, there's a hill that will take ye up tae the Royal Mile. That road will take ye tae the castle. It's called Castle Wynd, technically, and it's a steep walk tae get there, but not a long one."

The Cracked Spine sat in the middle of a short side of the rectangle. It was the second of three shops that were distinctly old but very cute. The shop's front windows couldn't possibly allow any light inside, though. Books were stacked against the window, high enough to leave only a few inches of clear space at the top, and messy enough to make me want to march inside and straighten the rows and stacks, to save the ones with the unquestionably broken bindings. I would take on the job eventually, but I didn't think anyone would appreciate me marching in with that singular task in mind. One step at a time.

There was a furniture store on one side of the bookshop and a French bakery on the other side. The bakery and furniture store looked small, and so did the main part of The Cracked Spine, though I wondered if the bookshop also spilled over to the space next door to it, in between it and the pastry shop. There was a storefront there without a name and with blacked-out windows. I wasn't sure why I was inclined to think it was part of the bookshop, but it's what I sensed. The bakery window was topped with a sign that simply said, "Patisserie," and through its window that's what I saw: colorful pastries and shelves full of fruits, cakes, and cream-filled danishes. My sweet tooth made my mouth water. I'd probably visit the bakery even before the castle.

There were two old chairs sitting up on a ledge behind the furniture shop's window, and a sign above it that said: "Fraser's Gently Used Furniture and Reupholstering Services." The storefronts weren't wide, so the sign's words required two lines.

Atop the bookshop's front window was a red aluminum overhang with yellow letters that said, "The Cracked Spine," on one line and "Book Purveyors" underneath. I liked the phrasing of book *purveyor*.

The road was narrow and so was the sidewalk. We were close enough that if anyone happened to walk out of the bookshop and glance over, they'd see me, the nervous redhead from Kansas, in the back of the cab. I swallowed and told my rapidly beating heart to slow down.

And then I glanced at the long part of the street on the other side, and a warm sense of destiny washed over me, calming my nerves to something tolerable. A window that wasn't even quite as wide as the others was trimmed in green-painted, ornately carved wood. Written in black letters surrounded by more green, the sign on the window read: "Delaney's Wee Pub, the Smallest Pub in Scotland."

My name was Delaney, and no matter the fact that I wasn't sure I'd ever visit the adorable pub, just seeing my name there made me think I'd made the right choice in answering the ad, that I'd found another good omen.

With a quick scan around the market, I noticed more pubs, a restaurant or two, small groceries, and a couple of shops with names followed by "Take Away."

"Does take away mean you get food and take it out of there?" I asked Elias.

"Aye. That one up on the other corner, the place called Castle

Rock, has some of my favorite fish and chips, tho' it's hard tae find bad fish and chips in Edinburra."

"Good to know. And what about buildings on top of the businesses? Are they flats?" Stretching high above the businesses, the building's tops were their oldest parts, made up of timeworn stone, skinny paned windows, and uneven rooftops that were peppered with spires and points and television antennae.

"Aye, most of them it looks like. Expensive, I'm sure."

I nodded. It would be wonderful to live this close to work, but though I was going to be paid well I didn't know the economy well enough yet to know what "expensive" meant.

I looked up toward the top of the high volcanic crag.

"I get to work next to the castle."

"Aye, lass," Elias said with a smile in the rearview mirror.

"And my hotel is just up there?" I nodded to our right.

"Aye, I can get ye right there." Elias put the stick shift into first.

"Actually, I have a favor, Elias. Would you mind dropping my bags off there for me? I don't think I can wait one more minute. I don't even want to take the time to check in. I want to see the bookshop." I opened my purse and found a twenty-pound and a ten-pound note. The meter said nineteen pounds, but the extra would be for the luggage drop.

"I'd be happy tae," Elias said. He took the money, wrinkled his nose at it, and gave me back the ten-pound note.

"Thank you," I said.

"Listen, ye ring me up, wee lass," Elias said. He scribbled a phone number onto his business card. "Ye shouldnae use my work number. Ring the number I wrote there. That's my mobile. I'll get yer bags delivered, but I'll also come get ye and tak ye wherever ye need tae go. I ken the missus would love tae have ye o'er for supper this evening. I can pick ye up whenever ye call."

I took the card and looked at the scribbled number. I didn't quite know how to respond. Fortunately, he jumped in.

"If ye call me for supper, I'll bring the missus with me so ye can see that I'm not a fleysome sort of bloke."

I smiled. "Thank you. I don't know what I'll be doing today or tonight. . . ."

"Aye. Just call me if ye need a ride. Supper can be whenever." He paused. "I dinnae want tae alarm ye, we're a wonderful city, but dinnae ye roam aboot at night alone. Go with someone or be sure ye call a cab, even if 'tisna mine. Be canny now."

"Thank you, Elias."

"Aye, ye're welcome." He tipped his cap.

It took much more courage than I thought it would to open the cab door and step out onto the narrow sidewalk. As Elias pulled away from the curb and drove up a short hill away from me, he honked the horn once and waved out his window. Immediately, I missed those eyes.

Then, I laughed at myself.

"Come on, Del, you can do this," I said as I rearranged my purse strap on my shoulder and made my way toward my bold new adventure.

TWO

A bell above the front door jingled as I pushed through. I stepped inside and then stopped so I could inspect my new place of work. The shop was empty of customers and booksellers, which gave me a welcome and solitary moment to soak in the atmosphere. If the name of the smallest pub in Scotland had given me a sense of comfort, the interior of the bookshop sealed the fates for sure. I was right where I was supposed to be. It wasn't a museum in the strictest sense of the word, but it was *like* a museum. For books. Sort of. And in a good if messy way.

The space wasn't huge, but it wasn't necessarily cramped either, unless you took into account that each and every shelf that held books was crowded with them, stacked neatly in some places, haphazardly in other places. I gritted my teeth and told myself not to look closely at the books for a moment so I could ignore their pleas for assistance, their bookish voices, long enough to see the rest of the shop.

A desk that served as the checkout counter sat to my left. It held a short, modern cash register, a couple of newspapers, and a few wobbly stacks of books; I ignored them too, curbing the urge to at least straighten them. I didn't see a computer anywhere.

The entire shop was probably about twelve feet wide and extended back about thirty feet. There was a stained-glass window on the back wall that illustrated a set of scales piled with coins, tipping the scales to the right. Light also came in from a space to the left of the window. I thought I was seeing light from a glass door or a tall window on the back side wall but it was difficult to tell from where I stood. The high ceiling was topped off with deep and curved moldings that were painted bright yellow, and worked well with the dark wood shelves and the two large dark wood book tables placed in the middle of the shop. The floor was swirled off-white and gold linoleum, or maybe that was marble? I squelched the desire to crouch and feel it.

A ladder on wheels was attached to the shelves on the long left wall, but there wasn't a ladder attached to the right wall. I wondered about that enough to take a step to see why the right wall didn't seem to extend back all the way, but my forward movement was halted.

"Can I help you?" a lightly accented voice said from somewhere, it seemed from above.

I looked around, even behind and out the front door.

"Hello? Can I help you?" the voice said again. Not only was his accent much less pronounced than Elias's it must have been attached to someone much younger.

"I don't know where you are," I said.

"Oh, of course. I'm up a wee bit, tae your right. You can't see me because the light fixture is in your way. Just another step or two and you'll spot me."

I stepped forward and peered around the old brass light

fixture hanging from the yellow ceiling to find a young man on a balcony. Surprisingly, he was dressed in Shakespearean clothing and stood over the wooden railing as he held open a large book and smiled down at me. He couldn't have even been twenty, and his clothing and his longish brown hair made me think I might have interrupted a performance.

"Hello," he said. "Can I help you?" he repeated again.

"Hi. I'm Delaney Nichols. I'm a new employee."

"You're Delaney? We weren't expecting you until tomorrow. I'm sorry. Half a moment. I'll be right down."

He closed the book and sat it on something behind him before descending the short flight of stairs to join me on the main level. I spied more packed bookshelves along the wall behind the small balcony.

"I'm Hamlet," he said as he extended a hand. "I work here too, well, part-time."

Kansas girls are typically brought up a little better than to hesitate when being offered a hand to shake, but I couldn't help myself.

"Your name's Hamlet?" I said before finally returning the friendly gesture.

He laughed. "Aye, 'tis. 'Tis what my parents named me."

"It suits you," I said as I smiled and glanced at the large ruffled collar adorning his jacket.

Hamlet laughed again. "I know. Oddly, I'm also an actor who will be performing in a Shakespearean play in the park this afternoon, thus the costume."

"I see. And let me guess. You'll be playing Hamlet?"

"No. Today it's Macduff. Today I get tae kill the other king. It's bad luck tae say his name but I expect you know who I mean."

"I do, and, darnit, you just told me the ending."

Hamlet didn't miss a beat, but waved away my false concern and said, "It's all rather confusing anyway. Mr. Shakespeare never did like tae be all that clear."

"So true."

I could see now that Hamlet most likely *was* still a teenager, though an older one. He was cute in the way that attracted angst-riddled teenage girls, thin with longish dark hair and intelligent brown eyes that surprisingly held only a small glimmer of artistic torture.

"Ms. Nichols, welcome tae Edinburgh. I am at yer service," Hamlet said with a respectful nod.

"Thank you. It's wonderful to be here. I'm sorry I'm early. I couldn't wait to see the place."

"Ye're welcome anytime."

The pause was brief and not all that uncomfortable.

"So, do you have any idea what I'll be doing?" I said.

Hamlet blinked. "I've no idea. Edwin will probably be here soon. We'll ring him in a minute if we need tae. Can I get you a cuppa—tea or coffee? Americans like coffee, Scots do too. We have some, though it's instant. I could run next door and get something better."

"No, I like both, but I would love a cup of tea. If you just want to point me in the direction of the kettle, I can get it myself. I don't mean to disturb your work."

"Come along. We'll make tea together. You should get a proper tour anyway. We'll have us a little blether until Edwin arrives."

Hamlet turned toward the stairs he'd come from. I hesitated long enough that he turned back again.

"This way," he said with a friendly smile. "This was a bank at one time. We've got some secret hidey-holes."

"I love hidey-holes," I said. I hoped I liked blethers too, whatever they were.

From the spot at the bottom of the stairs, I saw that the shop's right wall didn't, in fact, extend in a straight line. Beyond the stairway and balcony was another space, set back and squared-off. It was also filled with packed bookshelves, as well as two worn leather reading chairs and a rectangular table with four wooden chairs tucked underneath it. The table was covered with books and messy stacks of paper.

I followed Hamlet up the stairs where we turned left and walked into a short hallway past the small balcony. I wondered if at one time when the bank had been in business this had been some sort of crow's nest for a security guard to watch goings-on from a higher perch.

We walked down the hallway and Hamlet opened another door. He turned to me before leading me through and said, "This is actually part of the building next door. Edwin uses this space for offices up here on this level." He pointed down toward the bottom level. "Our kitchen, the toilet, and his warehouse are down there."

"A book warehouse?" I said.

"Oh, well, not only for books. Edwin didn't tell you about his collections?" Hamlet said.

"No, he didn't. Frankly, we didn't talk all that much about him or the shop. We talked mostly about me," I said.

"I see. Well, you'll find it quite fascinating, I'm sure," Hamlet said.

I heard doubt in his voice, like either he couldn't believe that Edwin hadn't told me about the warehouse or that I hadn't asked more questions, or maybe that I'd actually find its contents fascinating. He sent me a hesitant smile as he flipped up a light switch that was attached to an exposed bulb on the high, dingy ceiling.

This side of the wall was much less welcoming than the other side. We'd come out to another balcony and set of stairs, but he ignored the office hallway and took us down to the front part of the building with the blacked-out windows. The floors here were stained, and I silently hoped they weren't made of something as nice as marble. We'd left the scents of old books and ink back on the other side. This side also held hints of those pleasant smells, but it also carried a musty aroma tinged with what I guessed were some sugary scents that had sneaked in from the bakery. The scents weren't completely unpleasant, but surprising, and along with the shadowy space they made me think of an abandoned carnival that had served its last cotton candy years earlier.

Another hallway extended down the middle of the space and to the back wall. There was a window at the back, but it wasn't stained glass. It was tall and dirty and let in some light that was only able to stretch a short few feet into the hallway.

"This first door on our right is the toilet, and the next room is our wee kitchen. The door on our left is the warehouse. It's locked but I'm sure Edwin will give you your own key."

I looked at the warehouse door. It stood out much more than everything else. It was an imposing bright red, ornate, with carved designs and curlicues, and slightly larger than any ordinary door.

"I can't wait to see in there," I said quietly.

Hamlet didn't respond but led us into the kitchen. There was nothing fancy about it. A round table and two chairs filled up one corner, and the far wall was filled with a couple of shelves, a small refrigerator, tea and coffee supplies, two electric kettles, and a sink under a caged-off window.

"Wait, I thought the blacked-out window space was next to the pastry shop. How is there a window to the outside on that wall?"

"Aye, yes, there's a close in between us," Hamlet said as he reached for a kettle and held it under the faucet.

I moved next to him and looked out. "An alley?"

"Aye, a close is an alley. But we named them closes because all the buildings were so close together. There's not much space there. There are lots of tales tae go along with them. They have names, usually after someone who lived on them a long time ago or some sort of business that was located on them. This is Wardens Close. I suspect that a prison warden once lived here, but I'm not certain. Edwin will probably know." Hamlet paused and looked at me. "You do know that Old Town Edinburgh on the Royal Mile is a city built upon another city?"

"I don't understand."

"There's a whole maze of underground closes and tunnels below Edinburgh. Not here in Grassmarket, but the parts of Old Town up there." He nodded toward the direction of the castle. "We'll show you around and explain it better."

"Close. Interesting." I looked out the window again, at the bars. "Do people try to break in?"

"Edwin's big on security. With the warehouse and all, he's awful canny, particular, about those sorts of details."

"I'm dying to know what's in the warehouse."

"I'm sure he'll show you right away." Hamlet blinked. The kitchen was lit with a normal glass fixture, but it cast almost as many shadows as the exposed bulb had. I thought I saw something pinch Hamlet's eyes, but I couldn't be sure if it was the weird lighting or if something else bothered him.

"What?" I said. "There's more?"

He looked at me for a long beat and then smiled easily. "So much more, but it's all for Edwin tae share." He turned and plugged in the kettle. He gathered two mugs, a couple of tea bags, a carton of milk out of the small fridge, and then placed the items on the table.

"Have a seat," he said.

As I reached for one of the two chairs, the bell above the front door jingled. Or that's what I thought I heard. It was a distant but distinct ring.

"Ah, perhaps that's Edwin. Or Rosie, our other employee. Or a customer. Edwin makes appointments sometimes for something he's stored in the warehouse. I'll be right back."

"May I come with you?"

"Of course."

We'd barely reached this side of the wall's stairs when a high-pitched voice sounded: "Haaamlet, do come help me."

Hamlet picked up pace and I followed suit.

A woman had stopped halfway into the store. She held numerous items and had lots of colorful scarves wound around her neck.

"Rosie, hang on; let me grab something," Hamlet said as he quickened his pace again down the other stairs to get to her. I still kept up.

"Och, what a morning I've had. I'm sae sorry I'm tardy, but it couldnae be helped. It just couldnae be helped," Rosie said.

"Not a problem," Hamlet said as he took three full shopping bags from her hands. She still had other bags tucked under her arms.

"Ta, love. Aye, here, this one too. Oh, pardon me," she said

in my direction. I smiled as I revved up my weary brain so I
could translate her accent, which was much stronger than Hamlet's. "I'm all a fluster in front of a customer. Apologies, lassie."

"Oh, I'm not a customer," I said. "I work here. I'm Delaney
Nichols from America."

"The one from . . . Kansas?" Rosie said.

"Yes."

"How delightful, and ye're a wee bit of good news. I can use
some good news."

"It's good to meet you."

"Ye too. Now, here, hold Hector, and I'll tell ye both all
about my morning over a cuppa. I really could use some tea."
She handed me what I'd thought was a small brown rolled-up
scarf.

When the scarf licked my hand, I almost dropped it. I realized that she'd handed me a small dog that had only been disguised as winter wear.

"Oh, my." I smiled down at it through its bangs. It panted
back up at me; its pink tongue was the tiniest one I'd ever
seen.

"Ah, look there, he's taking a liking tae ye already," Rosie
said.

"I like him too," I said. It would have been impossible not
to immediately fall in love with the creature/dog/teddy bear/
scarf imposter, whatever it was.

"Good. Now, Hamlet, let's put a kettle on. I'll tell ye all
about my morning run-in." The kettle whistled, another far-off
distant sound like a late-night train. "Ye were prepared? Come
along then." Rosie walked past us to the back table. I caught
the scents of lavender and chocolate as she passed.

Hamlet put his hand on my arm.

"She's a wonderful lady, Delaney. You'll get used tae her," he said quietly.

"I have no doubt," I said.

Everything inside me was churning. I was a classic case of tired and wired. There was no more waiting, no more "it's almost here," no more anticipation. I was there, in the middle of a rare manuscript and bookshop, smack-dab somewhere in the middle of Grassmarket in Edinburgh, Scotland, and I'd just met two of the most fascinating coworkers I'd ever had. And I was holding an adorable dog. Not to mention that there was a mysterious warehouse close by. "I have no doubt at all."

"All right then. Here we go."

THREE

Rosie was old, probably closer to seventy than to sixty, but she wore her age well, proudly, with little attention given to her short, gray coarse hair that stuck up stubbornly in every direction. There was not a stitch of makeup on her face and her wrinkles looked as if she'd ordered them to fall so that they fanned out from her mouth and eyes in an appealing way. She was a lot smaller than I'd originally thought. When she took off her jacket and the scarves around her neck, she proved to be petite and skinny.

The shopping bags had also been filled with scarves. They were her creations. Before we got into the conversation and as he was helping her get comfortable in one of the chairs around the shop's back table, Hamlet explained that Rosie knitted scarves that were sold in a hair salon down the street.

I also learned that Hector went everywhere she went, and though he was hers, he had laid claim to everyone who worked at The Cracked Spine. He rested comfortably on my lap, welcoming the new girl I supposed, as Rosie explained what had happened to her that morning. I wasn't sure I'd ever be able to give the dog back to her.

"Och, t'was a horror!" she began, after which she shook her head slowly and then took a sip of tea. Hamlet and I looked at each other. Rosie continued, "I dinnae ken hou the driver didnae see that poor man. I mean we're all crossing at all points all the time. Intersections that dinnae make much sense. Usually, the coach drivers are sae aware."

"What happened, Rosie?" Hamlet said.

"I was walking down Candlemaker Row minding my own business as I usually do, hauling my scarves and holding tight tae Hector." At his name, Hector's small head rose briefly and his ears perked, but he relaxed again when he realized there was nothing important to attend to. "And right there, when I wasnae far from Greyfriars Bobby"—she paused and looked at me— "that's a statue of a dog, we'll show ye one of these days." She took a deep breath and continued, "I heard the screech of brakes, not just any brakes, mind, but big brakes. Big, loud, noisy brakes. I looked up tae see the coach—t'was one of our tourist coaches, double-decker, open top." She looked at me again, this time as if to see if I knew what she was talking about. I honestly couldn't recall if I'd seen one on the way to the shop or not, but I had a good idea of what she was describing so I nodded. "I looked up just in time tae see it come tae a crooked, lumbered, and infinitely long stop. In those small moments, I saw the man. He stood there in the road, not even at a crossing! Like a fool, he just stood there with his mouth open and his hands in the air. Why-oh-why dinnae he leap oot o' the way? Why didnae he cross at a crossing spot? I just dinnae understand." Rosie plunked her elbow on the table and then let her forehead fall into her hand.

The heft of Rosie's accent was somewhere between Hamlet's and Elias's. I understood her, but she'd spoken the last few sentences so quickly that I'd had to focus extra hard not to miss a word. I knew now that Elias had slowed his speaking just for me, but though she was undoubtedly a friendly person, I didn't think it would ever occur to Rosie to slow down. It would be my job to keep up.

Hamlet leaned forward and put his hand on her shoulder. "Are you all right, then?"

"I'm fine, Ham, but that coach, it hit him. It wasnae the driver's fault, not really, but no matter whosever fault t'was, I just dinnae ken if that man will make it."

"So you witnessed that it wasn't the driver's fault?"

"Aye, of course. I *saw* that the man was in the road, not a crosswalk. He was alone. Coach drivers are good at what they do. They stop when they're supposed tae stop, but when someone is in the middle of the road, and the streets aren't at normal angles over there . . ." Rosie's words trailed off. She blinked and her eyes unfocused as her attention moved to the tabletop in front of her. As an afterthought, she added, "At least, I'm fairly certain that's what I saw."

"But you're not one hundred percent certain?" Hamlet said after a long thoughtful pause.

"I *was* sure. When the police talked tae me I was as sure as I could be. There was no doot in my mind that I saw what I saw."

"But there's a chance you didn't?"

"I just dinnae ken, Hamlet," she said.

Rosie was probably in some shock, and it would be difficult for anyone to digest what she'd witnessed.

"Did you get the police officers' phone numbers?" I asked.

Rosie nodded and patted her pants pocket.

"If you think you saw something different, all you have to do is call them. They'll understand; they run into this sort of thing all the time. They understand that the mind can play tricks on people." I didn't really know if they'd understand or not. They probably hoped for only reliable witnesses, but I didn't think Rosie should torture herself over perhaps misinterpreting something so awful. Even if the police weren't happy with a changed story, certainly they were used to such a thing happening. I hoped.

"I suppose," Rosie said. She hadn't shed a tear yet, but I sensed she was on the verge.

"Delaney's right," Hamlet said. "I'm sorry you had tae see what you saw. I'm sure it was traumatic."

"Me too," Rosie said. "They hurried the man who was hit off in an ambulance. Do you think it would be oot of line for me tae stop by hospital and see if he's well enough for visitors?"

Hamlet's eyebrows came together again.

"I guess you could call the police and ask them if that's a good idea," I said.

"Och, I will. Today, I will call the police and let them know I might not have seen what I thought I saw and ask if it would be all right tae check in on the man. Oh, gracious, I do hope he lives."

"You know what you should do now, though?" Hamlet said, slapping the tops of his own breeches—I suddenly remembered the word for the type of knee-length tight pants he wore.

"What?" Rosie said.

"You should show Delaney the warehouse. I bet she'd love tae see what's in there."

"Oh, dear," Rosie said with an earnest sniffle, "I forgot all aboot the other thing I was tae remember. Edwin wilnae be in today. He has some . . . well, some family matters tae attend tae. I think he would like tae be the one tae show Delaney the warehouse, and he didnae think she'd be in until tomorrow. In fact, I think he'd be upset if either ye or I did it in his place. He's been blethering on so aboot how best he was tae bring her aboard."

"Oh," Hamlet said.

"Shall I ring him, Delaney?" Rosie said.

"No, not at all. I *wasn't* supposed to begin until tomorrow. And, frankly, I'm kind of tired. No, all of a sudden, I'm really beat. I'll grab some sleep so I can start off fresh tomorrow."

"Ye must be shattered, dear girl," Rosie said.

I blinked.

"*Extremely* tired," Hamlet said with a smile.

"Yes," I said.

"Tomorrow will also begin with an adventure," Rosie said before she bent forward and lowered her voice to a whisper. "Edwin's been called tae an auction."

"A book auction?" I said.

"I dinnae think so," Rosie said, now just above a whisper.

I blinked again.

"The auctions are . . . I suppose Edwin will want tae explain that tae you, too," Hamlet said.

When I looked at him he smiled easily again, but I was pretty sure I saw a glimmer of the artistic torture I'd noticed earlier. Pain. Perhaps something bigger than I'd thought it had been when I'd first noticed it. I sensed something was off between my new coworkers, but it was too soon to know if my instincts were correct or if jetlag was making me overly observant and sensitive. I hadn't even met Edwin yet. It was far too soon to be reading anything into anyone's behavior.

"I can't wait," I said sincerely as I shook off the wonky vibes.

"All right, weel, I'll check with the police and Hamlet will walk ye up tae yer hotel. Edwin will be in at around seven tomorrow. Will that work for ye?" Rosie said.

"Absolutely," I said.

The most difficult part of leaving was relinquishing Hector. I was promised that I'd see him again the next day.

When I stood from the chair I realized I was beyond shattered, tired all the way through, the crash now coming on fast and heavy.

Hamlet walked me up the hill to the hotel where I checked in and zigzagged my way through the building to find my comfortable room. I sent my parents a quick e-mail telling them I was safe and sound and would be in touch again soon. I was too tired to do anything else, even look out the windows that probably had a great view of the market. I noticed that it was only around noon when I put my head on the pillow.

I didn't wake again until my alarm sounded the next morning at five.

FOUR

He was all elbows. And long legs. Tall. Aristocratic came to mind, but I wasn't sure if that was because of the way he spoke—so beautifully accented and toned—or because of the way he carried his height.

Edwin MacAlister welcomed me with a hug, exclamations of how happy he was I'd made it in one piece, and a box of pastries from the bakery next door. I wasn't hungry and even a French pastry that had been created a mere North Sea away from France couldn't convince my taste buds to come back to life. I nibbled on something with lots of pastry cream, but I didn't really taste it.

I was rested, but deeply nervous.

We'd gone directly to the table in the back, where Hamlet and Rosie both veered by to grab a pastry before moving on to their projects. Rosie, much less distraught than the day before, wore one of her bright red scarves around her neck. I didn't sense a good moment to ask her if she'd visited the man in the hospital but I hoped to later. Hamlet rearranged items on the table and placed some pens in a short, wide drawer on the other side of it. I gathered that this was his work space, but he didn't mind clearing away a few items to make way for the pastry box. He wore old, faded jeans and a white shirt that tied loosely at the neck. Even when he wasn't dressed for a performance, it seemed he held somewhat true to Shakespearean characters.

I might have been watching Hamlet too closely, looking for the strain I thought I'd seen the day before, but I wondered if I caught a tense moment between him and Edwin. They greeted each other tersely and with a too quick release. However, I was now so nervous that I knew I still wasn't in any shape to accurately read what might be going on. I wished my instincts would stop nudging me to pay attention.

I'd woken up a wreck. It had started with the vexing realization that I'd slept almost seventeen hours without stirring once; I wasn't even sure I'd rolled over. That was a lot of sleep, a lot of time to lose. I'd never experienced jet lag, but if the hours I'd spent in a passed-out state had taken care of it like it seemed they had I'd be good to go. Once I relaxed a little.

Then the realities set in. I was starting my new job today. I was meeting my boss. I'd uprooted my life in one of the biggest ways possible. What if I didn't like Edwin or he didn't like me?

We'd arrived at the shop at the same time, and after the hug and friendly greeting, he held the door open and signaled me inside with the pastry box. We'd had nothing but an easy, cordial conversation, but I still couldn't quite relax.

"Today, Delaney, you will learn about one of the tasks I would like for you tae take over from me, very soon if possible, but it's a big task so you'll just need tae be perfectly honest with me as tae when you're ready."

"Of course," I said.

"We're going tae an auction. I'll someday give you the lee-way tae bid for me."

"I'll get to spend your money?" I smiled. Truthfully, the idea of spending someone else's money didn't sit quite right with me and my Midwestern make-your-own-way attitude, but I figured I needed to show some confidence.

"Aye, that's correct," he said without any hesitation at all. "I'm old. I'm not sick. In fact, I'm in the best of health, but I believe it's better tae be prepared than tae have tae scramble later. Don't you?"

"I do. What kind of auction? A book auction?"

"Not today. No, today it will be for something else, but I can't give you the details quite yet."

"Okay," I said. I didn't mention out loud that details might help me be able to take over sooner rather than later, but he got it.

"You will understand soon enough," he said quickly.

Edwin bit the inside of his cheek and inspected me. He was handsome like Cary Grant had been, or maybe more like Jimmy Stewart—classic and precisely groomed, but pale in the same way I'd noticed Hamlet and Rosie were pale, and topped with salt-and-pepper hair that was only salt in his thick eyebrows, which seemed brushed and plucked to perfection. "I've thought about the best way tae introduce you tae everything here at The Cracked Spine. I have a room, Delaney, that is full of things you will find interesting, and it's the place where you'll have a desk. But I think I won't show it tae you quite yet. I think it might be overwhelming at this point."

"Okay," I said again. I couldn't imagine why it would be overwhelming, but I liked hearing that my desk would be in the mysterious room. I remembered the red, ornate door, and since I was now mostly over the jet lag I wished I'd tried to convince Rosie to take me through it yesterday, and hoped there'd be enough time to see it later today.

"Very well, let's be off and we'll discuss more as we make our way." Edwin stood. "Rosie?"

"I'm up at the front," she responded.

"Will you ring Jenny? Tell her we'll meet her at the location I mentioned tae her yesterday."

The silence that followed was so heavy that I stood quickly and followed Edwin around the corner. Rosie was sitting behind the front desk and Hamlet stood frozen in place on the rolling ladder, his eyebrows close together as he peered at Edwin.

"Jenny's going tae the auction?" Rosie said.

"Aye, she is. It's part of our . . . new agreement," Edwin said. He turned to me. "Jenny is my sister, Delaney."

I nodded, but was more interested in the now blanched faces on the other bookshop employees.

"I . . . weel, I'll figure that . . . somehoo," Rosie stammered. Hector had been resting on the corner of the desk. He sat up and looked toward Edwin and me.

"Jenny didn't mention . . ." Hamlet said.

"You talked tae her?" Edwin said.

"Well . . . not really, it's not . . . That's brilliant, Edwin." Hamlet smiled unconvincingly.

Rosie rummaged around in a bag at her feet. A moment later, she pulled out a mobile phone and pushed some buttons. She seemed even more nervous than I felt.

Shortly, she held the phone away from her ear. "Should I leave a message?"

"Aye, do. I'm certain she'll get it. She'll be there on time." His voice was unsure.

Rosie left the message and I glanced sideways at her and Hamlet as I followed Edwin out of the shop. Rosie was on the verge of being distraught again, and Hamlet had turned his attention back to the books on the shelves.

They were deathly silent, those books. Briefly, I welcomed them into my mind, was willing to listen to them, hoped maybe they'd tell me something important, but their bookish voices weren't talking today. It was the first time that had ever happened, but certainly not the right time to ponder the reasons why. I quickened my pace to keep up with my new boss.

The good part about the tense moments inside the bookshop was that I was no longer thinking so much about myself and I wasn't nearly as nervous by the time Edwin opened his passenger-side car door for me—which was on the wrong side of the vehicle. My brain rebelled. Of all the things I thought I might have to get used to in Scotland, this was not one that had been at the top of the list. Of course, I'd known Scottish people drove on the other side of the road, but it seemed that fact should simply be something understood, not something that would take any sort of supreme effort to comprehend.

The car was a Citroën, a make I recognized because my high school history teacher drove one. His was white and from the '70s, and I thought Edwin's blue one was also from the '70s, but his was in much better shape. The low, curvy vehicle was made in France and always seemed like such a cool vehicle because such a cool teacher drove it. Edwin's ownership of one only made it cooler.

Once on the road and after I'd told myself to quit expecting the g-forces to come from the other direction I inspected my boss's serious and handsome profile.

I wanted to ask what was lying underneath the unspoken words in the bookshop but I couldn't, not so soon in our new employer/employee relationship. Maybe he'd volunteer something as the day went on.

"The locations for the auctions change all the time, Delaney," Edwin said as he guided the Citroën through a left turn. He was much less jerky with the wheel than the cabdriver Elias had been. "But we do have a favorite place. I can tell you now because we are in the auto, away from curious ears. Today we're going tae Craig House."

"The location's a secret?"

"Aye, very much so. I can't even tell Hamlet or Rosie, and they are two people I consider my family." He paused, tapped his finger on his lips, and then continued. "I've only recently told my sister, Jenny. You'll meet her today."

I mentally wrestled with the wording of my next question. Finally, I just went with the simple version. "Why hasn't Jenny been involved in the past?"

Edwin glanced at me briefly. "There's a history of difficulties with my sister. She's had some issues." He took a deep breath. "I don't want tae burden you with the details, but she chose a path that led her tae a life that someone like you could never imagine."

"I have a pretty good imagination, Edwin. I might have grown up on a farm, but I've seen a little grit and ugliness. What sort of choices did she make?" Actually, the only real grit and ugliness I'd seen was from books, television, and movies, but I hadn't been sheltered.

"Drugs. Evil workings, they are. For a long time the worst sort of drugs you can think of. Then the drugs that doctors, mostly bad doctors, prescribe."

"I see. I'm sorry." Edwin was at least seventy. "How old is she?"

He sent me a knowing smile. "Fifty-five, much younger than I am, but long old enough tae know better. It's a miracle she's made it this far. A few months back, she and I formed a sort of truce. She promised she'd left that life behind, and I told her I wanted us tae be closer, her tae be involved in my life, my business."

Drugs. The bad stuff and the bad prescribed stuff. I'd seen some of that, actually, and I knew that welcoming an addict, even a family member, more deeply into your life could be a challenge. But Edwin and Jenny were siblings, and bonds like that tended to thrive on the hope that trust wouldn't end up misplaced.

"How's it been going?" I asked.

"Well," he said doubtfully.

I waited. He finally looked at me again.

"Maybe not as well as I'd hoped," he conceded.

"I'm sorry," I said again.

"Don't worry yourself. I've given her a giant responsibility." He gulped so hard and in such an unsophisticated way that I could hear it, and I had an urge to put my hand on his arm and offer supportive words, but I didn't do either. "I hope she doesn't disappoint me. She and I argued yesterday, but I hope we mended things enough that today will be better."

"What did you argue about?" I asked. I sat up higher in the seat.

"Forgive me, lass, but I don't think that would be appropriate tae share."

"I understand."

"Here we are anyway. Craig House. It was at one time home

tae a psychiatric hospital. It's a lovely old estate, and private. One of our members is a surgeon who acquired the room for us. We all donate tae the upkeep as a thank-you."

"Sounds like an interesting place." I looked up at the large, red brick and gray stone building that reminded me of a hospital from another time with its rounded window tops, domed corners, and differing wings, sectioned off but still one with the original architecture. It was perched on a green hill and though it was beautiful, with the appropriate dark sky and murky camera filter it would make the perfect set for a scary movie.

"This part is Craig House. The other parts are a university now."

"It's old but well cared for."

"Aye, 'tis. There's history on every corner in Edinburgh. This house, like many others, is thought tae be haunted by the ghosts of its past. Of course when the ghosts were once psychiatric patients from a time when mental illness was treated with cruel and unusual methods, those ghosts are bound tae be a wee bit livelier. But before the hospital owned it, others lived here too. One was John Hill Burton, who was a fascinating man in his own right. He was, among other things, a Scottish historian. He was also secretary to the Prison Board of Scotland and prison commissioner. The way he did and presented his research was unique at the time, and he was well respected. I've heard stories about his ghost being one tae haunt the old place, along with the distressed hospital patients."

"You know your ghosts."

"I know my Scottish history. My . . . well, interests are a result of my love for my country. My country is as important to me as the oxygen I breathe. I will bore you at times, I'm sure."

"I doubt it. Have you ever seen a ghost?" I asked.

"I have, but not with enough definition tae know exactly who it was when it was alive. For me the ghosties are like charged waves in air, there one minute and gone the next, but leaving one with an unmistakable and memorable jolt."

I studied his profile again. There was no glimmer of jest in his eyes, no pull of a smile at his mouth.

"Where were you when you saw them, or sensed them?"

"Many places. I'm fairly sure we have one at The Cracked Spine, but he or she doesn't show themselves all that much. Hamlet hasn't seen them. I doubt you will. They seem tae be bothered by Rosie mostly. Sometimes things move of their own accord in her office. It's all very harmless."

"Oh. Okay."

Edwin laughed as he turned the key, silencing the engine to cooling clicks. "Have you never experienced something that made you wonder for a brief instant at its validity?"

"Hmm. Not things moving, really. When I was a kid I remember sensing some strange things, but that might have just been because I was a kid. And sometimes I hear books." I'd said the last part quickly and casually, and then held my breath.

"What do you mean?"

"Oh, just lines from books I've read, characters' words. They play in my head sometimes. Nothing really. I hope to run into a harmless ghost or two here. Maybe someday."

"Interesting," Edwin said.

I nodded but didn't say anything more as we both turned our attention to a burly gentleman walking our direction. He trod heavily, as if he was perturbed, and was dressed in a green and yellow kilt with, as I'd come to think of it, all the trimmings—a sporran around his waist, kilt hose that I would have just called socks with fringe, and a white shirt that reminded me of the one Hamlet had been wearing. The discussion Edwin and I had been having and the approaching man's Scottish postcard look made me wonder if we might be seeing a ghost. I looked for a sword or a dirk, but he held no weapon.

"Here we go, Delaney. Just follow along whatever I say or do. No one will be expecting you today. I hope there won't be too much of a kerfuffle, but watch yourself."

Edwin got out of the car and came around to my side to open my door. I hesitated a moment before getting out, but it wasn't because I was afraid.

I just happened to think the entire scene was wonderful and crazy enough to want to soak in every detail.

FIVE

"Benny, good tae see you," Edwin said as he extended his hand. "May I present Delaney Nichols from America. She's a new Cracked Spine family member. She'll be attending the auctions."

Benny scowled. "I thought yer sis was tae be the one a taken yer place some time doon the road, MacAlister," he said.

"No, Jenny is involved on her own. Now, please help me welcome Delaney. Delaney, this is Benny Milton. He organizes the Fleshmarket Batch auctions. We've shortened it tae just Fleshmarket though. Benny doesn't bid. He's a pub owner by trade, with a law enforcement background. Benny became a permanent fixture with us when he was investigating one of us, who turned out tae be innocent of all charges. He keeps us on the straight and narrow, and would report any of us tae the police with no second thought at all if he thought it necessary. He's a good man and friend."

I'd hit a mental speed bump when he'd said, "Fleshmarket Batch," but I caught up soon enough and extended my hand.

"Lass," Benny said a moment later as he reluctantly pulled his thumbs from the waistband of the kilt and shook my hand like he was both in a hurry and might need an extra arm to take home.

Benny was mostly bald with a few long stray pieces of black hair swooping dramatically back along the sides of his head, all hairs coming to a curled and pointed end at the back. He was big in a way that Kansas folks would describe as beefy. Thick everything, on the heavy side but not terribly so. His dark eyes were disturbingly intelligent and suspicious.

"Well, there, that wasn't so bad," Edwin said as he placed one big pat on Benny's shoulder.

"Come along then," Benny said after sending a sideways look toward Edwin. He turned and led the way to the doors, which were located at the end of a small walkway. We followed him in between two reddish brick pillars and then up a short stairway. Two giant white glass ball fixtures hung from the walkway's ceiling.

Benny pulled open one of the two doors and turned his attention back toward the road and parking spaces.

"Have you seen Jenny yet?" Edwin asked as he handed Benny his car keys.

"Noo, I havenae," Benny said. "I thought she'd be with ye."

"Would you please let her know I'm inside the moment you see her?" Edwin asked.

"Aye."

Edwin turned toward me. "Benny parks the cars elsewhere. He's a bit of a magician when it comes tae keeping us a secret."

Benny sniffed.

"I see," I said with a smile in Benny's direction. He didn't acknowledge it.

I followed Edwin inside, and then stopped in my tracks, needing another moment to soak in my surroundings.

"This is beautiful," I said as I looked up a wide stairway with a wooden railing and wood-paneled walls, not slat panel like in some of the older houses back home, but real wood panels, topped with carved arches.

"Aye, a lovely place," Edwin said. He looked back through the doors briefly. "Benny takes his security seriously. You'll see kilts here and there throughout Scotland but mostly for special occasions. To Benny, this is a special occasion."

I wondered if Benny took his security as seriously as Edwin did for his warehouse, but I just nodded.

"Come along, we're just up here."

I hurried after him, working hard to keep up with his long legs, and onto another floor with the same wood-paneled walls but with giant chandeliers above.

"What's the Fleshmarket Batch?" I said.

"Oh, aye, that's what we call ourselves, the Fleshmarket Batch. One of our founders had family that decades ago lived on Fleshmarket Close—a close is an . . . alley."

"Hamlet mentioned the closes to me. What about Batch?"

"Ah, I believe your word would be something like 'club.' "

"Fleshmarket, huh? Sounds gruesome."

"Aye. It was the location of the meat market that led to the slaughterhouse. Not pleasant images to ponder, but a reality from an older time."

I nodded as we reached the third floor. "Where is everyone?"

"They're either already inside or on their way. Come along."

Edwin now sauntered down the long hallway as if he didn't want to appear to be in a hurry even though I was sure he was. I followed and tried to keep my awe under control. Halfway down the hallway we turned toward a door on our right. Before he opened it, though, he looked in all directions, twice. Finally, he turned the old brass knob, and pushed through. I followed directly behind and he quickly and quietly closed the door behind us.

The room was expansive, decorated with the same polished wood paneling I'd already seen, but in here the floor was off-white marble with swirls of gold throughout, reminding me of an even more expensive version of the bookshop's floor. Tall windows offered a view of green grounds in one direction and more buildings and wings in the other. One half of the room was filled with puffy green upholstered chairs and a podium at the end of a middle aisle. The other side held a snack buffet with what looked like empty sterling silver serving dishes. That side was also populated by people. The space wasn't crowded, but there was a small group of three, and the low rumble of their conversation came to an immediate halt once they turned our direction and saw us . . . well, probably just me.

"Hello, friends!" Edwin said. He was exuberant but not overly cheery. "This is Delaney. She's from Kansas, in America. Please welcome her in the warmest of ways." My previous home was becoming a part of my name.

"I don't see Jenny yet," he said quietly to me as we walked toward the group. "But it looks as if everyone else is here. This isn't everyone in the group, mind, but it's the ones who were interested in the item up for bid today."

The introductions went okay, a little strained, but nothing that made me want to run out of the room and catch the next flight back home. No one had expected me to be there, but no kerfuffle ensued, or at least I didn't think so according to what I thought "kerfuffle" meant. Edwin left me to fend for myself but I didn't mind, and even a quick one-on-one with each of the three people would help me know them better.

If she'd been from England, Genevieve Begbie would have been straight out of a PBS television show about aristocracy and their servants. She was clearly Scottish though, and she was young in comparison to everyone else in the room. She was probably somewhere in her early fifties and dressed in clothes that made me think I shouldn't stand anywhere near her if I held food or drink. She wore her brown hair boyishly short with a small swoop to the right. Her firmly set mouth didn't smile when she shook my hand, but her eyes did a little bit, so I held out hope that she and I might get along okay, eventually.

"I thought dear Jenny would be coming with Edwin. You're a true surprise," she said, her smiling eyes holding steady with mine.

"I think she's coming on her own."

"I see. I do hope so. It's been so encouraging tae see her turning things around, though I think Edwin's given her a task that's too much tae try to handle," Genevieve said. The smile left her eyes so suddenly that I felt my eyebrows raise.

"Oh?" I said.

"She's been such a challenge tae that family. More than that family, I suppose. Gracious, I'm speaking out of turn," she said with no noticeable regret and with an accent so light I thought I might understand her even if she spoke quickly.

"How do you know the family?" I asked.

"Edwin's family and mine have been friends for decades. Our parents, grandparents were close, even though Edwin's parents were significantly older than mine. They're long dead now. And, Jenny and I were flatmates for a couple of years at university."

"It didn't go well?" It seemed like the only reasonable question to ask, considering her tone.

She laughed. "It went fine."

Evidently not, but Genevieve excused herself before I could ask more questions. I felt like I'd misjudged the earlier introductions. I'd thought maybe no one had expected me, but perhaps she'd been somehow prepared for my arrival, or maybe just prepared to say unflattering things to *someone* in regards to Jenny. I didn't necessarily feel like I'd been played, but perhaps used as a way to spread bad tidings. I wasn't going to spread anything, but in the back of my mind I started a list of things I wanted to uncover. I'd suddenly become much more interested in Edwin's family. Exploring his ancestors went on the list, right next to searching for the best spots to find ghosts.

I thought back to Edwin's unsophisticated gulp. Were he and Genevieve speaking about the same responsibility? What sort of monumental task had he given Jenny, and why did Genevieve think it might have been too much to handle? And, why had she brought it up to me so soon after our initial greeting? I looked toward the door, hoping Jenny would come through, but no one did at that moment.

"Hello, lass, you're a bright spot on our otherwise auld and cranky bunch. Welcome, it will be nice tae have some young blood," said another man as he introduced himself.

Hamilton Gordon also wore a kilt with all the trimmings today, but his color scheme was blue and yellow. He was adorable in the getup, in an almost-eighty-years-old, wrinkled and bald sort of way.

"It's great to be here. I think Jenny's on her way," I said reflexively. I cringed inwardly. I shouldn't have predicted that everyone would be looking for Jenny instead of me.

"Och, don't care who's here and who isn't. I've met the Mac-Alister lass a time or two and she's friendly enough. The more, the merrier, I say." He scanned the room. "Gracious, is there no whisky on the premises? Who has a gathering with Scottish people and doesn't think tae serve whisky? Disgraceful."

"Uh, I don't know," I said as I looked toward the buffet table. There were no whisky bottles in sight.

"I'll have tae find some on me own. Excuse me."

I sighed and turned my attention toward the man I still hadn't met. No time like the present, I supposed. I approached him as he turned away from Edwin. Whatever they'd been discussing, it seemed to have ended with a huff of disapproval from the man dressed in all gold. He wasn't handsome, but it seemed he'd worked hard to get that way. His build told me that he must have been close to Edwin's age, but the tight features on his face made me think he'd had a few plastic surgeries. Up close, I could also see the spaces in his head where hair plugs had been inserted. I had an urge to ask about the gold jacket and pants, inquire as to whether or not they had real gold threads in them, but I didn't.

"Hi," I said.

"Hello," he said with a forced smile.

"Delaney Nichols," I said.

"Birk Blackburn, at your service," he said with a small nod. "Welcome tae Edinburgh, Delaney. I'm one of the few outside the bookshop who knew you were coming tae join The Cracked Spine. I'm glad you made it safe and sound."

"You and Edwin are good friends then?"

"Aye," he said less than enthusiastically. "He told me about you when we completed a transaction a few weeks ago. Edwin mentioned that he wanted tae wait for you and your expertise, but he went ahead and purchased the item anyway. I'm sure he's mentioned it tae you." Birk's eyebrows rose in question, though his forehead didn't wrinkle.

"I, uh, he hasn't mentioned it yet."

"Aye?" He looked toward Edwin, who had moved across the room and was talking to Hamilton Milligan, and sent him a furrowed frown before he turned to me again. As with Genevieve, I got the sense that he was anxious to share something.

"It's a book of supreme greatness," he said quietly.

"Oh? What's the book?" I said. I knew I could have eventually figured out any book's value if that's what Birk meant as the reason for Edwin waiting for my arrival, but I wasn't an expert appraiser.

"Ask Edwin. He'll tell you. In fact, I suspect you'll be retrieving it today. He left it with his sister, and something tells me that's not working out as well as he'd hoped."

"Why isn't it working out? You won't tell me what the book is?"

"You'll have tae ask Edwin why it isn't working out. He won't give me the details. But the book"—he looked around furtively—"William Shakespeare."

"Okay." I caught myself before I rolled my eyes. The drama with which he'd said the bard's name could have landed him a starring role in one of his tragedies.

"It's one of his. One of his first ever. In fact, that's part of the title."

"I don't understand," I said.

"First Folio," Birk whispered.

The earth shifted. Birk couldn't possibly be speaking the truth, or at least the facts. Edwin had not purchased a copy of Shakespeare's First Folio from him. It wasn't possible. There

were only a couple hundred copies of the early 1600s manuscript still in existence. They were all accounted for and kept
mostly in museums. I'd dreamed of visiting the Folger Shakespeare Library in Washington, D.C., to put my eyes on at least
one of their twentysomething copies.

Except. Hadn't I recently heard that someone found a copy
in their attic? Had that been a true story? I couldn't quite remember.

First Folio was more than a book, it was an artifact.

I didn't notice that Birk had walked away because I'd fallen
into some sort of vacuum of disbelief, and my brain was working hard to understand the possible ramifications of such a
transaction, the possibility that the item actually existed.

The door to the room began to slowly swing open. I pulled
myself together and looked toward it. Everyone else in the room
did too. I hoped to see Jenny come through. I wanted to meet
the sister of my new boss, the person he'd allegedly trusted to
watch over something so outrageously valuable.

But it wasn't Jenny. The man who came through the doorway was probably close to Jenny's age, though, somewhere in
his fifties.

His most distinguishing feature wasn't his handsome face,
his red hair that almost matched mine, his dapper tuxedo, or
the cane he wielded. It was his black eye that made him stand
out from the crowd. Once inside, he closed the door behind
him, nodded sheepishly at the rest of us, and made his way to
one of the green puffy chairs. He sat down, angling his body
so that all we could see was his back.

"That's Monroe Ross." Edwin had stepped up to my right.
"I'd hoped maybe Jenny would have come with him."

"They're friends?" I said.

"Not exactly," he said. "They used to be together, a couple, but that was a long time ago. I'd hoped . . . I'd hoped maybe they could be friends again. I'm working on it. She's one of the few people he's comfortable around."

"What about the black eye?"

Edwin shrugged. "I haven't seen Monroe with a black eye for some time. Perhaps he's taken up his old ways. He used tae spend a fair amount of time in the pubs. But now he's not comfortable around a crowd. He has a difficult time, that's why he took a seat so quickly. He doesn't know you, Delaney. Perhaps you could befriend him."

Edwin walked away too quickly for me to ask him anything more, either about Monroe or the Folio. I could tell he was disappointed his sister hadn't shown up yet, but I didn't understand the exact reasons why. Did he think her absence was because of her addiction or the argument she'd had with him? Or something else?

His command had been clear, though. I was to befriend Monroe. Genevieve had wanted to dump some gossip my direction. And even though I sensed that he knew Edwin hadn't yet told me about the Folio, it had been Birk's priority to share the information. Was this the Scottish way, or was I being used as a conduit for moving information from one place to the next? If so, what direction was it all supposed to go? It didn't much matter. Whatever my job would turn into, I wasn't going to suddenly become a gossip. And I doubted I'd ever be convinced to do much of anything behind my boss's back. But I might be able to get to know Monroe easily enough.

Benny pushed through the door. The noise of his forceful shut—almost a slam but not quite—lingered in the big room.

"Awright, time tae get the shoo on the road," he said before he stood straight and folded his hands behind his back. Everyone seemed to know where to go. I thought a chair next to Monroe might not be a bad idea.

Leaving enough space to keep any introvert from bristling too much, I sat a couple of chairs away from him. I smiled in his direction. Just as I was about to introduce myself, he turned away, and Birk slammed a gavel on the podium.

"First item of business," Birk said into the microphone I hadn't noticed until then. "We need tae discuss our new member and if we'll welcome her or not."

I tried not to look surprised as Edwin took a seat directly next to me, on the other side from Monroe.

"We'll get this taken care of, Delaney," he said quietly. "Not tae worry."

I hoped he was right.

SIX

In fact, Edwin was correct, there was nothing to worry about. There were no votes and no real discussion. Hamilton Gordon might have found some whisky, because his words slurred a bit when he proclaimed that everyone in the group was free to bring whomever they trusted to the auctions, no questions needed to be asked.

No one had a problem with me becoming a part of the Fleshmarket Batch. Even Birk, who'd been the only one to act as if a discussion needed to take place, didn't seem to mind too much. It was easy. Maybe too easy, but I had other things to think about at the moment that seemed more important than the smooth slide into my new position among these strangers. Besides, maybe Hamilton had summed it up; maybe they all trusted one another's judgment enough not to probe deeply.

"As you all know, I brought the item up for bid today," Birk said.

He leaned over to the side of the podium, lifted up the large item that was covered by a thin red sheet, placed it on an easel, and then leaned back toward the microphone.

"It's original. I've had it verified. It's by James Tannock." He peeled away the sheet and exposed the painted portrait of a jowly man. The subject was older, big-nosed with a short and simple haircut that was combed straight, the ends slightly uneven but mostly stopping at mid-cheek level. I had no idea who he was. I didn't know the portrait. I didn't know the subject. I might have somehow heard of the painter, but I couldn't place him exactly.

However, it seemed I was the only uninformed person in the room. Ooohs and ahhs and murmured comments rumbled throughout.

"The artist, Tannock, was born in the late seventeen hundreds, I believe. He moved on tae London at some point, but he started his career as a house painter—oh, and maybe a shoemaker too if I remember correctly. He became successful," Edwin said quietly.

"Who's the subject of the portrait?" I asked.

"I'm not completely sure."

Edwin raised his hand.

"Edwin," Birk said.

"Is it Chalmers?" Edwin asked.

"Yes," Birk said.

Edwin leaned toward me again. "George Chalmers, Scottish political writer, and antiquarian . . . He has a distinct look, doesn't he? Rather weighty and bug-eyed. And . . ." His voice drifted as though his thoughts suddenly went a different direction.

"What?" I said.

"I'm . . . nothing."

I looked at him and had an urge to poke him in the ribs to continue, but I stopped myself.

"Birk, where did you get the portrait?" Genevieve asked.

"From a cousin in London," Birk said.

Edwin, Genevieve, and Hamilton laughed lightly.

Edwin said to me, "That's code for 'I'm not telling.'"

"Other than Benny's watchful eye, does everyone just trust that all these items are obtained legally?"

"Aye, we take it on faith. And as for how we obtain them, well, I suppose we have our connections. I'll show you some of that as time goes on."

"I see." I didn't see all the way, but I thought that I'd figure things out exactly how Edwin had just said—as time went on.

"Excuse me a minute. I have a question for Birk, but I don't want tae broadcast it tae the entire room. I'll be right back. You stay here." Edwin stood and made his way to the podium. Hamilton was already there, leaning over and inspecting the portrait with a large magnifying glass.

Monroe was still in his seat, still with his back mostly my direction.

I glanced over and smiled shyly at him, hoping I didn't look like I was trying to flirt. He craned his neck and looked directly at me, his black eye much meatier and rawer this close up, but didn't smile back. And then he looked away.

"Excuse me," I said.

He turned again and his eyebrows lifted in surprise.

"That looks like it hurts," I said as I pointed to my own eye.

"Not bad." He shrugged, but this time he didn't turn all the way away from me.

"Monroe, right?" I continued.

"Aye."

"I'm Delaney," I said. I didn't extend a hand. No need to cause him to have a heart attack.

"That's what I understand." He nodded toward the podium.

"Right. I'm curious, Monroe, is it okay to ask what you do for a living? Edwin didn't tell me whether I could ask or not."

If I hadn't looked like I was flirting a second earlier, I probably sounded like it now. This wasn't going exactly as I'd hoped, but I thought I could blame my rudeness on being a foreigner. Monroe didn't need to know that between my farmer father and my farmer's-wife mother, I'd been very well schooled on manners.

Monroe didn't hide his discomfort. He uncrossed and then recrossed his legs. His glance was only somewhat incredulous, but that might have been because of the black eye. I continued to smile in what I hoped was a friendly way.

"I suppose there are no rules regarding asking the question, but . . ."

I turned and faced him full on but kept my distance. "Okay, so, what do you do?"

"I'm a finance person. I help people with their money," he said a beat or two later.

"You must be very good at it," I said.

"I don't know."

"Where did you study? I mean, of course I went to the University of Kansas back home, but I'm not familiar with the universities around here."

That was an enormous lie. I knew them well. Even if I hadn't studied up on them before moving to Scotland, I would have been familiar with at least some of them. I didn't like playing the dumb American, but if it worked to get this man who my new boss had asked me to befriend to talk to me, I'd redeem myself later. I liked a good challenge.

"University of Edinburgh," he said.

"Oh!" I looked around to see if anyone was watching. No one was. I leaned a little closer to Monroe and he leaned a little closer to me too. This I considered a huge victory.

"That's where Edwin's sister, Jenny, went, right?" I had no idea where Jenny had gone to school, but it seemed like a good guess since they'd been a couple.

"She did. Jenny and I went tae school together. We were friends," Monroe said as he pulled back a little and out of our small shared space. I didn't think I'd lost him though.

"I think she was supposed to be here today. Edwin expected her," I said.

His eyebrows came together. "I didn't know she was tae be here today." Then he swallowed before rubbing his finger under his nose and turning away from me a tiny bit.

"You two still pretty good friends?" I said.

"No," he said too quickly. "Not really."

"I'm sorry. It's rough when friendships don't last."

Monroe nodded, but didn't look at me.

"How'd you get the shiner?" I asked.

"The what?"

"The black eye?"

"Ran into a door."

"No big bar brawl? I mean *pub* brawl?" I smiled at his lame reason.

"No, not this time." He looked at me and smiled sheepishly.

I think I could like Monroe Ross, and I hoped someday he might not be totally put off by me.

Before we could continue the conversation, we were interrupted by Benny, who held the portrait at the end of the aisle, seemingly just so the shy, somewhat agoraphobic Monroe could have a look.

Even though the man in the portrait wasn't handsome in the classic sense, he was interesting, and I had to give credit to the artist's ability to capture humor and intelligence in Mr. Chalmers's eyes. The portrait was in phenomenal condition. I wasn't an expert on brushstrokes, but it was unquestionably beautiful and from another time.

When Monroe seemed to be done looking at it, Benny turned and carried it back toward the front of the room.

I didn't waste a second. "When did you become a member of Fleshmarket?"

"Excuse me," Monroe said. He stood and walked to the back of the room, using the cane only as a prop, I thought. He parked himself close to a back wall.

I turned in the chair and watched him, but then turned around again when I realized he wasn't going to come back. I'd lost him. I didn't know if I'd done something wrong or if it was just that he was done with the conversation. If I chased him, he would probably leave the room altogether.

I tried not to feel too badly about his quick exodus from the chair, take it to mean something more about him than me, but it was difficult not to feel a little rejected.

Edwin took his seat again. I asked if he was interested in the portrait and if he wanted me to examine it more closely, but he wasn't interested in it and decided not to bid. He was distracted, probably wondering where his sister was, and I wasn't ready to make recommendations one way or another regarding what he should bid on.

The only thing to do now was get through the auction and, afterward, try to get some answers from Edwin. Birk was very good, and sounded just like any auctioneer I'd ever heard, but with a Scottish accent, which made everything sound better. However, though his accent was light, when he started speaking quickly my American ears struggled to keep up.

Genevieve Begbie won the auction, and Benny helped her carry her prize out to her car like it was just another item she'd picked up shopping that day, even though Edwin confirmed that I'd heard correctly—her winning bid had been fifty thousand pounds, close to eighty thousand American dollars. I didn't witness a money transfer and Genevieve didn't pull out her checkbook.

"How will she pay?" I asked Edwin quietly as we followed behind everyone down the grand hallway and staircase.

"It's all electronic transfer. Rosie handles all the money from our end."

When we were outside and she reached her car, Genevieve's eyes caught mine. I thought she might smile, but she didn't. She nodded and then looked at Birk, who had his head down as he inspected something on his mobile phone. I thought Genevieve was trying to tell me something, but the silent communication could have been my imagination. Before I could shrug or raise my eyebrows, she slipped into her red sports car. She revved the engine before backing away from the curb. Monroe and Hamilton followed suit.

Somehow, Benny had quickly gathered the cars from wherever he'd hidden them and lined them up outside the front doors. He handed each driver their keys and didn't offer much in the way of a farewell.

I told him it was nice to meet him, but he just huffed in my direction.

For such an easy incorporation into the group, I certainly wasn't left with a sense of comradery. It was too soon to judge, of course, and maybe too soon for the others to extend warmth my direction. Maybe I was expecting too much too quickly, but I hoped our next meetings would be less cryptic.

SEVEN

I didn't get to ask all the questions of Edwin I wanted to, but I did get one in.

"I'm concerned about my sister, Delaney. I'm going tae drop you at the shop and then I think I'll go look in on her."

"Do you want me to go with you?"

"No, I don't think so, but I have an idea. Ask Rosie tae show you the warehouse. You need tae see what's in there and then you'll understand the auctions better."

"That sounds great, but Edwin, can I ask you something?"

"Aye," he said too abruptly.

"Did you really buy a First Folio from Birk?"

"I did."

That was all he had to say? Just "I did"?

"How . . . I don't understand . . . they aren't . . ." I took a deep breath and let it out. "The First Folios are priceless, and most of the ones still in existence are accounted for, Edwin, and though there's a chance there are more out there, they aren't something that's typically just found. Was this something that was in Birk's possession? If so, how? Why wasn't it locked up somewhere safe, a library, a museum, a maximum-security vault?"

"Birk has a story of how he found the Folio. I don't believe him, but it's a better story than his cousin in London, I suppose. I'll let him tell it tae you someday."

"If you don't believe him, where do you think he got it? And do you think it's real?"

"I searched and found that none had been stolen or lost or damaged, so I don't know where he got it, Delaney. I do think it's real, but I was hoping tae have you help me know for certain."

"Is it in the warehouse?" I hoped beyond hope that the alleged Folio was locked up somewhere safe. If not a library or a museum or a bank vault somewhere, at least secure behind the red door at the shop.

"No, I gave it tae my sister, Jenny, tae care for it."

"Did she lock it up?"

"I don't know what she did with it. That was our argument yesterday. Well, part of our argument. We argued about other things first, but then about where she hid the Folio."

"Oh, my." Truth be told, I wanted to faint and cry. At least whimper a little.

"I know what you're thinking, Delaney, that I was stupid and careless, and you might be right, but perhaps if you understood my past with my sister, you'd know I was just trying tae rebuild something that broke a long time ago. Entrusting her with the manuscript was my way of telling her she was welcome into my life, that I believed that she'd moved on from her terrible past. I admit, it was probably a bad choice and one that I will regret forever, even if we find the Folio and are able tae mend our family anyway."

Edwin didn't need to explain anything to me, to anyone really, but I appreciated the gesture. He was correct that I hadn't walked a proverbial mile in his shoes, but I did think he'd made a terrible decision, no matter what the view from that walk might be. It wasn't my place to point that out, though. Besides, he seemed to be beating himself up well enough without anyone else's help.

"Do Rosie and Hamlet know?"

"They know I gave the Folio tae Jenny, but they don't know she wouldn't tell me where it was. I would appreciate if you didn't tell them that part. I would like tae do it myself. Tomorrow."

"Of course. Let me know what I can do to help," I said.

"I will."

I couldn't dwell on the Folio. Well, I could I supposed, but it wasn't going to do anyone any good for me to continue to be astounded by its possible existence and now disappearance. If the auction was any indication, I had stepped into a world that would hold many awe-inspiring items. I'd have to get used to it.

The rest of the short ride back to the shop was silent; both Edwin and I had fallen deep into our own thoughts. I didn't know what I could do to help him, unless just getting to work on something at the shop, perhaps in the warehouse, might help everyone.

He pulled the car up to the curb, and I hurried out before he could hop out too and open my door. I waved as he drove away, but he was probably too distracted to notice.

The bell above the door jingled as I went back into the store.

"Delaney! How did it go? What did ye think of yer first auction?" Rosie said, still in the chair behind the desk.

"Fine. We didn't bid on the item, but I got a good sense of how things are done."

"That's wonderful! How was Jenny?" Her smile flipped into a frown.

"She didn't make it there," I said as I moved to the corner of the desk and scratched behind Hector's ears.

"Oh. I'm sure Edwin was disappointed. However, it will help . . ."

"What will help?"

"Och, 'tis nothing."

I watched as her eyes squinted, unsquinted. She scratched above her ear and then her chin.

"You okay, Rosie?"

"Fine, lass. Just fine."

"Edwin said that you could go ahead and show me the warehouse, if you have time. I don't want to disturb a project."

"Yer not! That sounds delightful." She lifted Hector from the desk and tucked him under her arm.

"Where's Hamlet?"

"Gone for the day. He's here only part-time, the other times he's an actor and a university student. I believe he had some classes today, but I have a difficult time keeping up with the lad."

"He sounds busy."

"I think so."

We retraced the path up the balcony steps, over to the other side (I tried very hard not to let the idea of "the dark side" solidify in my mind, but I didn't think I was successful), and down to the middle dingier, darker hallway. Rosie didn't even acknowledge the upstairs offices before she'd flipped the switch that lit the naked bulb.

When she reached the red door I felt like the explorers who'd opened King Tut's tomb must have felt. Anticipation mixed with concern that the other side would be a bust.

With the drama I'd silently inspirited in my own mind, Rosie pulled a loaded key ring out of her pocket and flipped it a couple of times in her hand to sift for the appropriate key: it was oversized, turquoise blue, and had an old-fashioned curlicue endpiece.

Deftly, she inserted the key and turned it three times to the left before the lock loosened with a metallic slide and thunk; the noise was loud and attached to mechanisms that belonged on something more important than an ordinary old door. She pushed and reached around to a switch on the wall. A flip sounded and the room became illuminated.

"From what I heard about yer résumé, lass, this place is going tae feel like a wee bit of home."

I followed her inside.

I blinked a million or so times as I looked around and tried to digest all the things that were in the room. Or at least digest a few of them. There were so many.

The warehouse was not big, but it was tall in that it took up the entire back corner of the building. There was no second floor over this part, and two very small, high-up windows gave the room a sliver of natural light. The rest of the light came from three brass chandelier-like fixtures on the ceiling, and though the light seemed somewhat dim, it somehow managed to illuminate the entire room. Or more precisely, illuminate all the things on the shelves in the room.

An old, large, wooden desk filled the center of the space. Next to the desk was a modern worktable with a light panel over its top, just like one I'd used back at the museum in Wichita.

The worktable top was clear of clutter, but the desktop held a few messy piles of paper.

The walls were lined with black-painted steel shelves. One wall of shelves was filled with books—so many books. They were stacked willy-nilly and off-kilter, even worse than the books out front.

They cried out, begged to be straightened and organized, but I shut them out. For now. I'd get to them soon enough.

The other shelves were jam-packed too, but not with books. At first glance, I noticed an antique tube radio, a golden Pharaoh head (just like Tut's tomb—I realized the appropriateness of my earlier thought), an ornate mirror, a gilded and jeweled box, a whole shelf just for medieval weapons, bottles filled with liquid or powder or just empty . . . So many, many things. More things than I'd ever seen stored on the museum archive or storage shelves. Or perhaps it was that everything here was in total disarray. There was a preciseness to the shelves at a museum. There was the opposite of preciseness here.

"I don't understand," I said. Between the auction for a portrait and the inventory in this room, had I misinterpreted the nonanswers to my non-asked questions? Had my mind created the "bookshop" part of the answers? No, wait, the sign out front had said, "Book Purveyors," not museum or "Purveyors of Every Sort of Thing Under the Sun."

"This is Edwin's collection. Books are his first passion, but he loves things: old, valuable things. This is where he keeps some of them and then sometimes sells them, sometimes uses them tae barter."

"I still don't understand," I said. "Will I be organizing or acquiring these sorts of things, or archiving and preserving them, or helping him sell them?"

"Aye." Rosie nodded.

"Does he have someone he works with at a museum?" I asked.

"No, this is all his, not for display, but he kens he has some museum-quality pieces. 'Tis why ye're here."

As I looked around again, I thought about Edwin's carelessness regarding the Folio. I couldn't mention to Rosie that Jenny wasn't telling where she'd put it, but a tiny bit of why he'd been so trusting with something so valuable crept into my consciousness, a minuscule slice of understanding. Despite appearances, I didn't believe that Edwin didn't care about these things; it must have been something else. The only conclusion I could come to in the span of a few seconds was that Edwin MacAlister was silly rich. He was the type of person who had so much money that he could replace anything he wanted just by pulling out his checkbook, or calling Rosie to make the electronic transfer.

But not really. Folios weren't easy to find. Neither were medieval weapons.

"He loves these things?" I said.

Rosie sighed. "Aye, he does. Truly. He's a contradiction, Delaney. He's a gatherer, but not someone who can organize. I think he's become upset with himself and his care for his treasures, which is why he hired ye. He's a good man with a heart o' gold. He feeds and clothes many who canna afford it themselves, but he'll never tell ye aboot that. He's brilliant, but sometimes a wee taupie."

"Taupie?"

"What's the word? Scatterbrained? Does that sound right?"

"An absentminded-professor type?"

"Meebe, but good tae the core. His goodness gets him into trouble too, but I work tae keep him oot of it."

"How do you do that?"

"Nothing you need to fret aboot."

Oddly, the next question that came to my mind was, "Has that desk seen the likes of kings and queens?"

"Oh, aye! The advertisement. It has. It came from the court of William II."

"From the late sixteen hundreds? For real?"

"Aye."

The desk *had truly seen the likes of real kings and queens.* From the seventeenth century.

I felt the movement of my very soul as it teetered toward the brink.

"I need to sit down," I said as I beelined my way to the modern and clearly not overly valuable desk chair. I veered away from the ridiculously valuable desk that was obviously in need of at least a good dusting.

"Delaney, are ye awright?" Rosie said as she stepped toward the desk. Hector whined, a brief and high-pitched squeak.

I had an unreasonable urge to stop her, to tell her that no one should be so close to the desk until I had a chance to take care of it properly, or at least straighten the stacks of stuff atop it.

Then, as suddenly as it had gone away, reason came back and took over, and it hit me—I was overreacting. Perhaps it was the combination of everything that had happened, the travel, all the big life changes (in the hierarchy of stressful events, wasn't moving the number one? Moving to a different country surely pushed that even higher), but there truly was no need to feel panicked or out of control. I chuckled to myself. It wasn't my job to care for and preserve the entire world. I hadn't taken a "do no harm to old valuable things and report those who

don't" vow. These items belonged to someone else. Even though
I'd worked in a museum, inside Edwin's warehouse I'd probably never been around so many amazing things in my life. In
fact, perhaps no one in Wichita had. I could ignore the distressed characters in the books, at least for the time being.
They'd be there when I could get to them. Until this moment—
or at least until the moment that I'd accepted the job—these
things *hadn't* been my responsibility. And I still wasn't completely clear regarding the responsibilities anyway. I'd wanted
an adventure, and just when one was standing right before me,
exposing itself like it had been cloaked in a suspicious raincoat,
I'd panicked.

"I'm fine," I finally said. "I think all the travel might have
made me a little woozy for a second." I scooted a little closer
to the desk so I could put my elbows on it just to prove to
myself that I could do it. Unfortunately, I wasn't quite there
yet, and I retracted my elbows before they touched. I smiled
confidently at Rosie and gently patted the edge of the desk with
two fingers.

"Good," she said doubtfully. "Now, I'm not clear on exactly
everything ye will be doing, but this will be yer office. Ye get
both the desk and the worktable. Ye should feel honored; ye're
the first one other than Edwin, and long-dead Scottish royalty
of course, that will get tae work from that desk."

"Great," I said, freezing the smile in place.

"Now"—Rosie looked around and laughed—"I have no
idea what tae tell ye tae do, so ye may stay here and figure something oot on yer own, or ye can come up . . ."

The front bell over the door jingled distantly.

"Unless you need me, I think I'll stay in here awhile," I said.

"I'll be fine." Rosie and Hector hurried away, but she turned back a second later and brought me her key. "Never, ever, leave this room unlocked, even if ye just have tae go tae the toilet. Lock the door behind ye every time."

"Of course." I took the turquoise key. It was heavy and warm from Rosie's pocket.

"Come over tae the shop side when ye want tae," Rosie said before she turned to leave again.

I heard her footfalls up this side's stairs and then down the other side's, and the rumble of voices.

I spun the chair and looked at the shelves again.

"One bite at a time." I sighed.

Then I turned toward the wall of books, steadied myself, and said to their anxious bookish voices, "Bring it on."

EIGHT

I straightened one shelf of books. It wasn't easy to inspect the books, listen to their characters, *and* put them in some sort of order that wouldn't be too difficult to understand and use as a system for the entire shop. I came upon familiar authors like Defoe and Brontë, their characters' words talking in my head when I allowed them in, but there were others I'd never heard of. I spent way too much time reading and acquiring new voices.

I'd heard once about a Scottish writer named David Lyndsay, which was a pseudonym for a female writer, Mary Dods, a friend of Mary Shelley's. When I found a book *The Haunted Women* by David *Lindsay* on the shelf I grabbed it without noticing the difference in the spelling of the last name. I opened the book to a random page and read without context. Though I'm not sure when I'll go back and read the whole book, I did catch one character's words.

"Why should a married woman be a parasite?" she said.

I closed the book immediately, but the words would be in

my head forever and they'd find *their* perfect moments to speak to me. Once it had been read, there was no going back.

It was just a weird mind trick, some sort of photographic memory of printed words, mostly dialogue. I didn't have a photographic memory with anything else. I had a difficult time remembering birthdays. Numbers weren't my thing at all.

Sometimes it was a huge distraction. I could have entire conversations with the characters in my head. I could see them in my mind's eye almost as clearly as if they were standing in front of me. Before I learned to control the quirk, people thought I was prone to zoning out. Or worse.

My dad knew about the bookish voices; he's the one who named them. He'd been the one to pick me up from school when I was in fifth grade the day my teacher thought I'd had some sort of seizure. She'd tried to get my attention for "a good two minutes" but I was glassy-eyed and seemed incapable of responding. I knew enough not to tell her that I was ignoring her because I was having a conversation in my head with Henry from *The Boxcar Children,* a book that she'd read aloud from just that morning, and it was much more interesting than anything she had to say. Henry wasn't my first visitor, but he was the one who'd stuck around the longest up to that point, and he'd been the one to give me away.

Dad and I sat on the tailgate of his pickup in the school parking lot, me in a pink dress I wore just to spite Melanie Beamer because she'd told me, very meanly, that redheads should never wear pink, and Dad in his dirty overalls and mud-caked boots.

I can't remember exactly what I said, but after I insisted that I didn't need to go to the doctor I tried to explain how books talked to me. He said I just had a good imagination and a good memory. But I knew even at that young age that it was more than that, that the voices were so loud and clear, much more than I thought they were for the likes of Melanie Beamer and my other classmates. I'd read or heard about them once, and then there they were, like I had a stage in my head and they lurked behind the curtains ready to contribute when and how *they* thought it necessary. I told Dad I'd been able to find books I thought had been lost because in my head I'd asked the characters where they were hiding, and they'd told me, using their own words of course.

I remember the curiosity in his eyes as he peered down at me, the wrinkles around his eyes and his eyelashes dusted with dirt from his crops. He blinked and seemed to think a good long moment before he said the perfect words.

"Del-baby girl, I believe everything you're telling me, and I have an idea. It's okay to let them talk to you, but you gotta push them away when someone out here in the real world needs to talk. You just gotta. Nothing's wrong with you. Nothing at all, but you'll have to figure it out. We all have things we have to figure out. It comes with livin'. You're lucky that you know your thing now. You can start working on it right this minute."

There was no waver to his voice, no question, no doubt.

"Do we have to tell Mom?" I said.

"Not if you don't want to. In fact, we'll keep your bookish voices just between the two of us for as long as we can get away with it."

As far as I knew, my mom still didn't know about my secret. I had never been able to get the voices completely under control, but for the most part I had them where I wanted them. No one else had ever thought I was having a seizure. The few moments I'd zoned out briefly around my parents over the years,

Dad had looked at me with a question in his eyes. I'd just nod at him and he'd nod back. And then we moved on.

By the time I locked up the warehouse, and then told Rosie good-bye for the evening, I was starving. I went to Elias's favorite take-away spot, and ordered fish and chips with brown sauce, which was a vinegary liquid that I poured on the fried fish and potato pieces. I enjoyed my dinner as I sat on a red stool next to the front window of the small shop and people-watched. I concluded that there must be no "typical" Edinburghian. The city was populated by all ages, all races, and from the bits and pieces I heard more than a few different languages, though mostly Scottish-accented English.

Back in my room, I hadn't realized I was still tired but I fell asleep easily. However, I didn't rest well. Images of all the people I'd met and all the valuable items I'd seen throughout the day played like a frantic slide show through my dreams. It was exhausting, and I was relieved to wake up and get to work the next day.

My first coherent thought of the morning was that I needed a place to live. Edwin was paying for the hotel, but I was going to have to find something more permanent soon. I wanted to. As I pulled open the door of the bookshop I decided I would ask everyone for suggestions regarding an apartment. Or, as they called it, a flat.

But the look on Rosie's face made me forget my need for a home. She stood behind the desk as Hector sat on it and looked up at her. She was on the verge of some horrible emotion, but I didn't know if it would show itself with tears or a scream.

"Oh, no, what's wrong?" I hurried to the desk.

" 'Tis devastating news," she said as she deflated into the chair behind her.

"What is it?" My breath caught as my throat tightened.

"Jenny's gone." She looked at the mobile phone clutched tightly in her hand, and then at me. "Gone. Dead."

"Jenny? Edwin's sister, Jenny?"

"Aye. Gone."

"Oh, no," I said.

Rosie was correct. The news was devastating. I could have used my own chair, but I thought I should attend to Rosie first.

"I'm so sorry. You okay?" I said.

"I dinna ken, Delaney."

"Tea. How about I go get some tea? Or coffee?"

"Tea, coffee," she said as if she wasn't sure what the words meant.

The bell jingled as Hamlet came through the door.

"Oh, no. What is it?" he said the second he saw our faces.

———

Edwin sat in the inexpensive office chair on the other side of the desk, my desk as of yesterday. His attention was focused on nothing specific, his demeanor grim with his arms folded in front of his chest. Despite the current dire circumstances, I couldn't help but notice that he belonged in that room. It might have been made by him, but it was also made *for* him. All the items, all the books, the mess—for some reason his dapper figure belonged among the attic-like mishmash.

Not long after Hamlet had arrived at the shop, Edwin had come through the front door too, his eyes tight and too wide and shiny with despair and grief. He'd called Rosie on his way in to let her know that Jenny was dead, asking her to gather both Hamlet and me so he could share the details with us all together. We followed him to the warehouse, because that's where he wanted to go.

We set up three folding chairs on the other side of the desk and sat patiently while he gathered himself the best he could.

"It's the worst news possible, I suppose. When a loved one dies," he began.

"What happened, Edwin?" Rosie said.

"Jenny was killed, brutally. I found her."

The words were not softened by Edwin's pleasant accent. For a moment I thought it a terrible shame that the accent, as beautiful and lyrical as it was, could do nothing to make horrible news less horrible. My stomach plummeted and my throat tightened again. Even though I hadn't met Jenny, how could hearing such news not be devastating?

"No!" Rosie exclaimed. Tears finally flowed down her cheeks, the flood released. "Oh, Edwin."

Hamlet sat forward and leaned his elbows on his knees. From the profile view, I saw his face lose color so quickly I wondered if he might faint.

Keeping a slice of attention on both Rosie and Hamlet, in case either of them went down, I said, "I'm so very sorry, Edwin."

"It was an awful shock, as you can imagine. Yesterday, after I dropped you off, Delaney, I stopped by Jenny's flat. She didn't open the door. I have my own key, but I never tried tae use it before yesterday. But the door wasn't locked. I could just walk in." He blinked and continued. "It was such a mess. Though Jenny wasn't the best at keeping her flat tidy, this was much worse. At first, it didn't register that there might be a problem. I just wanted tae find Jenny. As I stepped over and around tumbled and strewn items, panic set in, and then I finally found her." Edwin paused again. He gathered his resolve and finished. "She was half in the hallway, half out of it toward her small kitchen. She'd been hit on the head, I believe. There was blood, and worse."

"Oh, no, no, no, this cannae be," Rosie said.

Hamlet was still silent, still leaning forward, but his cheeks weren't as alabaster as they had been a moment ago. Now there were small red splotches over them.

"I'm afraid there's more." Edwin sat up straight and took a deep breath in through his nose. "This is not the tragic part, but a part I'm afraid that all of us will have to deal with one way or another, particularly if the motive for my sister's murder was theft."

Hamlet sat up and with a weak voice said, "G'on."

"The Folio was gone. In fact"—he swallowed—"the day before yesterday she and I argued about it. She wouldn't tell me where she'd put it."

"I dinnae understand. Why wouldnae she tell ye?" Rosie said.

"Because she was angry with me. She said I was expecting too much from her, that she didn't want tae be such a part of the business, of my life. I insisted though. I kept telling her it would be good for her."

"Oh," Rosie said knowingly.

"Maybe . . ." Hamlet began, but he stopped himself quickly.

"What, Hamlet?" Edwin asked.

"I'm sorry, Edwin, the thought I had is unfair."

"I know what you were thinking, Hamlet, and on the contrary, your line of thinking is not only *not* unfair, it could be a real possibility," Edwin said.

I didn't know where the tissue came from that Rosie held to

her nose. She whimpered once. I wasn't sure what the noise meant. Was she reacting to whatever code Hamlet and Edwin were speaking in?

Edwin continued, directing his words to me. "Delaney, as I explained tae you, Jenny had struggled with dark demons, drugs. The possibly correct assumption that Hamlet might have made is that perhaps Jenny used the Folio tae barter for drugs. Perhaps she used it tae her own advantage even though I never would have guessed she was savvy enough tae do such a thing. Certainly, the people in her life who were the bad influences could never have understood what tae do with it."

I nodded as I had a memory of reading the First Folio in college—a copy made by modern means. I'd been one of the few people in my class who'd enjoyed what I'd come to call "Shakespeare in the Raw." My heart broke for Edwin, Rosie, Hamlet, and Jenny, but it also ached some at the idea that there might be an original Folio out there in the world being used as currency for drug transactions. The entire situation was a huge tragedy or dark comedy, and Shakespeare's characters didn't lack for either sort of commentary. At the moment I was working hard to keep their voices at bay. I neither wanted nor needed the distraction.

"I see," I said. "I'm just so sorry."

"I've shocked you in many ways," Edwin said. "I'm the one who's sorry. This was not what you bargained for when you decided tae come tae Edinburgh."

I shook my head. "No. What can we do to help you?"

"Thank you, Delaney, and I'm not sure. There will be an investigation into her murder, of course. I need tae make appropriate arrangements for Jenny, but I'm not sure when the police will release her body. I have many questions, but I know there will be an autopsy, and . . ." Edwin stopped abruptly.

"What is it?" Rosie asked.

Edwin's mouth became straight and tight. He sat forward and drummed his fingers on the desk as he stared off at nothing in particular to his left. He looked at us all again.

"I didn't tell the police about the Folio. I didn't mention it, and I don't want tae. I'm not going tae," Edwin said. "If the police come and talk tae any of you, please be honest with them. I would never ask anyone tae lie for me or for Jenny, but I thought you should all be aware that I will not be forthcoming in telling the police about the Folio."

I looked around. "Why?"

"I purchased it from Birk, as you know," Edwin said. I nodded. "His story is . . . less than believable regarding how he acquired it. He's a friend, the auctions are important. That's too arrogant a point on the matter, but I feel I need tae protect friends at this time. Maybe I'll tell the police, later when I have more information."

An image of Monroe Ross with his black eye formed in my mind. Did Edwin want to protect his Fleshmarket Batch friends, or perhaps look more closely at them without police interference? Neither Hamlet nor Rosie seemed to care that Edwin wasn't going to tell the police about the Folio, so I didn't push to understand. For now.

Hamlet shifted in his chair and everyone, including Hector, looked at him. I thought maybe he was going to express some of the same doubt I was having, but that wasn't it.

"I . . . uh, I was at her flat day before yesterday, Edwin. I was there. I think I should tell the police that. Don't you?"

"Why were you there?" Edwin asked.

"I stopped by tae check on her. Rosie mentioned that ye were attending to family matters that day, so I wondered if it was something tae do with Jenny. I thought I should check on her."

"How was she?" Edwin asked.

"She was fine," Hamlet said. "She was polite, but I got the impression that she didn't want me tae stick around for very long."

"She was in good shape?" Edwin had straightened even more and leaned forward so that his long arms reached almost the whole way across the desk.

"Aye, fine."

"How was the state of her place? Was it messy at all?"

"No more than usual. Nothing had been destroyed or torn up, if that's what you mean. I don't know where she kept the Folio and I didn't ask about it, but I didn't see it sitting out anywhere."

"Did she seem like she was worried about anything?"

Hamlet thought a long moment. "No, not worried really, but like I said I could tell she didn't want me tae stay. It was as if she had plans."

"And she didn't mention what those plans were?"

"No, and I didn't ask."

Edwin fell into thought again, his fingers drumming the desk, but more slowly and lightly now. Shortly, he looked at Hamlet again.

"Thank you for being concerned about her. Thank you for checking on her."

Hamlet nodded. "Of course. She was a friend, Edwin." Hamlet's voice faltered with emotion. He cleared his throat and the muscle in the back of his jaw pulsed.

I wanted to understand their relationships and how someone like Hamlet, someone so young, had befriended Edwin's
sister. Was working at The Cracked Spine really like becoming
part of a family? I'd felt some of that, of course, but I didn't
think Jenny had ever worked at the bookshop. And, even Edwin's *younger* sister would not have been youthful enough to
spend lots of time with a university student. I was curious. Unfortunately, now wasn't the right moment to ask about the
makeup of their relationships.

"She was a good person," Edwin said, "who made some terrible choices and sometimes couldn't find her way out of those
choices." Edwin's voice cracked. He put his hand up. "I'd like tae
know what happened tae my sister and if the Folio was somehow
responsible. I'm not going tae tell the police about it yet, but, aye,
Hamlet, I do think you should tell the police you stopped by
tae see her, and let them know she was fine at the time."

"Edwin," Rosie said, "the Folio wasnae the reason Jenny was
killed. If it was stolen then she must have told someone aboot
it. She knew she was supposed tae keep it a secret. It was not
the Folio's fault, Edwin."

She was truly saying that it wasn't Edwin's fault. She was
correct, of course, but her words weren't as comforting as she
probably hoped they were.

Edwin sat in silent thought for a long moment before he
said, "We shall take the day off today. The shop will be closed."
He looked at me and his eyebrows came together. "I'm sorry
about this bad beginning."

"Just let me know what I can do for you, Edwin."

"I will," Edwin said. He reached into his pocket and pulled
out a business card. "Hamlet, here is the contact information
for one of the inspectors that came tae the flat."

"I'll ring right away," Hamlet said as he reached for the card.

But Edwin pulled it back slightly. "Hamlet, I'm not going tae ask you not tae mention the Folio, but I would like tae ask you tae think about not mentioning it. You must do what you think is right, of course, and I hope you know me well enough tae know that your job does not depend upon that choice, but it is a . . . delicate situation, at best."

"Potentially illegal at worst," Rosie jumped in. "Hamlet, dinnae mention the Folio. We'll talk tae the police aboot it later if we feel like we need tae. Edwin paid for the Folio, but we still dinnae ken exactly where it came from. Or at least we have questions. Aye?"

I did not sense that Edwin and Rosie were strong-arming Hamlet. In fact, Edwin seemed to be treading lightly, and Rosie probably didn't know how to tread any way but her way, which was surely and heavily. Still, I didn't like the way they were thinking. It seemed so obvious to me—the police could potentially find Jenny's killer much more quickly if they knew a valuable item might have been part of the reason she was killed. If owning the Folio was illegal in the first place, perhaps the police would somehow overlook that detail with the greater picture of finding a killer in mind. Or, maybe not.

"I won't mention it unless they ask about it specifically," Hamlet said. "If they ask about it, that means they know about it. If they know about it, they might have already figured out that it could have had something tae do with Jenny's death. But I won't bring it up myself."

"Guid," Rosie said. Through her contributions to the conversation, she continued to cry, and tears were still rolling down her cheeks, but her focus had moved to the matter of the moment. A part of her was grieving, but another part of her was taking care of the family still living.

"Thank you," Edwin said. He took a deep breath and released it slowly. The sadness and stress still showed in the corners of his eyes and the pull of his mouth, but a tiny sense of relief was there too. One step at a time.

"I'm so sorry, everyone," I said. "I can tell you're all very close and this is a painful day. Would you like for me to leave the room so you can further discuss things in private?"

They all looked at me with genuine surprise, which in turn surprised me.

"Delaney, you are now a part of The Cracked Spine. You might not have the history we all have, but I picked you because I knew you would be a perfect fit. You're here and we're happy you're here. I'm sorry tae have such a tragedy be a part of your first few days, but we will get through this, and we will somehow come out stronger in the end."

Hector, being smarter than your average dog, stood from Rosie's lap and hopped to mine. He relaxed into a flat, brown, well-brushed mop.

"See, even Hector kens," Rosie said with a sniff.

I nodded and spent a moment hoping the adventure I had, indeed, found hadn't just become more dangerous than bold.

NINE

"There ye be," Elias said as he opened the cab back-passenger door and nodded toward the bookshop. "How's awthing . . . e-very-thing going?"

"Little rough at the shop. I'm not working today," I said.

"Lass, have ye been sacked awready?" Elias asked.

"No, we're closing for the day. There was a tragedy in the owner's family."

"I'm sae sairy," Elias said as he glanced at the store's darkened window that was still cluttered with books.

"Me too." I looked at the window too. I was the last one out. Edwin left right after he shared the news. Hamlet, Rosie, and Hector (it was again difficult to give him back to Rosie) left shortly after Edwin. With the blue key, I locked the warehouse door, and with a normal key that Rosie gave me I locked the front door. For a long few moments, I stood outside the shop wondering what to do. I'd wanted to stay there by myself and work, but Edwin had insisted that none of us work today. Finally, I found the card Elias had given me. He answered after the first ring and said he would be there to get me quickly. I thought that's what he said. I didn't quite catch the word he used for quickly.

"Hap in then," Elias said.

When I was in the familiar backseat, he leaned over and peered in the open window.

"What do ye say, denner with the Mrs.? I told her all about the fair and fiery lass from Kansas in America and she would sae love tae meet ye. She'll have denner-pieces ready by the time we get home."

I'd originally called him for a cab ride around town and maybe some direction on finding a flat, but it was close to noon and I was hungry. And, I was pretty sure that denner was the same thing I called lunch. Denner-pieces couldn't be too bad, could they?

"I hope she hasn't gone to too much trouble, but I would love to meet your wife."

"Braw!" Elias said. He said it with a smile, so I thought it was probably a happy exclamation. He hurried back to the other side and into the driver's seat.

"We dinnae live too far away, but it wouldnae be a short walk," Elias said as he started the cab.

We traveled west and then south a bit, through the building-packed downtown part of Edinburgh. I thought we'd passed some of the same buildings on the way to the shop two days earlier, but there were so many and there was so much traffic that I couldn't be sure. The modern still mixed with the old, in pleasant, interesting ways. I was still bothered and, frankly, confused by the vehicles on the left side of the road. My mind and the g-forces still fought against the reasoning of "that's just how it's done." At moments, I felt a queasy sickness because of it. I decided I shouldn't try to drive right away.

"There's the King's Theatre," Elias said as he slowed a few minutes later and pointed to our left. "Plays, pantomime. Aggie, that's me wife, she loves the theater. I'm nae much for it masel, but 'twas built in the early nineteen hundreds and I like the architecture."

The brown building stood out from the smaller shops around it. It wasn't a theater-in-the-round but looked like the perfect place to catch a little Shakespeare. Perhaps that was because the bard had been on my mind since yesterday.

Elias turned right at the theater, and the neighborhood transformed into a long row of small businesses followed by fairly narrow side-by-side houses.

"Most of these are guesthooses. Aggie and I have two and we rent them oot to veesitors. Some are permanent homes and they all have their awn wee gairdens. Aggie loves to putter in the gairden."

"Aggie's busy."

Elias laughed. "Aye, she's busier than anyone else I ken."

Elias pulled the cab into an open space next to the curb. I was surprised that there was only a little less traffic on this street than on the busier city streets we'd taken to get here.

"We're here then," he said. "Aggie and I hae the two end hooses and we have a wee cottage we live in behind them."

"It's perfect," I said.

Like the sign on the cab, there was a wooden hanging sign in the front garden space between the two connected houses that said: "McKenna Guesthouses."

"Follae me," Elias said.

I followed behind him as we made our way down a space that was bigger than a close, but not really an alley, that led to the back. You'd never know it from the street, but there were more houses back here. They were smaller and more cottage-like.

Elias opened the front screen door of the first cottage we came to. "Aggie, love, I'm home and I've brought the lass from Kansas in America."

"Good news, Elias. Bring her on back to the keetchen," a pleasant voice called from the back of the house.

"This way, Delaney," Elias said.

It was small—cozy, though not cramped, with plenty of windows to give the space a lit, warm feeling. We stepped directly into the living room, which was furnished with a small, well-used floral-print couch and chair, and a wall of filled bookshelves.

I gave the books a stern look. Not now. Not when I needed to make sure I was as polite as I could be.

A door was shut on the back wall of the room and a hall-way led to the right. As we stepped toward the hallway a woman leaned out from about halfway down and smiled.

"Hullo, Delaney," Aggie, I presumed, said as we stepped toward her and into the kitchen. "It is a pleasure tae meet ye. Welcome tae Edinburgh." She held up a mug as if to both greet and salute me.

Aggie was short and slightly plump; round but not heavy. Her gray hair was styled just like I remembered my grand-mother's had been styled. I had a flashback to when I was a child and I would go with my grandmother to the beauty parlor. Her "beautician" Clara always gave me a sucker and let me paint my own fingernails while Grandma stuck her head under the big-headed, loud dryer. Aggie wore a full apron that said, "Kiss the cook only if you plan on doing the dishes efterhaund."

"Nice to meet you too, Aggie," I said.

"Come, come sit and we'll have some denner. We're not

going tae either kidnap or poison ye, I promise. When Elias told me about his enthusiastic invitation, I thought ye might be right tae call the police." Aggie smiled warmly at her husband and then at me. "We're both happy tae welcome ye tae Scotland and tae our home."

The kitchen was long and narrow, but decked out in beautiful stainless steel appliances, white cabinets, and gray countertops. At the far end was a cubbyhole with a stacked washer and dryer, but at the end we were closest to, there were a round table and chairs that reminded me of my mom's country kitchen back in Kansas.

"You're very kind," I said as Aggie directed me to a chair.

"Not at all," Aggie said as she put a plate with a roll and what reminded me of pulled pork on the table in front of me. A denner-piece must be a sandwich. "Ye are an adventurous young woman. I cannae imagine picking up and moving my life tae a completely different country. Did ye ken anyone here?"

"No one. Do you know much about Kansas?" I said.

"Not really," Aggie said as she took a seat to my right. "Just what I learnt from the movie with Dorothy and Toto. Farms and twisters."

Elias sat on my left. He removed his hat and put it on the window seat behind him. A tattoo extended down from his short sleeve. I thought it was some sort of Celtic symbol, but I wasn't sure.

"About right. Kansas is a pretty place—lots of wide-open spaces. And the people there are wonderful. You'll never find better people no matter where or how far you search, but it's not the most exciting place. I admit, before now I haven't been all that adventurous but I was looking for an adventure. And I can't imagine a better place to find one than Scotland."

"Ye may be right," Aggie said.

I thought I saw the edge of a tattoo on her arm too, but it was well covered by her sleeve and I didn't want to stare.

Using a fork, I took a bite of the meat. "This is delicious."

"It's an easy denner and one of Elias's favorites. Actually, his true favorite is our very own haggis, but I didn't want tae spring that on ye just yet."

"I'd like to try it. Someday." I smiled.

She continued an easy pause later. "How do ye like the bookshop? Will ye enjoy your coworkers?"

"I love the shop and I think I'll feel the same about the coworkers. So far, they've been wonderful and welcoming."

"Aggie, love, Delaney was telling me that they had a tragedy," Elias chimed in.

"At the shop?"

"The owner's sister was killed. Brutally," I said.

Elias and Aggie had put together their own denner-pieces and they both held them halfway in the air, as they blinked at what I'd said.

Aggie put hers back down first. "Murdered?"

"Yes."

"That *is* a terrible tragedy," she said. She glanced at Elias as they shared a look of concern.

"My boss's name is Edwin MacAlister. His sister's name was Jenny. I believe she had some issues with drug addiction."

"I think I heard about that this mornin' on the television," Aggie said. "I'm good with names. I think I mynd the name Jennifer MacAlister. Aye, they said they were investigating. I read that her building was located in a rougher neighborhood."

"I wish I knew what happened," I said, briefly letting my

mind wonder as to why someone with so much money lived in a rougher neighborhood. But then I realized that Jenny might not have had the same sort of money that Edwin had. If that were true, the inequality might explain some of their difficulties.

"I suppose we'll hear more as time goes on," Aggie said.

"If she lived a less than desirable part o' toun . . . ," Elias said. "Ye mentioned drug problems?"

"Yes."

Elias and Aggie nodded knowingly.

"I'm sairy for yer boss," Aggie said.

Before I could stop myself, I said, "Elias, is there any chance your cab is available for hire this afternoon? I'd like to see some more of Edinburgh, including the place where Jenny lived. I'm curious. And, I need to find an apart . . . a flat of my own too."

Elias and Aggie exchanged looks again, but I couldn't quite read them.

"My cab and I are baith available, and if ye're going tae explore that particular area, I'd like tae be the one tae show it tae ye," Elias said. He looked at Aggie once again. She nodded. "My love and I have something else we'd like tae talk tae ye about."

"Okay."

"We have a locus . . . a place"—he nodded back toward the other side of the house—"next door that we'd like for ye tae consider."

"I don't understand," I said.

"Delaney," Aggie said as she put her hand over mine, "we have an identical cottage behind our guesthoose next door.

Ye couldnae see it, but ye get tae it by walking around this one. We dinnae buy these guesthooses. My family did and now they are mine and Elias's. We are fortunate tae have them and the cottages behind them. We dinnae live in a fancy hoose, and ye wouldnae either, but our home is plenty for us. We thought ye might enjoy a wee one of yer own."

"I, uh . . ." I had no idea what to say.

"Just have a leuk at it first," Aggie said. "It's simple, we leuk for the right person tae live in the cottage. It became available a couple of months ago. We have never ignored our instincts on this and we've never been wrong. We'd be honored if ye would consider looking at the hoose."

"I, uh," I said again. I was struck at least incoherent if not speechless.

Elias and Aggie looked at me, their smiles hesitant but warm. They didn't strike me as lonely people, so I didn't think they were just looking for someone to talk to. Maybe it was exactly as Aggie had said. Maybe they listened to their guts about who they wanted to live in the space next to them. Their gut instincts weren't off. I was tidy and fairly quiet, bookishly nerdy, and I minded my own business, or spent my time talking to the bookish voices in my head. They weren't noisy conversations.

"I'd love to take a look," I said.

"Oh, good," Elias said as Aggie's smile turned less hesitant and much more confident. If she wanted to cook me in the oven, it looked like I was hers for the basting.

We commenced gobbling up the rest of the sandwiches. It was an unexpected and shared moment of excitement, a moment I would look back on many times and realize that it was then, as we sat around the table and hurried to eat the sandwiches, that we lost the wary politeness that was reserved for strangers. After you gobble lunch together, something very important is bound to change.

After the dishes were done, Aggie led us out and around their cottage. And, true to her word, there was another one on the other side of it and directly behind the other guesthouse. It was almost identical to the one I'd just had lunch in, though maybe even a little better taken care of on the outside. The furniture in the living room wasn't as used, though it still had a country flair. The door on the back wall of the living room was open wide in this one; it led to the bedroom, which turned out to be surprisingly larger than I would have expected, furnished with a wrought iron–framed queen-sized bed, a dresser, an armoire, and a reading corner with a tall lamp and a cushioned, old leather chair and ottoman.

The kitchen was in the same spot but it wasn't as new as the other one, and that was fine.

"This cooker is an auld one, but I think it makes cakes better than mine does," Aggie said as she pointed at the old white appliance that I would have called a range.

"It's great," I said. "Really great."

Aggie and Elias smiled at each other.

"This way then," Aggie said.

Farther down the hall from the kitchen we found the bathroom. It was bland but also bigger than I would have guessed.

"And this"—Aggie pointed up and above the doorway that was just past the bathroom and led to a small shared courtyard between the two houses—"is your electricity. Ye have to put clinkers, money, in it."

I looked at the strange wired contraption that reminded me

of something from an old black-and-white movie about Thomas Edison, blinked, and again said, "I don't understand."

"Aye, ye have to feed it coins and it will power the hoose. It's an efficient system and should only cost ye about ten pounds a month."

"Really?"

"Aye. Ye do need tae pay attention tae it though. Ye dinnae want tae be in the middle o' something and be caught without power."

"I see." I'd never heard of anything like it, but I thought I'd be able to handle it okay.

"Come out tae the courtyard," Elias said. He stepped around Aggie and me and pushed open the back door that faced the other cottage's back door.

There was a wooden deck and a matching fence, both looking as if they'd only recently been restained. The deck was only big enough to hold a small table and four wicker chairs with well-used pillow seats. There were also about twenty large flowerpots along the border, making the entire deck one large container garden.

"I . . . ," I began. "It's really perfect. I love it."

Elias's and Aggie's faces lit with their warmest smiles yet.

"Byous! Wonderful," Aggie said.

"How much?" I asked.

They looked at each other again and then back at me. I was afraid they would say "nothing." Unfortunately, that would have forced me to walk away from this perfect opportunity.

Elias quoted a rent amount that was almost too good to be true, but just almost, and enough to keep me on the line.

"I'll take it!"

"Braw!" Elias said.

I looked around at my new home and neighbors and another sense of rightness washed over me.

So far, not too bad on tackling the adventure. If only my people back in Kansas could see me now.

TEN

I hadn't unpacked much at the hotel so it was easy to repack my bags and take them down to Elias's cab out front. The small hotel lobby was full of visitors from Sweden who were checking in. It was long past checkout time and I didn't want Edwin to pay for that night, so I quickly gave the clerk my credit card and then scooted out of the way.

Elias reloaded my bags into his cab, and directed me to the front passenger seat, and then we set off on a guided tour of Edinburgh. There was so much to see that it was difficult to digest much of anything, but the castle on the hill made a good reference point. I didn't think I could get too lost if I could spot the castle and make my way from there.

He drove up the curved hill on the other side of the hotel, past a bagel shop, a cigar shop, a place with a sign that said, "The Cadies and Witchery Tours," a whisky shop, and even a pizza restaurant that was sit-down and dine-in, not just take-away. At the top of the hill he turned left. A short moment later we were conveniently stopped at a traffic light.

"This is the Royal Mile," he said as he nodded to the cross

street in front of us. "Up tae yer left, ye could get tae the castle. Go right and ye'll get tae Holyrood Palace and the gantin—I mean *ugly* parliament biggin, uh, building. 'Tis an eyesore, let me tell ye."

"But everything else is beautiful!" I said as I looked as many directions as I could.

Mostly, it was old architecture up and down the long sloped road. Buildings made of brown and gray stone and adorned with tall windows and peaked and corniced roof lines. The buildings were tall, and they all had small businesses on their bottom floors—restaurants, souvenir shops, pubs, their upper floors holding what I determined were flats, business offices, art galleries, and government offices.

"A mile, huh?" I said.

"A wee bit more than a mile," Elias said. "Almost another two hundred of yer American yards. Ye'll want to explore it all. Venture doon the closes—uh, the *alleys,* I believe ye call them."

I spotted a couple of the closes, the narrow passageways, each of which had a sign above it.

"I've heard about the closes. Do you know where the Flesh-market Close is located?"

" 'Tis somewhere directly oof the Royal Mile, but I'm nae sure which direction. Aggie would ken exactly."

"Maybe I'll make a day of exploring some of them this weekend."

"Aye. Ye'll enjoy every meenit of it. I have one more place to show ye afore we take a leuk at the flat where that poor lass was killed," Elias said.

Elias crossed through the intersection and then took a couple of left turns.

"Ah, a spot in front," Elias said. "I'll just stop a minute, but ye'll want tae spend some time in there later, I'm shuir, particularly since ye're working at a bookshop and used tae work at a museum. There, have a leuk."

The building was tall, formed with some of the same sturdy stones I'd already seen. It looked like a miniature castle with a turret atop the front corner and old double wooden doors at the bottom.

"It's wonderful. What is it?"

" 'Tis the Writers' Museum. Scotland is proud of those inside. Robert Burns, Sir Walter Scott, and Robert Louis Stevenson."

"Ooooh," I exclaimed, my hand involuntarily going to the door handle even though I knew there wouldn't be time to tour it today.

As I looked wide-eyed at the building, I soaked in the entirety of the moment—a museum devoted to Burns, Scott, and Stevenson; could there be a better potential heaven on earth? I closed my eyes and decided to let them into my head for a second. Their voices were clear and sure.

"The best laid schemes 'o mice and men," Robert Burns said.

"Oh, what a tangled web we weave, when first we practice to deceive," said Sir Walter.

"I travel not to go anywhere, but to go. I travel for travel's sake. The great affair is to move," said Robert Louis Stevenson.

"Delaney, lass?" Elias said as he put his hand on my arm.

My eyes popped open. "Oh, I'm sorry. I was . . . taking it all in." I could have listened to them for hours. Some other day.

"S'aw right. I was saying, ye do ken that Edinburgh is a national city of books or some such thing?"

"I do." I smiled at Elias. "I think there are over fifty book-shops in Edinburgh. That in itself is amazing."

"Aye, 'tis. I didn't ken that. Fifty?" Elias frowned. "Dinnae tell Aggie. If she ken there were that many, I expect I'd have tae take her tae each and every one."

I laughed. "Deal." I looked back out at the museum. "I can't wait to visit this museum but I'll need a full day at least." And I'd need to do this tour on my own.

"Aye."

I sighed and relaxed into the seat. "Could we go to Jenny's now?"

"I s'pose."

"You'd rather not, huh?"

Elias shrugged. "All has been gaun well. I'm superstitious enough not tae want tae test our guid luck. Driving tae leuk at a murder victim's home might play havoc with our guid fortune. Scots are a freitie bunch."

"Freitie?"

"Superstitious," Elias said.

"We'll make it quick?" I said hopefully. I wasn't superstitious in the strictest sense of the word, but I had a few rituals. I also didn't sense that there would be anything wrong or even par-ticularly dangerous about driving past Jenny's flat.

Elias shot me a patient smile. "Awright."

The drive was slow because the traffic became too thick to zip anywhere. I took the opportunity to ask a question that had been on my mind since the morning.

"Elias, what would I do if I wanted to find addresses of people who live in Edinburgh? Are there phone books?"

"Who do ye want tae find?"

"Some friends of my boss's."

"Ye cannae ask him?"

"No, not right now."

"If ye'd like, ye can give me the names and I can ask Aggie tae help. She kens how tae find people."

"Thanks," I said, without committing one way or the other. I wanted the addresses of the members of Fleshmarket. I didn't think I should give their names to anyone else, at least until I understood the secrecy within the group better.

"Ah, we're here. The lass lived a bit on the outskirts of the city," Elias said as we came upon an area with less traffic that reminded me more of a residential neighborhood in Wichita than part of an old historical town. "Up forrit, there is the building that was listed as the address."

The building was much more modern than what I'd seen in the city proper. It was five stories and made of white, light brown, and dark brown brick. It reminded me of a bigger version of the 1970s apartment buildings back in Kansas. Each flat had a wrought iron and thin plywood-paneled fence around a small balcony. The surrounding neighborhood was somewhat bleak but not dirty.

"It looks pretty safe to me," I said.

Elias looked around. He didn't seem all that concerned, but he was very aware.

"We're probably awright during the day."

From the outside, of course, there was no way to tell which flat had been Jenny's. I was surprised that I was suddenly overwhelmed with the need to know exactly which one was hers, to connect with her that way.

"Elias, could you wait here a second? I'd like to go inside and talk to the landlord."

"Hou? Now, why would ye want tae do something like that?"

he said. He lifted his hat and then put it back on his head, causing the tufts of gray hair to fluff.

I shrugged. "I could pretend to be looking for a flat."

"Ye think the murder victim's flat will be available?" Elias said, his voice high with disbelief.

"No, not really, but maybe I could just get a feel for the place, a sense of Jenny."

"I dinnae understand, lass," Elias said.

"I'm not sure I do either," I said as I looked back at the building. "I'd just like to go inside for a minute. I'm sure it's safe. It's daylight, and whoever murdered Jenny isn't lurking nearby." Well, if they were, still, it *was* daylight.

Elias sighed. "Let me come in with ye."

"No, it will be more awkward with two of us. It'll be okay with just me. This won't be dangerous. Look, there's someone coming out of the building right now."

An old woman cloaked in a frayed rain jacket and a plastic head scarf exited the front doors. She moved as if she was irritated about something, quick but labored steps down the walkway, directly toward us. I watched her but I didn't think she noticed us until she was almost directly upon the cab.

"Och, what are ye doin' just sittin' there?" she said as her eyes landed on mine.

"Sorry, I was just wondering . . ." I began.

"Spit it oot."

"I was just wondering if this was where the woman was murdered."

"Do ye ken how tae read?"

"Yes."

"Are ye civilized enough tae get the newspaper?"

"Yes," I said, keeping out the details of why I didn't have one of my own yet.

"Then ye can read aboot it in the paper like civilized people do. People have been comin' 'round ere all day. I'm tired of it."

Elias's cab was the only vehicle in the area that could potentially contain curious stalkers. I looked around, but didn't see any other suspicious characters.

"Weel, they were all mostly here this morning," she said with a click of her teeth.

"Did you know the victim?" I asked.

She looked at me with hard eyes, as if she couldn't believe I would ask such a question. I remained silent, but my toes curled a little.

A moment later her eyes softened and lit with amusement. It was kind of creepy.

"Aye, I ken the hiely wumman," she said. "I wilnae sae she deserved what she got, but it wasnae a big surprise."

I wasn't sure what she meant, but I forged on, not wanting to miss my chance. "Why wasn't it a surprise?"

"Pretendin' tae be something she wasna. Living here instead of some place for rich people, like her brother." The old woman blinked and withered. "I shouldnae be sain such things. Now go on, get yerselves oot of here. There's nothing tae see." She turned abruptly and walked away, her steps slower but no less determined.

"There ye have it, I s'pose," Elias said.

"What is hiely?"

"Snooty."

"Please, just give me a second, Elias," I said as I opened the door and hurried out of the cab. I closed the door and leaned into the open window. "I promise I'll be fine. I'm just going inside for a minute. I won't go into anyone's place. I'll just knock on the landlord's door."

"Gracious, lass, the thought that ye might do such a thing hadnae even occurred tae me. I think I should come in with ye."

"No, it will be better this way, I promise. I'll be right back."

Elias looked at me a long moment.

"I won't do anything dangerous, Elias. I promise."

"Aggie will have my hide, but go on. Make it quick."

"Thanks."

I hurried up the walkway and opened the building door. There was no security, either in the form of a guard or a simple buzzer. I could just walk directly inside.

The entryway and attached hallway were both clean. The walls were beige and the carpets brown, the colors consistent with the outside brick colors. There weren't any strange smells and it was so quiet. No screaming babies or adults, no loud music, nothing. There was a faint scent of disinfectant, which wasn't unpleasant.

The landlord's flat was easy to find. It was the second one on my left and it had a sign posted on the door that said, "Manager."

I hesitated and thought about the story I was going to tell. After running it through my mind quickly a couple of times, I decided I could easily handle it.

I knocked.

There was no answer, so I knocked again. Still, no answer.

I peered down the hallway. There were ten doors on each side. I'd counted five stories. Fifty flats?

Nothing seemed out of place on this floor. I didn't see any

sign that this building had recently been the scene of a horrible murder. There was no crime scene tape fluttering outside a door.

For a moment I thought about checking out the other floors, but if I was gone too long, I knew Elias would come searching for me. I didn't want to worry him more than I already had. Besides, I shouldn't be roaming around a place I was unfamiliar with anyway. No matter how much I wanted to.

I turned away from the manager's door.

"Need something?" a voice said from behind me.

I gasped at the sudden and gruff voice.

"Sairy," the man in his underwear and robe said. He hadn't bothered to tie the robe closed.

He stood in the open doorway of the flat that had been on my right and behind me as I'd been looking down the long hallway. He must have had the quietest door in all of Edinburgh. I hadn't heard a squeak or even a slight whistle of air movement.

"Oh. Yes, I was looking for the manager," I said in my best recover voice.

"He's nae around much." He pulled the ties of the robe forward and closed the show. He wasn't old but he was at the far end of middle age with uneven salt-and-pepper hair, a matching short and scraggly beard, and heavily sagging eyes.

"I see. Well, I can stop by another time. When do you think would be all right?"

He shrugged.

"Do you know if the building has any available flats?" I forged on.

"Ye're from the United States, are ye?"

"I am. I'll be staying awhile."

He nodded, and the eyes above the heavy sags squinted.

"Aye, there are plenty of available flats, but I'd recommend ye find another place. There are better places."

"I need cheap."

He shrugged again. "Ye'll get cheap here, but spend a wee bit more and get something a wee bit better. Just by the looks of ye, if ye were my daughter I wouldnae want ye living here."

"Why?"

He shrugged again, but didn't say anything.

"Okay, well, thank you," I said after the silence had gone on too long.

"Ye're welcome. Have a lovely evenin'." He closed the door without making hardly any sound at all.

I stood in the hallway another moment and thought about what I should do next. The only thing that came to me was that I should rejoin Elias in the cab. I also concluded that if the owners of the building advertised their vacancies, they should include how achingly quiet the whole place seemed to be.

Which, frankly, was odd.

Quiet didn't usually go along with places that were troublesome, or places that new arrivals from America should stay away from.

Maybe I'd just hit it at a quiet time. Late afternoon was quiet time? It would be difficult to know without another visit, which I wasn't prepared to schedule at the moment, particularly as I glanced again at the robe man's door and sensed that he was watching me through the peephole.

I hurried out of the building.

Elias had gotten out of the cab and was pacing the sidewalk in front of it. When he turned and saw me, he looked relieved.

"How'd it go?" he asked.

"Fine. No problems at all."

"Did ye inquire aboot the flat?"

"No, the manager didn't answer, but it's not the sort of place I want to live anyway. The place I've got is much better," I teased.

" 'Tis a fact. Come along, lass, let's go home."

Elias held the door again and I scooted into the passenger seat. I held on tight and was glad there were seat belts in the front because the drive home was more like the drive from the airport; however, it was good to have a real home to hurry to.

ELEVEN

I stepped off the bus with a sense of satisfaction I hadn't felt in some time. Of course, the shop was kind of a straight shot from my new home, but Aggie had still painstakingly drawn me a map and written out the exact bus number I was to board. And, of course, she'd walked me to the bus and stepped up and onto it behind me. She'd said to the driver, "Ye will make sure this young lass gets off at the Grassmarket stop. She will probably be able tae handle the trip just fine, but it will be on yer shoulders if something happens tae her."

Aggie and Elias had discussed the best way for me to get to and from work. They decided I needed some independence—this was a good conclusion for them to come to because as I'd been listening to their discussion I'd been trying to figure out a way to remind them that I was a grown-up. They got there. Thankfully. And, the bus driver knew enough to just nod and say, "Aye, ma'am," to Aggie.

He glanced at me in his large observation mirror and we shared an understanding smile. He'd probably had lots of mothers step aboard and make sure their little ones were watched over carefully. The fact that I wasn't so little and that Aggie wasn't my mother didn't much matter.

It was a cool-ish day, and still cloudy. I thought it might rain today, not just drizzle, but I wasn't sure. Another typical Edinburgh day, according to what I'd heard. Except the temperature was probably a little higher than normal, at around sixty-five degrees, which Elias had explained was a little over eighteen degrees Celsius. I'd get used to the weather conversion much quicker than I would the driving on the wrong side of the road.

I was comfortable in nice slacks and a blouse. It seemed like appropriate working attire. Though I wasn't sure—in the three days I'd been at the shop it hadn't been discussed. It hadn't been a priority. I would ask Rosie today to make sure I was acceptable.

I'd had an issue with the warm water in my shower, but Elias said he'd fix it by the time I got home that evening. Other than that, I'd been extremely cozy in my new home. I'd e-mailed my parents late last night again, and I imagined their relief and happiness at all the good news. Of course, I left out the part about Jenny's murder. I'd share that with them later. Maybe. I needed to buy a new cell phone—a mobile phone with UK service—but I wasn't sure when that was going to happen.

I was at the shop by 7:30, and I thought I saw movement in the back as I peered in the window. It looked like Rosie was already there. As I pulled my face and hand away from the glass, another reflection directly next to me came into view.

"Oh," I said. "Excuse me. I didn't expect . . ."

"Pardon me," the man said.

I couldn't help myself. I had to inspect him. Surely, he was used to it by now. He was beautiful, but in a manly, Scottish kind of way. Had he perhaps stepped out of a book, a Scottish folktale? Had my imagination finally stepped over and into the abyss? Was I now hearing *and* seeing three-dimensional forms, more than just as part of a daydream?

He was probably over six feet tall, but not by much. His dark curly hair was a little longer in the back but not mullet-worthy. His face was friendly, but rough—that was probably the early morning shadow that most likely sprouted the second after he finished shaving. His eyes were cobalt blue—that was the word that came to my mind when I saw them. Cobalt.

He wore a red and blue kilt, but for some reason it took on a whole new meaning today. On him, a kilt wasn't just interesting, it was . . . *interesting*.

"Pardon me," he said again after he gave me my time of inspection. "I didn't mean tae sneak up on you."

"No problem," I said.

He maneuvered himself so that he could reach for the handle and pull the door open.

"You're not from here, are you?" he said. "This is a lovely bookshop. Please, go on in."

I stepped inside and he followed.

"It is a terrific place. I'm from America, but I'll be working here for a while."

"You're the one from Kansas in America? I forgot you were arriving this week. I'm Tom Fletcher. I own the pub a couple doors down. Delaney's Wee Pub." He extended his hand.

It was warm and strong.

"Hi, I'm Delaney. I mean, I'm Delaney too. Not your Delaney obviously. I mean, I saw the name of your pub and I thought it was a fun coincidence." I sighed.

Tom laughed. "They didn't tell me your name. They've just been calling you The American."

I didn't realize we were still holding hands. He smiled—almost sheepishly—and pulled his hand away. I had a sense that something pushed me from behind and wanted me to step closer to him. I resisted but it wasn't easy.

"I'm glad you're real," I said before I could stop the words from propelling out of my mouth.

He cocked his head and blinked and then smiled.

Silly American.

"I'm glad you're real too, Delaney. Please come by the pub anytime. If you haven't tried Scottish whisky, you must. At least a sip. On me."

I wasn't much of a drinker, but I'd heard plenty about Scottish whisky and I looked forward to trying it.

"Thank you, I will take you up on that soon."

"Good. I look forward tae it," Tom said.

"Delaney, ye're here," Rosie said as she appeared from the back corner. "Hello, Tom. Have ye met Delaney?"

"Aye, just now."

"Guid. Yer book is right here." She grabbed a book from the back table and brought it toward us.

"Ta, Rosie, what do I owe you?" Tom said.

I tried to see the title of the book, but it had been wrapped in brown paper.

"Not a thing. Edwin wants ye tae have it. No, no argument. Edwin was firm. Ye wilnae pay for this one."

"Thank you. I'll thank him properly when I see him. And, I heard about his sister. I'm so very sorry. Is there anything I can do?"

"It's a tragedy, but we'll get through."

"Don't hesitate tae let me know if any of you need anything. I'm just a couple doors away."

"Thank you, lad. Now, Delaney, I'm afraid I need yer help. We've got tae find another book. It's one that Edwin promised a customer he'd have delivered earlier this week. That task was understandably forgotten. But, Edwin wants tae get it delivered today. He files things in such a fashion that even he cannae remember where he put it. I'd like tae find it before the morning gets away from us. Good tae see ye, Tom."

He nodded. "Nice tae meet you, Delaney," Tom said with another smile. He didn't seem bothered by Rosie's dismissal. "I look forward tae seeing you again."

"Me too. Nice to meet you too," I said, forcing my eyes to keep looking up and not down at Tom's knees and sock-clad calves.

As he exited, Rosie seemed to notice the look I gave him when I freed my eyes to roam at will.

Rosie laughed. "I've ken Tom Fletcher for sae many years that I tend tae forget what he can do tae a female's pulse rate. I thought I saw a bit of that being returned by him, in fact. Hmm, not a bad idea, ye and Tom."

I blushed. "I'm sorry. I need to be more professional. Men don't wear kilts in Kansas. It was an . . . interesting sight. We have much more serious things going on though."

"Not a'tall. It's good not tae think about those serious things every single moment." She paused and blinked hard. "Ye have good timing. I believe he's available, though I wouldnae set my hopes too high. None of us around here think Tom's the type tae settle down and marry."

"Oh! I hadn't even thought . . ."

"No, ye'll need tae get past those knees tae do that, I suppose." Rosie smiled again.

I blushed a little more.

"Ah, dinnae fash yerself, we'll see where it all goes. For now, we need tae find that book. Hamlet's looking in the warehouse, I've been everywhere else, or so I thought. Maybe yer eyes will help me."

"What's the book?"

"*The Adventures of Roderick Random* by Tobias Smollett, a Scottish writer from the eighteenth century. The copy that Edwin recently acquired isnae valuable, a reprint long after the original publish date, but it's apparently in good condition."

I'd never even heard of the author, let alone knew any of his characters' words. My mind was blank. There were no voices giving me any sort of indication where the book was hiding. I'd have to rely on other measures of investigation.

I remembered the organization, or anti-organization as it might have been, from the messy shelf in the warehouse. At first I'd thought everything had just been thrown onto it, but in fact there had been a vague method to the mad stacking.

It reminded me of deciphering a code with few tangible connections. I hadn't pinpointed the code exactly, but I'd gained a small sense that there was *something* there, something intuitive that I might not be able to define quite yet, but I had an inkling.

"Give me a second, Rosie," I said.

She nodded and stood back a little.

I didn't do much of anything except look around, and think about the books on the shelves. There were so many and as I looked even more closely at them it was apparent that there were too many on each shelf, their covers and bindings more squished together than cracked. I added more tasks to my mental to-do list, and then refocused on the current task at hand.

Was there a collection of themes, or perhaps of general

ideas? What had Edwin been thinking when he was placing *The Adventures of Roderick Random* on the shelf?

I turned to Rosie and said, "Can you tell me what kind of book it is—comedy, drama?"

"Oh, something silly, I think."

"A parody?"

"Mebbe."

"Maybe that's it, or maybe that's it for this one." I went to the ladder against the left wall and rolled it to the middle of the wall of shelves. It was more than the fact that it might be in the P's for parody. It wouldn't have been that simple, I decided. I climbed three rungs. As my eyes scanned the crowded shelves where the P's (for whatever) should be, I did, in fact see some books by authors with last names that began with the letter, but I skimmed over those.

"Which century again?" I said down to Rosie, who stood at the bottom of the ladder.

"Eighteenth, though I cannae be more helpful than that."

"That's good." Without much specific intent I moved my eyes over an imaginary calendar, over the centuries, and when I thought I'd reached the eighteenth, my eyes slowed and only a moment later, and by what I thought was mere beginner's luck, landed directly on the book we were searching for. "Got it."

"Not possible," Rosie said.

I wrested the book out from its tight confines and carried it down the ladder and handed it to Rosie. She looked at me with wide, surprised eyes.

"How did ye do that?"

I looked back up the ladder and then at her. "I'm not sure I know, or that I can explain."

She laughed. "Goodness, Edwin certainly ken what he was doing when he hired ye."

That moment was even more satisfying than mastering my bus stop correctly. I smiled and didn't even mind the blush that warmed my cheeks.

"Come along. Let's make sure it's in the shape it needs tae be in. Hamlet will be glad tae stop searching."

"How's Edwin? Everyone?" I asked as I hurried to follow behind her.

"Hamlet and I are staying busy. I havenae spoken to Edwin yet today."

"Am I late? I'm sorry if I am."

"Not at all. Ye can set yer own hours. Hamlet and I needed tae stop thinking about Jenny. I rang him at six this morning and he was as awake as I was. We decided tae come intae work."

"Any news on . . . the killer?"

"Not that I ken."

Though my new home was comfortable, I'd also spent a few restless overnight moments. Jenny's murder weighed heavy on my mind too. Somewhere in the middle of the night I'd come to the conclusion that I needed to somehow ease into asking Rosie and Hamlet more questions about Edwin's sister as well as the members of Fleshmarket.

The bell above the front door jingled as we reached the top of this side's stairs, before I could formulate something that might appropriately begin the questioning process.

"Perhaps that's Ed . . ." Rosie said as we leaned over the balcony and peered toward the door. "I guess not."

Two men had come into the store and were already making their way toward us. Judging by their uniforms, they were with the police. Their demeanor made it clear that they weren't there for a book.

"Can we help ye?" Rosie said as I followed her back down the stairs.

"We're looking for Edwin MacAlister," the tall man said.

"He's not here at the moment, but he should be in soon. Can I give him a message?" Rosie said.

The taller of the two was thin, almost lanky, but not quite. He had bags under his light blue eyes, but I didn't think it was because he was tired. They looked like a regular part of his long, pleasant face. His pale skin tone and freckles and red pate gave us lots in common.

The other man wasn't, in fact, all that short, just shorter than his partner. He was taller than my five feet, six inches by a good three inches. His face wasn't as pleasant as the tall man's, but that was because he was trying hard not to be friendly. His brown eyes were suspicious. His wide shoulders topped off what looked like a weight lifter's muscled body that had been wrapped in a thin layer of baby fat. Somehow it wasn't an unpleasant combination on him.

They both wore dark uniforms with insignias that meant nothing to me, but I caught Rosie's eyes scanning them.

"I'm Chief Inspector Morgan, this is Inspector Winters," the freckled one said, his voice higher than I expected, making his light accent somewhat singsongy. "We have a few questions we'd like tae ask Mr. MacAlister. When exactly is he expected?"

"Any minute now, I s'pose," Rosie said. "May I ask what this is regarding?"

Inspectors Morgan and Winters looked at each other again before Morgan continued.

"We just have a few questions," he said. He pulled out a card and handed it to Rosie. "Please ask him tae ring us when he arrives. We'll make further arrangements with him."

"Certainly." Rosie took the card.

The inspectors turned to leave, but then stopped by the door. Winters turned around and squinted at Rosie.

"You all work with rare things, correct?" he said.

"Aye, our specialty is the rare book and manuscript trade," Rosie said.

"How valuable is your stuff?"

Rosie blinked. "The value varies. It depends on sae many things."

"Some worth millions of dollars?"

"Weel, that would be *extremely* rare," Rosie said noncommittally.

"And, you have a young lad by the name of Hamlet working here. Correct?"

"Aye," Rosie said.

"Please have Mr. MacAlister ring us as soon as possible."

"I will."

The inspector stood still a moment and waited for her to say more, but she had nothing more to add.

"Thank you," Morgan said. Winters glared a moment before they left, but he didn't add anything either.

The bell jingled as the door closed behind them.

"That wasnae comforting," Rosie said.

"Do you think they know about the Folio? Maybe Hamlet did say something to the police. Is that what that was about? Do you know if he talked to them about visiting Jenny?" I stopped speaking. I wasn't exactly easing into anything.

"He did talk tae them, but I doubt that was it. I ken that Hamlet didnae say anything about the Folio. They were probably talking generalities, and were confirming that we ken him. It's well known that Edwin is rich. There are stories, blether . . . gossip and such. Mebbe they were fishing, but not for anything specific. Mebbe."

"Rosie, I know he said he didn't, but did Edwin obtain the Folio illegally? He said Birk's story is unbelievable, but maybe there's no real story to tell," I said.

Rosie sighed and twisted her mouth. "I'm not exactly sure, Delaney. Edwin isnae a criminal, but there are times that I'm certain he's had tae skirt the law tae obtain something that might not be meant tae be owned by an individual person. Ye ken, perhaps the item belongs in a museum or some such thing. Of course, we all have our faults, and as I told ye one of Edwin's is that he's a bit taupie, or scatterbrained. But he is generous and trusting tae a fault. Though he loves his things, he cares for people much more. Sometimes I think it's just a fun, though perhaps careless, game for him, finding and buying things, but he wouldnae harm anyone or . . . what's an American phrase? Rip them off. No, he wouldnae rip anyone off. Or outright steal."

"I understand," I said. "The Folio though. Is it really one that had yet to be discovered?"

"I think so." Rosie nodded.

"My goodness, that would be something." My heart fluttered but didn't plummet at the news this time.

Quietly, Othello appeared in my mind and spoke whispery words: *"O, balmy breath, that dost almost persuade Justice to break her sword!"*

He was talking about not killing Desdemona because her kiss was so sweet, but I heard him for his willingness not to do what needed to be done. Was I willing to be swayed or just look the other way every now and then? How much of that was I going to be asked to do?

I pushed Othello back to the book he'd come from. It wasn't a stretch that there would be a copy of the play somewhere in the store.

"And the Folio *would* be something tae kill someone for, I suppose," Rosie added. "I'm sure Edwin will never forgive himself for his sister's murder. He will always think the Folio somehow had something tae do with her death whether it was directly related or not. He will always think that giving it tae her sealed her demise."

"But it might not have," I said hopefully.

"We may never ken. He cannae tell the police everything he should tell them tae make sure they investigate thoroughly. Perhaps other people would be placed in harm's way, Delaney, not just him, not just us. Ye've met some of those people at the auction. As time goes on it will become clearer tae ye as to why Edwin can't offer up the information about the Folio to the police. At least not yet."

"What about those people?" I said. "Do you know Monroe Ross?"

"Aye."

"He used to date Jenny, right? And he had a black eye at the auction."

Rosie blinked. "And ye think the black eye might have come from Jenny trying to fight him off?"

"I don't know."

"I dinnae think so, Delaney," Rosie said, but she paused thoughtfully before she continued. "They were together many years ago. Monroe used to brawl in the pubs a bit. Mebbe that's what happened to him."

"Edwin said that was a long time ago. That he hasn't done that in years. Monroe said he ran into a door, but I didn't believe him."

"Aye, but . . . no, I dinnae think he was in the pubs. Let's talk tae Edwin about it." She turned and started walking toward the stairs. "Besides, if any of the Fleshmarket members had reason tae kill Jenny, it was probably a woman named Genevieve. Was she there?"

"Genevieve Begbie? Yes, she was there. Why would she have wanted Jenny dead?" I hurried behind Rosie.

"Och, that was a wee bit of a whid . . . an exaggeration on my part, but Genevieve never forgave Jenny."

"For what?" I said as we reached the top of the stairs again.

Rosie stopped and faced me. "Jenny took Monroe's heart, took him right from Genevieve. 'Twas an ugly state of affairs, and 'twas when Monroe left Jenny a year or so later that her downward spiral began. All a long time ago, but I dinnae think Genevieve ever forgave Jenny, and I always thought she was somehow pleased about Ginny's downfall." Rosie blinked and then waved her hand in front of her mouth. "Delaney, ye've got me sayin' things I shouldnae be sayin', or even thinking about. It wouldnae be possible that Monroe or Genevieve had anything tae do with Jenny's murder. Not possible."

As Rosie turned and continued through the doorway, I took a steadying breath. The questions had come naturally. Now, I just had to figure out how to ask more of them and how to get a few addresses.

If Rosie wouldn't help, I bet Hamlet would, I thought as I followed Rosie's footsteps over to the dark side.

TWELVE

Edwin arrived only a few minutes after we relieved Hamlet of his search duty in the warehouse. I didn't have a chance to ask about addresses or anything else, but by what must have been the same sort of fortuitous magic that brought us together so easily and quickly via the Internet advertisement, Edwin and I were again on the same wavelength.

After our somber greetings and Rosie's delivery of the message from the police, Edwin explained that the book I'd found was for Birk, the man dressed in gold at the auction, and asked me if I'd like to go with him to deliver it. There was something about the way he asked that made me think the errand was more than a simple book delivery.

"Of course," I said.

We were silent as he steered the Citroën through the city. I decided that the only time I'd known the real Edwin was on our first phone call, my interview. So much had fallen apart since I'd arrived that my boss had transformed from his clever, delightful, and witty phone self to a brother in mourning. I felt terrible for him, but I knew there wasn't much I could do or say to help him move through the process.

"Edwin," I said, interrupting the quiet.

"Aye?"

"Why are we delivering this to Birk?"

"It's the book he wanted."

"No, I mean, why us? You and me. If book delivery is one of my tasks, I'm happy to do it, but something tells me there's more. Do you think he had something to do with Jenny's murder?"

He glanced at me briefly, his eyebrows high. "Gracious, Delaney, how did you come tae think such a thing?"

"Just because, I suppose. Do you want to let me in on what we're trying to get out of him, or why you think he might have somehow been involved?"

Edwin smiled my direction, but turned his sad eyes back to the road again quickly. "You're a clever lass. Tae be clear, I don't think Birk murdered my sister, but if she was killed because of the Folio, I want tae know the real story of how and where it came from. I think there's not one thing wrong with you learning the real story with me."

"Did Birk know Jenny?"

"Aye. All of my friends knew my sister."

I nodded and paused briefly. "What about Monroe and his black eye?"

"I don't know where Monroe received his black eye, but I don't think it was a blow from Jenny's fist, if that's what you're asking."

"What about Genevieve?"

"Genevieve Begbie?"

"Yes, Rosie mentioned that Genevieve and Jenny had a rough time."

"Rosie, such blether. No, that was decades ago."

"Broken hearts sometimes stay broken, even after decades pass."

"No," Edwin said, but I heard a tinge of doubt in his voice.

I let him think through the rudimentary ideas I'd thrown out.

"Did you have a chance to call the police?" I asked a moment later, though I knew he hadn't. We'd been in the same room since Rosie had given him the message, and I hadn't seen him on a phone.

"No, I will though."

"Do you think Hamlet told them about the Folio?"

"No, I know he didn't." All doubt was gone from his voice. I nodded. If he was sure, I was sure too. At least for now.

We'd traveled toward the northwest part of Edinburgh, and the castle was nowhere in sight. A moment or two after turning into a clearly affluent neighborhood, Edwin steered the Citroën up a steep and curved driveway. The grass next to the driveway was green and groomed to perfection, and seemingly endless. There were no big trees, but there were a few precisely manicured shrubs here and there, and the lawn might have stretched all the way to the sea for all I could tell.

"Oh, my goodness," I said when we turned another curve and then reached the top of the hill. I'd never seen anything like the house, no, mansion—or was it a castle? No, not a castle. It was a mansion that verged on being a castle, probably something like Edwin's home estate.

"This place is stunning," I said.

"Aye, it's quite nice," Edwin said genuinely after we got out of the car. "Come along."

I carried the book and followed Edwin the rest of the way up the curved driveway and then onto a granite walkway. I didn't want to be intimidated, but I couldn't help it. It seemed like my clothes and shoes didn't fit quite right, like I'd been transported to another planet instead of just another country. I gave myself a silent pep talk and waited next to Edwin as he knocked an even rhythm with the giant golden knocker on one of the two wide, also gold, front doors.

Edwin leaned over and quietly said, "Birk's a direct descendant of our own King Henry. He might mention that to you if he didn't already at the auction. Don't act impressed, or he'll go on and on."

"Birk Blackburn. Sounds like a pirate's name."

"Oh, lass, don't tell him that. He would like the idea too much, manipulate it into something romantic and legendary."

The door opened.

"Edwin, my friend, I am so sorry about Jenny. My heart is breaking for you," Birk said. He glanced my direction and nodded once.

Again, Birk was clad in mostly gold. His robe was gold silk with red trim; the pipe in his hand was carved from dark wood, but was also trimmed in gold. The tobacco scent was pleasant, but I stifled an urge to wrinkle my nose as a thick pocket of aroma traveled directly toward my nostrils.

"Thank you, Birk," Edwin said. "We've brought your book."

"Welcome. Come in." Birk stood back as the door swung wider and then back another step as I entered. The inside of the house matched the man. Everything seemed unbearably ostentatious and gilded in gold. There was no way all the extravagant items I saw could possibly be real, genuine gold, could they? I'd never known anyone who had real gold picture frames, real gold tiles on the walls, along with golden accented tables and chairs. It was unreal.

"Wow," I said because I couldn't help myself.

"Aye, it's quite a place isn't it?" Birk said proudly.

"Yes, Birk, quite a place," Edwin said.

I didn't think that the thread of irritation I heard in Edwin's voice and Birk's false manner could be because of jealousy, but they didn't *behave* as if they were friends. No, that wasn't it, I realized. They behaved as if they were friends, but spoke to each other in unfriendly tones. I needed to gain a clearer understanding of their relationship.

Birk's eyes landed on the book I held. I handed it to him, suddenly realizing I'd been holding on to it very tightly.

"Lovely. Come in. I have whisky or tea or coffee. And I must tell you about King Henry. On this day of mourning it might be the cheer-up we all need." Birk looked at me with a hint of his dazzling smile.

I didn't want whisky, and the idea that I wanted to wait to try it in Tom's pub ran through my mind. I didn't want to be rude, though. I glanced at Edwin and he took the lead.

"Coffee would be perfect," Edwin said.

Birk clapped his hands together with two hard hits. I waited for some lights to turn off or on, but instead a woman entered through a side hallway.

"Aye?" she said. Her eyes were dull and bored and framed by lots of sagging skin. Her roundish body didn't seem as old as her face, but I thought she must have been in her sixties. She was dressed in a classic maid's outfit—conservative black dress, white apron, white cap.

"Coffee and something sweet, please, Ingy," Birk said.

"Aye, sir," she said before she turned and shuffled away.

"Ingy's been with me forever. I'm very fond of her," Birk said.

I'd seen no sign of fondness from either of them but I nodded and smiled.

"Come, please sit down," Birk said as he stepped through an entryway to his right. The room was big, cavernous, and filled with even more gold stuff—the fireplace mantel, the mirror frame, the furniture armrests, some threads through the large rug, and the corner pieces on the bookshelves, just to note a few.

"Have a seat, Delaney," Edwin said.

I sat on one of the chairs, Edwin on another. Birk sat on a couch and crossed his legs, one of his hairy calves becoming exposed. If he decided to change positions, I really hoped he had underwear on, but something about Birk told me he might not like underwear.

He was the second man I'd seen in his robe. Was it a Scottish thing, or a coincidence?

"Thank you for the book, Edwin. You really didn't need tae bring it out today. It could have waited," Birk said. He'd set the book on the couch and gingerly opened the cover with his index finger. It wasn't an extremely valuable copy, but I appreciated the careful maneuver.

"I'm sorry about the delay, Birk. I should have brought it a couple days ago, and then circumstances caused some distraction."

Birk closed the book and gave his full attention to Edwin. "Such tragic news."

"Aye, well, thank you for your condolences, but I have an

ulterior motive for coming out today. As I explained tae you at the auction, Delaney will be taking over most of my duties. I think it's best tae begin training someone when I'm healthy."

"I understand," Birk said as he sat up a little straighter. I saw more of his knee, but everything else remained covered. He looked at me. "Edwin MacAlister doesn't trust many people with his secrets, Delaney. You must be very special."

"I hope I can be what he needs me to be. And I have a question," I said.

"Aye?" Birk said.

Edwin jumped in before I could ask. "I know you told her about the Folio, Birk, but I haven't told her how you found it. I want tae make sure the story is true. If it isn't, I hope you'll tell us the true version today." Edwin looked at me. "According tae Birk, it was something discovered in the depths of one of our old and haunted places. We have lots of secrets, hidden places, and as I've mentioned lots of ghosts."

"I can't wait to explore," I said as the hair stood up on my arms.

"Actually, it was one of my acquaintances who found the item, and then put it in a place where I had tae search for it," Birk said with an unequivocal tone. "We don't know where it had been for so long before that. I was sent on a treasure hunt. And my story is true."

"Treasure hunt?" I said.

"That's what we were all told," Edwin said.

"And, that's certainly what happened," Birk said, his mouth pinched obstinately.

"Oh?" I said as expectantly as I could.

Then Birk said something that surprised me. I saw a flash of the same surprise in Edwin's eyes, but he recovered quickly.

"So, have you seen it? What do you think? Edwin wanted you tae see it," Birk said. He sat forward on the couch and lowered his voice now.

"Not yet," I said as evenly as possible, wishing Edwin had prepped me better.

It was that moment when I realized that what I'd learned about my boss, from our interview and Rosie's blether, was an incomplete picture. On our original call, he was curious, listened intently. According to Rosie, Edwin was good-hearted but scatterbrained, perhaps even somewhat foolish. I'd known on some level he was also smart, but it became clear at that moment that he was very smart. Edwin hadn't prepped me for this conversation because he wanted spontaneity. It was his way of judging whether or not Birk knew the Folio was missing.

The disappointment showed in Birk's face, though I wasn't sure who he was more disappointed in, me or Edwin. Nevertheless, it was genuine, and out of the corner of my eye I saw Edwin tilt his head just enough to acknowledge to himself that Birk, in fact, most likely didn't know the Folio was missing.

"So, it's a real First Folio? That's quite a discovery," I said.

"Birk says it is," Edwin said. "I believe it is."

"It's real," Birk said. "Look it over, front tae back. I will gladly give back every pound paid for it and put it back up for auction if there are any concerns or questions, or even if you change your mind, Edwin. I know many bidders regretted not continuing tae participate in the auction. Bring it back tae me this afternoon. I'll have the money."

Edwin's shoulders relaxed slightly. Another sign. "Thank you, Birk. I appreciate that, but I'm going tae keep it."

"Why didn't you just have Delaney look at it before you came here?" Birk asked.

Edwin shrugged.

"I don't understand. You're baurmie, old man, a fool," Birk said, but then he smiled a big white toothy grin, and I thought I finally saw the friendship between the two men.

Edwin's mobile phone jingled.

"Excuse me a minute," he said as he stood, pulled the phone out of his pocket, and left the room.

"Birk, please tell me the whole story of how you obtained the Folio," I said as his eyes tracked Edwin's departure.

Birk sat back and put the pipe in his mouth. He held the mouthpiece with his teeth a moment. Then he closed his lips around the pipe, lit it, and pulled and puffed once.

"How much do you know about Edinburgh?" he said.

I laughed. "Very little, really, but I'm excited to learn more. I did some research before arriving, but barely scratched the surface."

"You know how haunted we are, or you have some idea?"

"Well, I suppose."

"Aye, we're haunted tae the very core of our buried bones. History, battles fought, both lost and won. Good, bad. We're a mix of it all. You'll see. You'll come upon a ghostie or two while you're here. Everyone does."

He was so sincere that I held back the conspiratorial wink or doubtful agreement that would usually go with such comments.

"All right," I said as the hair tickled on my arm again.

"Anyway, what if the Folio was found in a place that was underground, a place where no one has lived for a long time?" He leaned forward and lowered his voice again. "A place that we show tae tourists now. There's probably a tour going through there right this minute, in fact."

I nodded. "Interesting."

"What would you think about a ghost leading the way tae the treasure, perhaps leading a weary soul who thought they might be beginning tae lose their faculties, tae hear voices?"

I swallowed. Having my own cast of voices in my head had never made me think I was losing my faculties, but maybe it should have.

"I'm not exactly sure," I said.

"A fine character sought me out as I was indulging in my fa-vorite breakfast at a lovely place called Elephants and Bagels—you must try them. Anyway, this man came up tae me. He was much more than a wee bit down on his luck. His clothes were torn and filthy. Actually 'torn' and 'filthy' might be adequate words for the rest of him too, but I don't want tae sound cruel. He approached me as I exited the store. I thought he was a simple beggar and though I don't tend tae give money tae many beggars, there was something about his eyes that made me stop and listen tae him when he pulled on my sleeve and told me he had something he wanted tae tell me.

"He told me his story. He told me he'd found the manuscript, though he just called it a magical book, as he was trespassing, tailing along on a tour he snuck into to escape the rain one day. He told me that once inside and as they trailed down into the depths, voices guided him directly tae it, and then the voices told him tae find me and tell me where it was located, that I should retrieve it."

It was very far-fetched, certainly, but a part of me wanted to believe it was true. Magic books, voices directing the way.

"What made you put it up for auction?" I asked.

"I had it for over three years, Delaney. I was doing nothing with it. I thought about giving it tae a legitimate museum, but

I have friends like Edwin who I was sure would want tae own it. I thought more of my friends than I did of the greater good, I realize that and I fully admit it, but there it is."

Interesting. And three years was long enough to keep anyone from finding the mystery man in the restaurant, but it wouldn't do me much good to point out the holes in the story.

Birk glanced toward the hallway. I could hear Edwin's voice but it was quiet, as if he'd moved well past the entryway. Birk sat even farther forward on the couch. He leaned toward me and said quietly, "Delaney, you've got tae do something about Edwin."

I blinked. "I don't understand."

"We're all worried about him. Of course, saddened that Jenny was killed, but before that tragedy occurred we were worried. He gave the Folio tae his sister tae care for. He told me that in confidence, but his desire tae include Jenny more in his life and business had worried us all. He told me he was going tae retrieve the Folio from her, but it never should have been left in her care. When we heard you were being hired, Genevieve and I—and others—hoped you would also watch closely over our friend and his decisions. I'll leave it at that for now, but please be on the lookout. And frankly"—he sent another anxious look toward the hallway—"none of us are the least bit surprised about Jenny."

"How well did you know her?" I said.

"Since she was born. Edwin and I were childhood friends."

"Who do you think might have killed her?" I said.

"Och, one of her drug friends, certainly. She made some terrible choices."

"But she was doing better, right? Even if you didn't think she should be involved in Edwin's life, she was doing better?"

Birk shook his head slowly. "I don't think she was doing much better. None of us do."

"I don't understand. I didn't know her. How would her being more a part of Edwin's life cause problems? Did she behave obnoxiously?"

"On the contrary. She was the picture of social propriety."

"Why didn't you want her involved then?"

"History." Birk looked at me with sad eyes. "Things I can't relay tae you because you weren't here over the years. You didn't see the damage caused, the hearts broken, the friendships tattered, the trust broken apart. Hard feelings that have been protected and perhaps buried for years. There's no need for Edwin tae have included Jenny in his business other than he was trying to mend his own broken trusts with her. He shouldn't have included the rest of us, some who might not have wanted tae think about his sister or forgive her."

"You didn't want to forgive her?"

"Not me."

"Morgan Ross and Genevieve Begbie, maybe?" I said.

"Aye," he said as though he was impressed.

"If I wanted to talk to Mr. Ross and Ms. Begbie, how would I find them?"

Birk looked at me a long moment. As he was contemplating my question, Ingy brought in a golden tray adorned with a golden coffee carafe, gold cups, and a gold plate piled with shortbread cookies.

"Ingy," Birk said quietly after he glanced out to the hallway once again, "please write down the contact information for Morgan Ross and Genevieve Begbie. Sneak the piece of paper with their addresses and phone numbers into Ms. Nichols's possession without Edwin noticing. Please. And add my phone number too. Just in case."

"Oh, I wasn't . . ." I began.

Birk winked at me. Ingy looked back and forth between Birk and me, her sad eyes drooping a tiny bit more, before she set the tray on a side table next to Birk and left the room.

"Looks like I'll be serving," Birk said as he stood and reached for the carafe. "Coffee?"

Edwin rejoined us but didn't offer up what the phone call was about. We drank coffee and ate cookies as Birk made me tell him all about Kansas. He was fascinated by farm life, by my work in the museum. Before long, the conversation flowed easily between the three of us. I caught Edwin observing the interaction between Birk and me a time or two.

As we left, I realized I liked Birk, but I still didn't trust him. He probably felt the same about me. I wasn't going to be his spy, but I hoped that's not what he'd been asking. There was a chance his concern for Edwin was genuine and based upon the affection of a lifelong friendship. I would watch for disturbing signs from my new boss, but I wouldn't report back to Birk.

I also didn't trust Genevieve and Monroe, but I didn't think Birk thought that was my reason for wanting to contact them. I was grateful for the folded piece of paper that Ingy slipped into my hand as we were all gathered by the front door. Edwin gave Ingy a questioning glance but didn't inquire as to why she was standing so close to me for a moment while not offering up any sort of farewell to either him or me. I hadn't planned on being so secretive, but it didn't seem like a bad idea. At least for now.

As Edwin drove the Citroën away from the mansion, I

glanced in the car's side mirror. Birk stood in the open golden doorway as he puffed on his pipe much more seriously now.

I didn't think he could see me looking, or my smile as I noticed Ingy next to him, one hand on her hip and her other hand's index finger pointing at him as adamantly as she spoke. She wasn't happy. Birk didn't seem to care.

"Where to now?" I said.

"How about Jenny's flat?" Edwin said.

"Good idea."

I'd slipped the paper in my pocket and it beckoned me to give it a look, but I resisted. I felt a little disloyal to my new boss, but not too much. I suddenly decided that it was far too soon to know who to trust.

THIRTEEN

The route Edwin took to Jenny's flat was slightly different than the route Elias had taken, but I was still able to orient myself using the castle. I liked how quickly I seemed to be catching on to a few locations. I didn't admit to Edwin that I'd been at Jenny's the day before.

"She lived there, in that brown building," Edwin said as he stopped out front in almost the identical spot Elias had stopped.

I felt guilty enough about my lie of omission that I just made a noncommittal sound as I looked at the building too. Today, the clouds weren't as ominous. It currently wasn't raining, but the whole place still seemed spooky.

"Let's see if we can get inside," Edwin said. "The police should be done. Perhaps we can make a better search of it. I doubt we'll find any clues the police didn't find, but if the Folio is there, some place I didn't see it, we can at least rule out that it had something tae do with her death."

I looked at Edwin.

"You really did think that Birk might have had something to

do with her death, didn't you? I mean because of the Folio. Did you think he wanted the Folio back and killed Jenny to get it?"

"I wasn't sure, Delaney. I hoped not, but he's a crafty fellow. I told Rosie and Hamlet that Jenny had the Folio and then you of course, and there's no doubt in my mind that they and you didn't have anything tae do with her death. I just had tae see for myself if I could catch Birk off guard, if he would act suspicious when I asked the questions. I've known him for so long that I thought I would be able tae read his face, perhaps a flash of guilt in his eyes. But I saw nothing that made me suspicious. I don't think I'm being naive. I just had tae see for myself. Does that make sense?"

"Yes," I said. "If it's any help, I don't think he has any idea the Folio has gone missing. I got no sense that he now had it in his possession."

He nodded and then turned off the engine. "Come along, let's go talk tae the manager."

I followed Edwin inside the brown, dreary building. We were greeted by the same quiet I'd noticed the day before, but it was much less eerie when I had someone with me.

Only a few moments after Edwin's enthusiastic knock on his door, the manager opened it wide. Since I'd seen a couple of men dressed in their robes when they opened their doors I was a little surprised to find this one fully clothed.

"Ah, Edwin," he said as he hiked up his jeans and then extended his hand. "I'm sae sairy aboot yer sister. Come in, come in."

The manager looked at me and nodded with a questioning glance. I just smiled.

"Thanks, Harry. Delaney, this is the building manager, Harry Boyd. Harry, this is my new employee, Delaney Nichols."

He shook my hand but still didn't smile. He was dressed in jeans and a T-shirt that had a small oily stain over the right shoulder. There was a glimmer to the stain that made me think it had landed there recently. He was blondish and pale but the stubble on his face was dark. The combination, along with his big, muscular arms and big thighs, made him seem tough in a stereotypical neighborhood bully kind of way.

"We'd like tae go up to Jenny's flat if that's all right," Edwin continued.

"Dinnae mynd a bit." Harry shrugged. "The police told me I could clear it oot anytime. I was going tae call you later today tae discuss that with ye. I was hoping ye'd take whatever of Jenny's ye wanted. I can sell whatever ye dinnae want tae keep. I'm really sairy, Edwin."

"Thank you, Harry." Edwin swallowed hard. "I didn't bring my key tae the flat. Would you mind letting us in?"

"Dinnae mind," he said again. He produced a large key ring that must have been uncomfortable in the back pocket it came from. "Let's go."

Harry stepped out of his flat and pulled the door closed. He somehow found the correct key on his chock-full key ring and had the door locked quicker than I could have handled it with only one key.

As we turned, we were greeted by the man who lived across the hall. He was still in his robe, or in it again, but I suspected "still" was more accurate.

He looked only at me as he took a sip of something from the mug he held. I didn't see steam so it wasn't a warm drink.

"Good afternoon," I said, hoping he wouldn't give me away.

"Afternoon," he said. He looked at Harry and Edwin and

then backed into his flat with two long steps, closing the door behind him.

"Ah, ignore him," Harry said. "The man is nosier than an old biddy with nothing better tae do. I dinnae ken how he always kens when someone is oot here, but he opens the door and greets them in his robe. I've asked him tae stop, but he doesnae care tae listen."

I walked behind Edwin and Harry and mouthed "Thank you" to the peephole in case he was watching.

Harry led the way to the elevator and up to the third floor. There wasn't any conversation, but our silence wasn't strained.

The third floor was similar to the first floor, achingly silent.

"It sure is quiet around here," I said.

"We have an unusual amount of quiet residents," Harry said. "Makes my job more pleasant, not telling people tae shut up and keep it doon all the time."

The third floor also looked just like the first floor except for a couple of leftover pieces of crime scene tape over one door.

Harry peeled them off and said, "I kept it on there just in case. I doot anyone will be curious enough tae break in and look around, but I thought it might help deter the curious. I'll leave it taped tae the wall if ye want tae put it back up when ye're done. I wilnae try tae rent out the place for a wee bit. Jenny was paid up through this month and next."

"She was?" Edwin said.

"Aye. She'd been keeping up with her rent these last six months or so. I havenae had tae call ye once."

"No, you haven't. I hadn't thought about that. That's good tae know."

"Uh-huh," Harry said as he pushed open the door. "Do

whatever ye need tae do in there. Just close the door when ye're done. It'll lock. Put up the tape if ye want."

"We will. Thank you, Harry."

"Aye," he said.

He left us inside the flat, closing the door behind him.

"This is it. It's a mess right now, but Jenny usually kept it a wee bit neater," Edwin said, his voice shaky. "Down the hallway tae the left is where her body was, and I suspect there might still be bloodstains there. Just stay in this part if you'd prefer."

I nodded and looked around. It *was* a mess, items strewn everywhere, furniture off its mark. "Did the police do this?"

"Some, but it was mostly like this when I came in and found her. It was the first thing I noticed and caused me immediate concern. Even on her worst days, Jenny wasn't this messy," he said with a sad sigh.

"This can't be easy, Edwin," I said. "Are you sure you want to be here?"

"Aye, Delaney. You are correct. I'm in a tough spot though. There might be something here that the police overlooked because they don't have the whole story. If we find something— anything—that would lead tae Jenny's killer, I will hand it over and do my best tae explain the rest tae them if the Folio is involved. I want tae be here. I want tae do this. I feel like I have tae."

"Even after visiting with Birk, you don't feel like you can tell the police about the Folio? I don't understand, Edwin. Birk would tell them the same story, wouldn't he? I don't think he could be suspected of anything nefarious; well, that could be proven at least. You telling them about the Folio wouldn't implicate him, I don't think."

"I agree, but I need tae take the steps I need tae take. I want tae explore all the avenues first. I know that doesn't make sense tae someone who doesn't have the history, but it's more than Birk, it's my business, perhaps the entire Fleshmarket Batch. It's not my intention *not* tae talk tae the police about the Folio, Delaney, but I need tae make sure . . . that I really need tae let them in on that part of my life. It's a long, important history with many people that could be changed forever if I don't handle it correctly. Does that make sense?"

"Not completely," I said.

"Can you trust me a wee bit longer?" he asked.

I thought before I answered. What I suspected was that he just didn't want the police to have the Folio, that he wanted it in his hands before they had a chance to get it into theirs. Greed. My idea didn't fit with the man I was getting to know, but neither did his reasons for not talking to the police. There was more, something else, but he wasn't going to tell me what it was yet.

"Yes," I finally said.

"Very good. Let's get tae work."

The couch cushions weren't all the way upturned, but they were off-kilter enough to know that they'd been looked under. Any drawers—in tables and the television entertainment center—were open, some of their contents sticking up awkwardly. The exposed surfaces were also strewn with items. And there was a small stack of pieces of torn paper by the front right foot of the couch. I gulped.

"Edwin, the pieces of paper?" I said.

"Not the Folio," he said. "I saw them after I found Jenny. I didn't check them all, but none of what I saw was part of it.

Mostly magazine scraps, but I don't understand why they're there."

I hurried to them and glanced through them quickly. Edwin had been correct; it seemed like a magazine ad for makeup had been torn up and piled together. I couldn't imagine there was anything important among the scraps so I moved on.

The furniture reminded me of a somewhat modern Kansas country home. Big floral prints over comfortable cushions. The coffee and side tables were white wood that had been antiqued.

The living room was neither spacious nor cramped. The small patio deck and balcony were directly off the living room, and the sliding glass doors that led outside let lots of light inside. The kitchen was on the opposite side from the patio doors; it was a small square space. From my vantage point I assessed that you could stand in the middle of the kitchen and touch all the appliances and shelves just by turning in a circle. The counter space was decent though, with stools on this side that made for the only sit-down eating space.

The polished wood floor was covered in throw rugs that clearly weren't where they were supposed to be.

"I'll go back tae the bedroom," Edwin said. "Why don't you see if there's anything tae see in here."

Edwin disappeared down the hallway that I wasn't sure whether or not I would traverse. I didn't want to see a blood-stain. I took a left and started my search at the television entertainment center. The TV was a modern flat-screen just like the one in my hotel room had been.

I looked all around it, even lifting it a bit off its small stand, only to find a light layer of dust beneath.

The entertainment center was simply an old set of drawers.

The drawers were already opened. I looked inside each one. Chances were pretty slim that I would find anything helpful, but it was worth a scrutinizing look. Each drawer had similar items throughout. CDs, DVDs, paperbacks, notebooks, magazines. Nothing was neat or organized, though I couldn't tell if the mess had been there before the police search or if it was a result of it. I saw no sign of drugs or of drug paraphernalia, but if there had been any, the police would probably have taken it away.

I gave up on those drawers and tried the ones on the coffee table and the two tables on each side of the couch. The same sorts of things were in those too. Nothing interesting anywhere. I lifted cushions and I looked under furniture. I lifted throw rugs, and still nothing.

The kitchen was next. It didn't look like Jenny was much of a cook; I found only one skillet, one pot, and a few wooden spoons that didn't look to have been used at all. Four stacked plates and a number of mismatched mugs were lined up on the bottom shelf of the first cabinet. Again, nothing interesting.

But as I closed the door to that particular cabinet, a buzz of intuition froze me in place. I'd seen something, but I wasn't sure exactly what it was. I opened the door again. There was nothing special about the four plates. They were stacked evenly and I felt no need to shift their positions.

I closed the door.

And then opened it again.

What was it? What was I seeing in this cabinet that was setting off my intuitive alarms?

Each mug was different. Some were decorated with different colors and patterns; some had sayings written on them. There was even one from the Edinburgh Castle. I moved its handle slightly so I could see the full picture.

My eyes moved over the rest of the mugs, and then stopped on one that was decorated with different colored squares that looked like confetti. I pulled it out of the cabinet and turned it over in my hands a few times. There was something about this one. . . .

And then it suddenly became clear. Though the mess throughout the drawers of the entertainment center in the living room had been random, there had been something that, in fact, did stand out.

I sat the mug on the counter, left the cabinet door opened, and went back to the drawers. In each of the six of them, I found some of what I was looking for. Little pieces of light purple paper that reminded me of the confetti on the cup, most of which at first glance seemed to have some handwriting on them. These were not part of the makeup ad that I'd found on the floor.

I gathered all that I could find. There were only about five pieces per drawer, but once I had them all in the palm of my hand it seemed like they belonged together, like they'd originally been one piece of paper that had had something written on it.

I would have liked to place the small pieces on a flat surface and try to put the puzzle together, but again my intuition buzzed. Maybe this was something I should do on my own. The piece of paper in my pocket beckoned again, but I ignored it. Maybe Edwin didn't need to know about it *or* what I had found until I really knew if I'd found something. If the police had cleared the place, surely I didn't need to ask for their permission to take the torn scraps.

I slipped them into my pocket with the note just as Edwin came back into the room, his face drawn and sad.

"Did you find anything?" he asked.

"Nothing. You?"

"Not one thing. I am certain that the Folio isn't here."

"I didn't get a chance to look into every single space in the kitchen. Maybe we should do that together."

I placed the confetti mug back onto its shelf and closed the door. Edwin didn't seem to notice. Even if he'd discovered something that might have been important to Jenny's murder, I doubted he would have truly seen it, if it would have made its way through his grief. However, I didn't doubt that he was aware enough to have seen the Folio if it had been hiding in any of the places he'd searched.

Briefly I wondered if he had found something and hid it somewhere on himself or if he had deposited something some-where on the premises. Perhaps I was being used as some sort of witness to an unclear alibi. I would have noticed the Folio on him though. It would be too big to slip into a pocket or under a shirt. I realized I'd never know if he left something some-where, but if the police asked I'd have to say that he was out of my sight for some time.

Together we searched all the other nooks and crannies in the kitchen and found nothing more exciting than a unique can opener with an S-shaped handle that was still in the plastic package.

We left the flat very close to how we'd found it, except for the pieces of paper I'd hidden in my pocket. If they led to any-thing I'd tell Edwin. Or the police. Someone.

I watched as he closed the door and confirmed that it was locked. His face was still sad, genuinely so, I thought.

"I have another idea, Delaney," he said as he turned and moved purposefully toward the neighbor's door. He knocked a couple of quick taps and folded his hands behind his back as we waited.

Again, I expected a man in a robe to answer the door, but I wasn't even close.

"Yeah?" the woman said. She'd opened the door with one hand and was trying to slip on a high-heeled shoe with the other. "Oh, yeah, I know who you are. You're Jenny's brother. I'm really sorry about Jenny." She finished with the shoe, stood straight, and smoothed her short white skirt. She had a thick, distinctly American accent.

"I am. Edwin MacAlister," he said as he extended his hand.

"Right." She hesitated, but manners got the best of her. Mostly. She didn't offer her name, but she did shake hands. She looked at me briefly, but it was clear that I was the unimportant part of the equation. "Can I help you with something?" Her voice was cold.

She wasn't exactly rough looking, but she was almost rough looking with badly bleached hair and thick eye makeup. She was probably in her fifties, but trying to look like she was still in her thirties. Her plan was failing, and though she wasn't very pleasant, I felt a little sorry for her being on the losing end of the battle.

"I was wondering if perhaps you talked tae Jenny somewhere close tae the time she was killed, or if maybe you heard anything strange the day she was killed. I think there was a struggle in there"—Edwin nodded toward Jenny's flat—"and I'm hoping someone heard something that might be valuable tae the police's investigation."

"Well," she said, sarcasm lining the way she drew out the

word. "I talked to the police and I told them what I heard and what I saw."

When she didn't continue, Edwin jumped in again. "Any chance you would share with us what that was? I'd be mighty grateful."

The woman messed with her earring and looked at Edwin a long moment before she gave in. "I heard a couple of bumps. Like a *thump-thump* around the time they think she might have been killed. And the only thing I saw was a visitor the night before. I'd seen him stop by a time or two. Young guy with long hair. He was dressed in goofy, puffy shorts and everything. Jenny told me once that he was a good friend."

It must have been Hamlet, but we'd already known that Hamlet had visited her the day before Edwin found her.

"The sounds—the *thump-thump*—did they come from inside the space or from the wall, like someone was pounding on it?" Edwin asked.

"No, the noise came from inside the apartment," she said with a sigh.

"We're sorry tae take your time, but we do appreciate you talking tae us," Edwin said.

I wished I knew what to do to ease her impatience, but she was either just naturally the way she was or she didn't like Edwin. They obviously hadn't met before, so her reactions to him could have been based upon something Jenny had said to her, or the snooty impression the old woman had expressed about Jenny when I was out front with Elias.

"I'm Delaney Nichols," I jumped in. "Do you mind if I ask if you and Jenny were friends?"

She looked at me, giving me her full attention for the first time since the door had opened. It looked like the maneuver had taken some big effort. Maybe the American tie would help. "We were neighbors for about ten years. I knew the family she came from. I knew about the money. I knew how selfish you were with it." She turned and glared at Edwin. "I knew her well enough."

I cleared my throat. "Did she, by chance, convey anything to you about being scared of anyone, someone? Had she mentioned a fight? Maybe not even recently. Maybe you'd heard people arguing next door before?"

Her face changed, as if I'd finally said something that wasn't worthy of sarcasm.

"Yes, actually, there was an argument in there about a week and a half ago. The police didn't ask me about that and I didn't even think about it. But, yes, there was some yelling. I think."

"One voice Jenny? The other?" I said.

"Yeah, I'm pretty sure one of the voices belonged to Jenny, but I don't know who the other voice belonged to. It was a male voice."

"You didn't recognize it at all?" I said.

"I just can't be sure. It might have sounded familiar, but I wouldn't want to say just in case I'm wrong."

"Well, as you know, we're not the police. It wouldn't hurt to tell us," I said. A zip of anticipation ran up my spine.

She thought a moment and then shook her head. "No, I don't think so, but I might call the police and tell them. I think that would be a better option." She smoothed her skirt again. We'd lost her attention. "Look, I need to finish getting ready."

"Thank you again for your time," Edwin said just before the door closed.

For a long, silent moment Edwin stood still with his hands behind his back as he stared at the beige carpet on the floor. I remained quiet too and waited.

Shortly, he looked up at me. "Thank you for taking over, Delaney. I'm sorry you had tae be exposed tae a wee bit of my family's dirty laundry, but I assure you the entire story isn't quite what the young lady just intimated."

I smiled. I don't know why, but it felt like the right thing to do. "She wasn't all that young," I said quietly just in case she was listening on the other side of the door.

Edwin smiled too. It wasn't the most grown-up behavior, but it alleviated some uncomfortable tension.

"Indeed," Edwin said. "Come along, I'd like tae try the neighbor on the other side and then we'll be done with this unpleasant duty."

The other neighbor was not in his robe either, though he didn't wear much more. His name was Waldo (I sensed that wasn't his real name), and he was evidently a weight lifter who thought it was necessary to show off the fruits of his weight-lifting labor. He wore a tight tank top and cutoff denim shorts—way cut off. The whites of his front pockets peeked out from under the frayed legs.

"Ooch, it's shite for certain," he said. I wasn't sure I'd be able to understand much of what he said so I listened hard. "I dinnae ken her weel a t'all. Nice enough but tae auld fer me tae be friends with, if ye ken what I mean." He winked.

Edwin stared at him like he couldn't quite understand him either, or he just didn't want to.

"Did you hear anything strange coming from Jenny's apartment recently, or in the last little while?" I asked.

Waldo shrugged—but it wasn't an I-don't-know shrug, it was more an I-don't-care shrug. "Ye hear stuff in the buildin' aaul the time."

"Really?" I couldn't help but counter. "This place seems very quiet to me."

" 'Tis not. Well, 'tis except for when it 'tisn't." Waldo scratched his head. "I mean, there's noise and stuff, but 'tis inside and when it's inside it's quieter." He waved his hand through the air as if to erase everything he'd just said.

"What's going on inside to cause so much noise?" I asked.

"Not a thing," Waldo said.

But for a brief instant, the big, burly guy looked scared. Maybe not scared, but a little worried. He recovered quickly.

"Look, I 'ave stuff I havta do. I dinna ken her weel and I 'ave no idea what happened tae her. I'm sairry she got herself kil't."

"Got herself?" I stepped forward, suddenly prepared to put my foot in the door if he made a motion to close it. "How did she 'get herself' killed?"

"Jest an expression," he said with too-wide eyes.

Yes, it was an expression, but there was more weight to the words when he'd said them. Perhaps I'd heard frustration or anger, but he'd made it more than just an expression.

I had no idea how to get him to tell me more. I looked at Edwin, who'd already finished with the overly muscled Waldo, his eyes aimed down the hallway. I stepped back.

" 'Ave a nice day," he said, before he shut the door with authority.

And again, it became so very quiet.

What a strange place.

"Come on, Delaney, I wouldn't think anything he said would be reliable," Edwin said.

I couldn't have agreed more, but I sensed Waldo knew more than he wanted to share. As I walked with Edwin to the elevator, down through the first-floor hallway of the building, and then out to the Citroën, I could not let go of the one thing that I continued to notice: the quiet. It was like one of my insistent characters from a book. It was as if it was raising its hand and waving desperately my direction. *Pick me, pick me.* I wanted to understand it better. I wanted to know the quiet. I wanted it to talk to me. But how does one make the quiet speak?

FOURTEEN

Both Hamlet and Rosie were busy when we returned to The Cracked Spine. To Edwin's obvious dismay, Inspectors Winter and Morgan had returned as well. Edwin and I shook off some moisture from the rain that had begun as we left the apartment building. We wiped our feet as we noticed the inspectors standing near the ladder in the middle of the shop. Edwin quietly grumbled some irritation before he spoke to them.

"Inspectors, I was just about tae give you a ring. Come along over tae my office," Edwin said to the two men who stood with identical thumbs-in-front-belts poses. I wondered if they knew they did that.

"Delaney," Edwin lowered his voice again. "Just jump in and see what Hamlet and Rosie might need help with. I'll talk tae the inspectors."

I nodded. Rosie looked to be in the middle of something about numbers with a man in a very wet rain hat. Rosie and the dripping man were both peering at an item on the front desk, their heads so close together that the top of the hat almost touched the top of Rosie's short hair. Hector was standing on the desk in between them and glanced down at the item too, or at least that's what I thought he was doing; hard to tell with the bangs.

Hamlet nodded welcomingly when I looked his direction. He was toward the back corner table. It seemed cloaked in shadow from dark-cloud-diffused light coming in through the stained-glass window. The ceiling fixture's age was showing, the artificial light only *almost* reaching to the back of the shop. I walked over and joined Hamlet and the customer he was talking to. As I approached I heard her say with a soft voice, "Dear lad, ye dinnae seem tae understand, that book is something I must have."

"I do understand, Mrs. Tuttle," Hamlet said. "We just haven't been able tae track down a copy for you yet. Delaney, this is Mrs. Tuttle."

Mrs. Tuttle was short; there was probably less than five full feet of her. She was old, and she wore enough makeup that she either couldn't see well to put it on or she was trying to hide her age, but failing even more than Jenny's neighbor had.

"Delaney?" Mrs. Tuttle turned her full attention to me.

"Yes, ma'am. How can I help?"

"Och, ye sound American."

"I am. I'm from a small town, but I recently lived in Wichita, Kansas."

"Kansas! I've been tae Kansas, though never tae Wichita. I was in Topeka for a glassblowers convention." Her eyes lit brightly, encircled in her thick mascara and cracking layers of bright blue eye shadow.

"I have lots of relatives in Topeka."

"That makes my day sae much better. Tae talk tae someone from America, who knows a place I visited. Brilliant!" She let the smile sag. "Except Hamlet here still hasnae found my book and I'm old, Delaney. I doubt I'll have much longer tae wait."

"What's the book?"

"It's called *Boggle the Mind* and it's by an author named Philomena Reyes," she said slowly, so I could catch each important word.

"I'm sorry, but I've never heard of it," I said.

"It exists," Hamlet said. "Well, it existed. It was a book that was published in hardback sixty years ago by a now long-gone publishing house that was located in Glasgow. The first and only print run was one hundred copies, and Mrs. Tuttle received one of the books as a gift when she was younger. Over the years she lost the book and would like tae have a replacement copy."

"Aye," Mrs. Tuttle said. "Delaney, the book was given tae me by a boy, my first love. He left Glasgow shortly afterward, and moved to Spain. I never heard from him again, but later I discovered that I hadn't heard from him because my parents destroyed his, well, oor, letters. By the time I knew the truth, 'twas far too late. I couldnae find him. Having a copy of the book would bring me a wee bit of him, enough tae hold on tae for my remaining time at least."

"That's a great story," I said. I paused and looked at Hamlet, who only lifted his eyebrows in defeat. I turned back to Mrs. Tuttle. "Have you thought about writing it down, the story of the boy and the book, and the letters? You could write what *might* have been in them."

"Why, no, I'm not a writer."

"I bet you are. The way you told just that little part of the story, with so much heartfelt emotion, I have to think that you would write it perfectly. Writing down your story might help until Hamlet finds your book. I have no doubt that he has searched high and low for it, Mrs. Tuttle." I looked at him.

"And I will keep searching until I find it," he said as he put his hand on her arm. "I promise."

Mrs. Tuttle pursed her lips and sighed through her nose. "I believe ye. I'm just impatient for it, that's all. But ye do have a good point, Delaney. Perhaps the story will make a good distraction for a time. But, ye'll help him search, won't ye?"

"I will help Hamlet in any way I can."

"Oh, guid. That would be very guid. Thank ye, both." She paused, and didn't seem to want to end the conversation. She pursed her lips, her red lipstick dotting some of the wrinkles around her mouth, and then turned to me again. "Do ye ken aboot the blown-glass store in Topeka?"

"No, where is it located?"

"On Ross Road. I dinnae ken why I remember that, but I do."

Unfortunately, further conversation about either Mrs. Tuttle's book or the blown-glass store in Topeka was interrupted by the police inspectors.

"He explained that he was at her flat. We knew . . . ," Edwin said as he followed the uniformed men who were making their way toward Hamlet, Mrs. Tuttle, and me.

However, the inspectors kept their eyes only on Hamlet.

"Young man, would you please come with us?" Inspector Morgan said.

"Why?" Hamlet asked, his eyes wide, his youth showing for the first time since I'd met him.

"We'd like tae talk tae you about your relationship with Jenny MacAlister," Inspector Morgan continued.

"They were friends, just friends. You make it sound like there could be more. There wasn't," Edwin said. He turned to Hamlet. "You told the police that you'd visited Jenny the night before she was killed, didn't you?"

"Aye, of course," Hamlet said.

"See," Edwin said to the inspectors. "He's told you everything he knows. Hamlet, I'm sorry."

"It's not a problem, Edwin, I did tell them everything I know. At least I told the other officers, the ones who were at the station when I went in. I didn't call them. I thought going in would be better," Hamlet said.

"Why do you need to talk to him?" I interjected.

Rosie, with Hector over her arm, and the customer with the wet hat had come up behind and were observing the scene with their own sets of big, round eyes.

"Ma'am, this is police business. If you'll excuse us," the tall inspector said.

"I told them about our trip to Jenny's flat," Edwin said to me with a look that I thought emphasized that the police still didn't know about the Folio. "I mentioned that one of the neighbors had seen Hamlet there the night before Jenny died and that the neighbor also mentioned an argument she thought she heard a week and a half ago. I said that's what they should investigate, the argument. I didn't mean for them tae assume those incidents were in any way related, but they jumped tae that conclusion, I'm afraid. I'm sorry, Hamlet," Edwin said again.

"Please come with us, young man. We just have a few questions for you."

"Is he under arrest?" I said, though I didn't know if the laws about willingly going with the police were the same in Scotland as they were in America.

"Not yet," Inspector Morgan said.

"Hamlet, I don't think you have to go with them," I said.

Hamlet looked at me, at Edwin, and then Rosie, and finally Mrs. Tuttle, who was obviously no shrinking violet. Her arthritis-ridden fists were balled at her sides and she was shooting venomous, blue eye-shadowed looks at the inspectors.

"No, I'll go. I'll straighten it all out," Hamlet said. "I'll be back shortly. There's nothing tae think I did anything wrong. We didn't fight, Jenny and I. Never. I'll go explain. It'll be better there than here." He smiled at Mrs. Tuttle.

"I'll go with you," I said. It wasn't until after the words were out that I looked at Edwin.

He nodded confusingly.

"No, Delaney, you don't have tae go," Hamlet said.

"I think it is a lovely idea," Rosie said. "She'll come back tae the shop with ye when ye're done."

The two inspectors looked at each other but didn't seem to be able to come up with a good reason why I shouldn't join them.

"Very well. Let's go." Inspector Morgan led the way. He kept his hand on Hamlet's arm and guided him to the police vehicle out front. The rain had stopped, but more was coming if the still-dark clouds were any indication.

Just after Hamlet was deposited in the backseat, Inspector Morgan assisted more than guided me next to Hamlet. As I glanced out the window right before we pulled away from the curb, I saw Edwin, Rosie, the customers, and Hector watching from outside the shop. I also saw one other observer.

In front of the bar of my same name stood a very handsome man, though he wasn't wearing a kilt this time. Tom had probably watched the entire display, including my escorted trip into the police car.

He rubbed his chin as his eyebrows came close together. For a moment I thought I might have ruined any chance to get to know him, but just as the car jutted out into the street I was sure I saw a wave of amusement pass over his face.

My bold inner rebel patted me on the back.

FIFTEEN

If I had my bearings correct I thought the police station was located down the hill on the Royal Mile. In fact, we were close enough to the water and coastline that I saw a currently unpopulated beach at the end of the road and small, foamy, dark waves hitting the shoreline. The station was inside a small, old brick building with a clock tower rising up its middle turret. The sign above the door said, "Monticello Police Station."

We were taken inside where I was directed to sit on a reception area bench and wait.

Hamlet had calmed some from his initial fear, but he was still intimidated by being hauled off by the police. He'd gone willingly, but still, going with the police was always scary.

The station's architecture was like a lot of other buildings I'd seen, medieval, probably Roman, which I thought was just ornate enough to be regal but not enough to be froufrou.

Even the simple wooden bench I sat on was old, probably crafted in the early 1900s. Its two seat spots were worn shiny and dark but the rest of the lighter-colored wood looked old and tired. "Jessie loves Billy" had been scratched into the armrest next to me. I wondered how someone had managed to deface police property as a number of police officers sat so close, each of them taking their fair share of turns to glance in my direction.

Soon after we arrived and Hamlet was taken down a hallway, Inspector Winters appeared from behind a wall that extended back from a pillar.

"The young lad told me you're from America and that you just arrived. Welcome tae Scotland. Coffee?" he said as he offered me a Styrofoam cup.

I didn't like either him or the taller, skinnier Inspector Morgan, and my protective sensibilities for Hamlet had been quickly armed. But I didn't think I should decline the offer of coffee.

"Sure. Thank you."

I took the cup and Inspector Winters sat down beside me on the bench. There was plenty of room, but I suddenly felt crowded and I moved over a little.

"What do you think of our fair country? How do you like Edinburgh?" he said.

"So far, I like the country and the city, though I haven't seen much of it yet. Jenny's murder has made the first part of my experience heartbreaking."

"I'm certain," he said.

Inspector Winters looked around the station, toward the space behind the front reception desk. I looked too but didn't see anything interesting so I turned my attention back to him. He smiled, almost shyly. I wondered if I was being set up for something, though I couldn't imagine what it might be.

"I'll tell you now that I don't suspect either Edwin MacAlister or the young lad we brought in of killing Jenny MacAlister."

"Oh, well, that's good. I'm glad to hear it," I said, but I didn't really believe him. "Then why did Hamlet have to come in?"

"My partner isn't of the same mind. He thinks that someone at The Cracked Spine was involved."

"Why?"

Inspector Winters shrugged, his beefy shoulders somehow moving in what seemed like slow motion.

"There are reputations to consider," Inspector Winters said. "You might not be aware of them yet since you're new tae Scotland, but there's a MacAlister reputation, and the lad currently being questioned has a sketchy history."

"Oh, yeah?" I said after I swallowed a gulp of the lukewarm coffee.

"Aye. Legend has it that one night Jenny MacAlister took off from the family estate with a carload full of all sorts of treasures. Gold candlesticks and the like being among her haul. Or so the story goes. I suspect it was something less impressive, like some small trinkets or just money, but the story of a big bag bursting at the seams with invaluable treasures works better. Anyway, she ran off and sold everything for drugs. That was it. Right then and there she turned into an addict. Of course, we all know that there's more tae her story of becoming what she became, but again, the story's better with some extra drama added."

"Legend? Edwin, Jenny, their family, they are all so well-known that there are legends about them? There are stories? People talk about them?"

"Aye. You've come tae work for one of our better-known citizens. You didn't know?"

"He's not known of at all in Kansas."

"Well, maybe not by you, but I bet someone else there has heard of him."

"Maybe. Go on," I said.

"All right. Jenny was both disowned and disinherited by her parents. In fact, so much so that when they gave everything tae Edwin, they included lots of legal caveats that prevented him from giving her even one single pound or he shall have tae forfeit the whole lot tae the Scottish government."

"That's strange."

"Aye, 'tis, but his parents were wealthy beyond imagination and they had pull with everyone in Scotland."

I nodded, as the close relationship of politics and money in both my home country and my new one were almost boringly redundant. Some things were the same the world over.

"It was shortly after Jenny's departure that her parents set everything in motion and they died shortly after that. If only Jenny had behaved herself a few more years, she would have been set."

"Or just a rich addict," I said.

Inspector Winters looked all around and then leaned a little closer to me. "It's said that he—Edwin MacAlister—has a secret room full of things Jenny stole, both from her parents' house and others. It's said that he opened The Cracked Spine so he could find a way tae give her money without breaking any of the legal obligations his parents put into place, that the old woman who works there cooks the books—och, I suppose that's not a good expression tae use for a bookshop—knows how tae work the numbers so that she hid the money Edwin gave Jenny."

"I see," I said. I took another sip as I thought back to the moments before Edwin and I left the shop for the auction. Rosie seemed befuddled by Edwin including Jenny in the auctions. Was she stumped at how to work the numbers or was it something else?

Inspector Winters sat back. "Has he shown you the room?"

"No, I don't know anything about a room like that," I said. "I think it's just all fodder . . . wait, you all call it blether. It's all blether."

"Aye, I think so too," he said with a wink.

"What about Hamlet and his sketchy past? What did you mean by that?"

"He had a rough childhood, has a record from those days. My partner is convinced that Hamlet's past run-ins with the law make him a prime suspect in Jenny's murder. He was at her flat the night before she was killed, and we . . . my partner thinks the lad is hiding something. Would you know if he's hiding something important?"

"No, nothing. But. What kind of run-ins, specifically?" I asked.

"Can't say. It would be against the law for me tae tell you. Maybe someone at the shop will tell you." Inspector Winters smiled. I didn't want to like him. His trickery was poorly executed, but I sensed that he hadn't tried all that hard to trick me into anything, just manipulate me to seek some of my own truth. I appreciated the style more than any strong-arm techniques he might have tried.

"Excuse me. I need tae get back. Call me if you feel a need tae share anything important with me." He stood and handed me a business card before he moved through a short swinging door. He looked back once more and tipped an imaginary hat my direction before disappearing down the hallway.

Shoot, I liked him. And though it might not be a bad idea to have a police officer as a friend in my new city and country, I didn't want to like him right at this moment.

I looked around. There were officers on the other side of the swinging door, but they didn't seem interested in what I was doing. I reached into my pocket and pulled out the note from Ingy along with some of the small pieces of purple paper. Carefully I put the small pieces back into my pocket and then unfolded the note.

As Birk had instructed Ingy to do, she'd listed the addresses and phone numbers of Monroe Ross, Genevieve Begbie, and Birk Blackburn. Ingy's handwriting was wobbly but clear enough. She also added some lines at the bottom of the paper. It said: *Ms. Begbie will be giving a lecture late this afternoon at the university. She's an expert on vases, or some such silliness.*

The note also listed the time and location of the lecture.

Just as I was tucking the note back into my pocket, this time into a pocket without the small pieces of paper, Hamlet appeared from behind the wall and pillar. He looked no worse for the wear. There was no visible evidence that he'd been interrogated or waterboarded. He looked somewhat put-out, but not harmed or harried at all.

"Hi," I said as he came through the swinging door. "You okay?"

"I'm fine." He looked back toward the now empty hallway. "Come on, I'll buy you a cup of coffee and tell you what happened."

I didn't know if I was more excited about his release or the chance to spend some time talking to him privately.

"Sounds good to me," I said.

We hurried up the Royal Mile, through intermittent rain, to a café called Leaftide. Its tall front windows were lined with green paint and the door was old-world wood. The inside was small but still roomy enough that Hamlet and I could find a table in a back corner and not feel cramped or eavesdropped upon. Inside it smelled like coffee and vinegar, a combination I wouldn't have guessed to be as appealing as it was. The outside smells had reminded me of a Kansas storm, fresh and sharp with ozone—until we'd passed through a pocket of sea air that had wafted up the hill. I'd never smelled such a thing and I knew I would remember it and forever tie it to the memory of the day I went with Hamlet to the police station.

Hamlet ordered us both coffees and some pieces of a chocolatey cheesecake that were delicious and light, each bite melting on my tongue.

"They asked me about Edwin and about my friendship with Jenny. They asked why I visited her the night before she was killed," Hamlet said. "One of the inspectors was mostly quiet and then left the room, but the other one, Inspector Morgan, thinks I was somehow involved in Jenny's murder, I'm sure. He doesn't have any proof, and I didn't do anything tae Jenny so he won't find any proof. I don't think he'll stop looking though."

"What did they want to know about Edwin?" I asked.

"They think he knows more than he's telling. He is, but I didn't tell them about the Folio. I wouldn't have, even if Edwin and Rosie hadn't asked me not tae, but not for the same reasons they have."

"What are your reasons?"

"Tae protect Jenny. Edwin's been good to me. I care deeply about him and Rosie, but neither of them seem tae want tae protect Jenny's reputation as much as they want tae protect the people involved with the auctions. I care about *her* too. She told Edwin she hid the Folio. What if she did something worse than hiding it?"

"I did sense that Edwin wasn't sharing all his reasons for not going to the police, Hamlet. Maybe he really is thinking that way too. But, I guess I need to understand why Jenny's reputation needs protecting. What could she have done with the Folio?" Honestly, I wondered how her reputation could be more important at this point than the extremely valuable Folio. She was gone, sadly, but finding the Folio should now be a priority. She wasn't my family though, and I hadn't known her so I didn't have any warm and fuzzy memories to counterbalance the bad things I'd heard, and I was probably judging too much.

"I don't really know," he said, his youthfulness now showing in his wide eyes for the second time since I'd met him. "But I think that we, as the family we are, need tae do whatever we can tae protect Jenny's reputation, at least until we know the truth."

I nodded, hiding my disagreement. "What do you know about the members of the Fleshmarket Batch?"

"I don't know who they all are, but I know some of them. Birk comes into the shop, a couple others have been Edwin's friends for a long time."

"Were many of them friends with Jenny?"

"Oh. I don't . . . oh, aye, Jenny was friends with some of them, but that was years ago."

"Wasn't there a romance or something? Broken hearts?"

Hamlet's eyebrows came together. "Aye, there was, but that

was a *long* time ago. I suppose I've heard the stories, but it was before my time. Monroe Ross and Genevieve Begbie, those are the names that come tae mind. I don't know all the details."

"Do you think that maybe one of them, or both of them, could have still been angry enough to hurt Jenny?"

"No, that was . . . a long, long time ago," he repeated.

"Right. But Edwin was bringing Jenny back into his life, into the business. Maybe there was some buried resentment rearing its ugly head?"

"I don't think so," Hamlet said slowly.

"What do you think happened to Jenny?"

"I don't know, but it had tae be one of the drug people in her life. There were plenty. The building she lived in is full of trouble."

I didn't know if Hamlet knew I'd been to Jenny's building so I didn't ask about the quiet I'd noticed. "She wasn't sober? The building holds temptations?" I asked.

"Aye. And Jenny had been sober for some time, though I don't think she was the night I visited. I didn't tell Edwin. It seemed like the wrong thing tae say as he was telling us about her murder."

I nodded. "Why did she live where she lived?"

"I suppose a desire tae live the way she wanted tae live no matter what Edwin wanted. You have tae understand how bad their relationship was not all that long ago. It was venomous bad. Edwin found a way tae pay her bills, but she didn't want him tae. She resented it. Finally, he worked behind the scenes, talked tae her landlord and asked him tae call directly if there were rent issues. Edwin's getting older, Delaney. I truly don't believe he's ill, but his hiring you and his attempts tae heal the relationship with his sister are ways of putting his life in order,

I think. He should never have given her the Folio. Never. He knows that. It was . . . just his *big* way of doing things."

"How did she pay her own bills if Edwin wasn't helping?"

"She cleaned houses for a time, but that was a while ago. Other than that, I have no idea." He shrugged.

I took a long, thoughtful sip of coffee. It was much better than the police station's. "Hamlet, how old are you and how did you get to The Cracked Spine?"

He perked up a bit. "I'm nineteen. I was adopted, not legally but in a real way nonetheless, by Edwin and Rosie and Hector, and Jenny for that matter, four years ago when I was fifteen and living on the streets."

"Oh. That sounds rough."

"It was. I was a regular Charles Dickens character, with the dirty face, thieving ways, and everything, but in Scotland instead of England."

"What happened?"

"My family was killed when I was ten. I didn't do well in the government system so I ran away and lived on the streets. I spent most of my days in bookshops around Edinburgh, other cities too, but mostly Edinburgh, reading as many books as I could and then stealing food from wherever, whenever I could get away with it. Other, terrible things too, but I don't like tae dwell on those. Rosie approached me one day. I was on the floor by the front window shelves. I was reading something I can't even remember now, and I thought she was going tae kick me out of the shop and tell me never tae come back again. Instead, she took me out for a wappin . . . enormous meal. I ate every bit of it and then she set me up a bedroll in her office where I stayed the night. The next morning she introduced me tae Edwin. I told him everything, all the ugly details about what happened tae my family and how poorly I'd handled the ugliness. He took me tae his estate and got me cleaned up. He set me up in a flat not far from here for a while. I finished all my primary school. Now that I'm at university, I live in a dormitory and work at The Cracked Spine tae pay my bills. Edwin pays me enough so that I can afford everything. He pays me too much for the job I do. I owe him, but he'd never say that. Edwin and Rosie and Hector—and now you, if you stick around—will always be my family, informally adopted though they might be."

"I'm planning on sticking around, and I'm honored. I'm also sorry about your birth family. No matter how well things are going for you right now, all that had to be very hard."

"It was." Hamlet stared up toward the ceiling thoughtfully, into the past. I could see remnants of pain on his artistic face, but I could also see that he'd worked to hold on to good memories; I hoped there were some genuinely happy ones. "Anyway, when I first knew Edwin, I also met Jenny and she was sober. She remained sober for a full year, and she became something like a mother tae me. But her experiences gave her and me a lot in common. We connected on a different level, a level that knew about hard times. I was fond of her."

"My first day at the shop I thought I saw a strain in the way you talked about Edwin, and then in the way you two greeted each other the next day. Have you and he had problems lately?"

"Oh. That. Aye, I suppose, in a way. I didn't want him to give the Folio tae Jenny. When he first told Rosie and me what he'd done, I didn't hide my surprise. I told him it was a bad idea."

"It was. You were right."

"Aye, but I shouldn't have handled it with quite so much . . . surprise. I still feel bad about it."

"Was Edwin angry at you?"

"Not really, but it's the first time I spoke out against something. I think we're both just trying tae figure out how tae accept that I might sometimes have a differing opinion about something. Rosie told me that I should always speak up even if I disagree. She said it's part of growing up."

"It is."

"Aye, I suppose."

I took another sip. "Hamlet, did Jenny steal all the stuff that's in the warehouse?"

"Ah, you've heard the legend. No, she didn't steal any of it. I know she didn't live a lawful life, and I don't know *exactly* where Edwin gets all his things, but Jenny didn't steal any of them. They weren't a sibling team of thieves, though it's a fine story and one that keeps people talking."

As we finished the coffee and cakes, we moved onto more pleasant conversation topics. He, like Birk, was interested in my farm life in Kansas. I told him about milking cows, feeding chickens, and all the laborious hours it took to run a farm. As I talked, the tension from his visit with the police dissipated almost completely.

"I suppose we should get back tae Rosie," Hamlet said with a glance at the time on his phone as the waitress picked up our plates. "She'll be worried."

It wasn't raining when we left, but almost drizzling as we continued back up the Royal Mile and then down the curved hill to Grassmarket and The Cracked Spine, where only Rosie remained to greet us and question Hamlet probably more thoroughly than the police had. It was cool and wet outside, but pleasant and I didn't mind the frizz my hair took on.

I didn't doubt *all* that Hamlet had told me. Exactly. I didn't think Edwin and Jenny were a sibling team of thieves. In fact, I didn't really think Edwin was a thief in the strictest definition of the word.

But there were a lot of secrets in the air. I felt like I'd only been able to grab on to the tails of a couple of them. No one owed me their full stories, but something told me that Jenny's killer lurked amid all those secrets.

At around four o'clock and as Rosie called an early end to the workday, she, Hamlet, and I went our separate ways, and I realized I'd just have to keep looking.

SIXTEEN

By myself, I took a bus to McEwan Hall on the University of Edinburgh campus. The university was the other direction from my new cottage and not too far from the bookshop. Though I still wasn't on a UK phone plan, I thought it was worth paying a little extra to do some quick research. Easily I pulled up maps and bus routes on my phone as I sat on a bench in the Grassmarket square. I didn't want to bother Elias and I thought I could handle the short trip on my own, particularly if I found a friendly bus driver. It had drizzled again, but the sky was now clear, and the sun wasn't setting yet. It was cool but comfortable if I kept my jacket on.

Not only was the bus driver friendly, so were the three university students I sat next to on the bus. I explained where I was going and they directed me, even pointing to the correct door I should use to reach the building's reception hall.

"Is nothing in Edinburgh ugly?" I said as I peered out the bus window at the domed building, done Italian Renaissance style with brown stone blocks, decorative pillars, and oversized dark wood doors.

"Aye," one of them said. "Have ye seen the parliament building? An eyesore, for sure."

"I'll have to check it out," I said, remembering Elias's similar opinion.

I thanked them and then found my way inside and up a ramped marble hallway. I needed to turn left to get to the reception hall, but the main hall was to my right. The access doors were wide open, and I couldn't miss the chance to peek inside.

One of the students had told me that McEwan was the graduating hall for the university, and it was nothing like any graduating hall I'd ever seen in person. It was old world and churchlike, vast with murals and a giant pipe organ. Reverent and oozing with the smarts of the people it had accommodated with a diploma. I didn't see anyone around but I didn't have time to linger. I was already a few minutes late to Genevieve's lecture.

Regretfully, I turned back and made my way to the reception hall. I put my ear to another oversized wooden door and heard a voice inside. Gently I pulled the door open.

It was a conference room, longer than wide with wood-paneled walls similar to what I'd seen at Craig House and a giant rug mostly embroidered with red. I'd come in the doors at the back of the crowded room. Genevieve was behind a podium at the front, and rows of wooden, straight-backed chairs were filled with interested onlookers as was the leftover standing room. I was able to wedge my way in between and to the side of a couple of tall men without disturbing anyone's view. Genevieve didn't seem to notice me.

Her expertise was in Ming vases. I loved old things, but I had no idea there could be a crowded room full of people interested in what she—anyone—had to say about them, but everyone listened with rapt attention. She was personable, humorous (even though I didn't quite catch all the words that brought on the laugher), and beautiful in a white suit with a long jacket, black trim, and black buttons.

I wasn't sure why I was there. I wanted to talk to her, but I didn't know what I wanted to ask, specifically. I thought I'd just play it by ear. I decided that approaching her after the lecture was a much better plan than simply calling her or arriving at her house unannounced.

As I watched and shifted my weight back and forth between my feet, I scanned the room. Fortunately, not everyone was dressed to the nines or I would have stood out for something other than my coloring. However, most people were precisely groomed and carried with them an air of affluence. I suddenly felt self-conscious about the frizz I'd been okay with earlier and I smoothed my hair with my hand.

My eyes landed on a shoulder in the back row, not far from where I stood, but on the other side of the room. I couldn't see anything but the shoulder, but there was something about the way it slanted away from the person next to it that seemed familiar. I leaned forward, sticking my head out from between the tall men, and recognized the slanted man, who was wearing sunglasses.

Monroe Ross.

Him being here would be like crossing off two items on my to-do list. That is, if I could get over to him, and if he would talk to me.

I quietly excuse-me'd my way through the people. There wasn't much room in the space between Monroe's chair and the wall, but I squeezed my way into it and crouched.

"Hi," I said, keeping my voice low.

He looked at me and even though he wore sunglasses, I could tell he was aghast at both my maneuver to invade his space and my impolite interjection of friendly conversation.

"Miss Nichols, hello," he said with a quick nod.

"She's amazing isn't she?" I said with my own nod toward Genevieve.

"Very much so." He put his finger to his lips to shush me.

"Oh, sure. It's good to see you," I said.

He nodded again and turned his full attention back to Genevieve. I stood and remained in the space next to him. It wasn't my intention to irritate Monroe Ross. I knew it wasn't necessarily polite to start a conversation with someone when a lecture was going on. But I'd known introverts like Monroe before, and I knew that if I didn't stick close to him—but far enough away that his space wasn't invaded—he would dart away without me having the chance to talk to him. He would dart away from everyone, not just me, but probably particularly me at this point. I'd have to try to mend our friendship later, when I knew for sure he had nothing to do with Jenny's murder.

The lecture flew by. Learning about Ming vases was just the kind of thing a girl who used to work in a museum and now works in a place with a room full of secret treasures enjoys. Had I not been so distracted by my imprecise plans, I might have taken notes.

Genevieve received a standing ovation, and true to my prediction Monroe tried to step past me and leave just as the ovation started. I grabbed the sleeve of his coat, too forcefully, and asked if he had a minute.

"Aye, I suppose," he said after a long moment's contemplation.

"Let's go to the hallway," I requested.

Genevieve would be busy with one-on-one questions for a few minutes at least.

The hallway was wide and I led us away from the main doors, giving us room and little chance to be bumped or interrupted. I let go of his sleeve and kept an extra distance between us. He relaxed a little bit.

"What can I do for you, Miss Nichols?" he asked.

"First, please call me Delaney. Second, I'm worried about Edwin. It's no surprise that he's taking his sister's murder very hard. Who wouldn't? He has little trust in the police, and I'm just trying to understand his sister better. Maybe I can help him get through the grieving, or maybe something I find out could jar a memory loose for him so that he can give the police a direction to look for her killer." It wasn't a complete lie, and it didn't make complete sense, but if Monroe didn't think too much he might not see the holes. Mostly, I counted on Birk's comments about him and others being worried about Edwin. I could pretend to be reporting in.

"I don't know how I can help, Delaney," he said.

"Do you have a description of his sister as you knew her? What can you tell me about her?" I asked.

"Oh, well, it was a long time ago that I truly knew her. She was kind, funny, a handsome woman who you would think was pretty when you got tae know her."

"That's a beautiful way to be described," I said.

He shrugged, and the light from a ceiling fixture blinked over the lenses of his sunglasses.

"When was the very last time you talked to her? A week or so ago, maybe a week and a half, right? You two argued in her flat?" I said.

Monroe Ross froze. It had been a complete guess, a stab in

the dark. I didn't have one clue as to the identity of the man who'd argued with Jenny a week or two ago, or if Jenny's American neighbor had been telling the truth about hearing an argument that included a male voice. I was just going to ask the same question to every man I thought it could have been. I'd come up with the question as I'd sat on the bench waiting for the bus. I'd started to dial Birk to ask him, but the bus had arrived before I could hit the Call button.

Had I been that lucky to have found the right person on my first ask?

"We didn't argue," he said, thawing slightly. "Not really."

"Oh, okay. But you were there a week and a half ago, right?"

He pinched his mouth.

"What did you talk about?"

"It's not relevant," he said.

"Right, I'm sure, but maybe there's a clue about Jenny's personality in there. Was she sober?"

"Aye."

"Why did you go over to her flat?"

"She called me," he said, stopping short.

"Why? Was it out of the blue? Had you not spoken in some time?"

"It's not relevant, Delaney, not in the least."

"Was that the last time you saw her, the last time you spoke to her?"

"Aye," he lied. Maybe.

I tried to figure out how to ask another question he would answer. He was ready now, though, and wasn't going to let his body language give him away again. Out of the corner of my eye, toward the doors where the lecture attendees were exiting,

I saw a brown flash amid the crowd. I jerked my attention in that direction. Had I seen what my subconscious thought I'd seen?

A young man's figure dressed in a Shakespearean costume and topped off with a brown ponytail.

"Was Hamlet at the lecture?" I asked.

"Not that I saw," Monroe said.

The crowd was just big enough that I could no longer spot what I thought I'd seen.

"Wait here a second," I said. "Please."

Monroe made a noncommittal sound.

I hurried toward the crowd and moved with it down the hallway and then out the same doors I'd originally come through. Once outside, the group dispersed in a few different directions.

I didn't see him though. I wasn't sure why I'd felt the need to chase after him, but it had seemed important at the moment. I wished I hadn't made the effort. I turned and hurried back toward the reception hall.

To no surprise, Monroe hadn't waited. And Genevieve was gone too, the reception hall empty except for a gentleman rearranging chairs.

"Help ye?" he said.

"I was looking for the woman who gave the lecture," I said.

"Gone. Left a wee moment ago."

"I must have missed her. I was even by the door," I said.

"She might have gone oot the other way, through the main hall. She left with her expensive vase and a gentleman in sunglasses. A security guard escorted them. Odd, someone wearing sunglasses when they're inside. Sairy."

"Yeah, odd," I said. "Thank you."

Once again I left the room and then the building. I hopped

on a bus and pulled out my phone to make sure I was going in the right direction.

I made it home just fine, though my mind was preoccupied with the day's activities and potential discoveries, making the ride nowhere nearly as satisfying as the one I'd taken that morning.

SEVENTEEN

Since it was the middle of summer in Edinburgh, my cottage had great natural light all the way up until about 9:30 at night if it wasn't too cloudy. It wasn't quite 8:00 when I took a lamp from one of the bedside tables and set it on the kitchen table, plugging it into an outlet low enough on the wall that the cord stretched straight. I had put enough money in my power machine to keep me going for a few days.

I spread out the pieces of purple paper. I'd brought a pair of tweezers with me from home and I grabbed them out of my bag and used them to arrange and rearrange the pieces, hoping I'd be able to come up with something quickly.

At first there was no making sense of the shapes and the ink lines and curves over them, but then I had a thought. I rounded up a paper towel and tore it down to the approximate size I thought the purple pieces had been when they were all together. Of course, I had no way of knowing yet if I was missing any pieces: big, small, whatever, but I guessed the best I could.

I tore the newly sized paper towel in half, and then continued the same maneuver until the napkin's smaller pieces closely matched the purple smaller pieces.

And I came to no good conclusion about anything at all. I wasn't even sure what I'd intended, except maybe to just get a feel for the tearing of the paper. I got no feel, no sense of anything. Just about the time my eyes got tired of looking at all the nonsense, a voice that wasn't from a book sounded in my head.

Borders first. There's simply no other way, Delaney. Let this be your first puzzle lesson, and remember to let it apply to life too. You just can't know what you've got until you know where to begin.

It was my father's voice and though I'd first heard the words when I was about five, I was pretty sure the memory was spot-on. My stomach ached briefly when I realized how much I suddenly missed my parents. I needed to get a new phone and call them soon.

"Borders. Maybe that will work. Thanks, Dad," I said aloud.

With the tweezers I extracted what I thought were the border pieces and placed them a good foot away from the others. And then with a patience even I didn't know I had, I somehow placed the pieces side by side to make something that resembled a border, at least a border with one corner and one middle piece missing.

I still couldn't make out anything at all. Except I was satisfied to have created a good beginning. There was no draft through the cottage, but I didn't want to risk it. I grabbed a glass bowl from one of the kitchen shelves and turned it over on the border to keep it from being disturbed, and then I got to work trying to find some inner pieces, picking up the bowl only to test whether or not something fit.

My patience ran clear out after I'd only come up with what I thought might be two of the top inner pieces. I was perhaps seeing the beginnings of an O or a Y.

I was glad for the knock on my back door so I had an excuse to give up, at least for a little while.

"Hello, dear girl, Aggie wants tae ken if ye'd like tae join us for a late supper. We're just getting 'round tae it ourselves, and neither of us have shown ye where the local stores are. We'd love your company."

"I accept," I said. "But only if you let me make you some meals when I get my feet under me better."

"Would be our distinct pleasure and honor."

I hesitated. "Elias, are you or Aggie any good at puzzles?"

"Gracious, lass, I'm not good at much of anything, but Aggie's my counter and is good at just about everything, puzzles included. Why?"

"After supper, I have something I want to show her. Maybe she can help."

"She'd be tickled, I'm sure."

Supper was a surprise with my first real taste of haggis (I did not hate it, but I did not love it either), tatties and neeps, which were basically potatoes and turnips. I really liked them, even though I didn't think I liked turnips. Aggie had put what I guessed was nutmeg on the neeps, which gave them an appealing flavor. Both Elias and Aggie laughed when I managed only half the haggis, and said they'd get me converted eventually.

After we cleaned up, they joined me in my cottage. I hadn't had much of a chance to personalize it beyond making my own sort of mess by opening the two suitcases and rifling through them enough to make a couple of piles of clothes and other things. My new landlords didn't seem to notice the mess as we all sat around the kitchen table.

"Well, ye've got some of the border," Aggie said as she peered through her reading glasses at the pieces of paper. "Gracious, it's a little more difficult when all the pieces have such unusual shapes and sizes. And something tells me there are pieces missing."

"The writing on them might help," I said doubtfully.

"Hmm. Mebbe," Aggie said, but then she moved her face a bit closer. "Ye might have something."

Using the tweezers, Aggie picked up a piece of paper and placed it in the top right corner, under a border piece. She grabbed another piece and placed it next to the first.

"That might be the letters 'r-r-y,'" she said.

"I think that's more than possible," Elias said as he stood over her shoulder.

"That's amazing, Aggie," I said. "I didn't see that at all."

A moment later Aggie's shoulder twitched. Elias looked at me with raised eyebrows. "Shall we perhaps catch a television show?"

"I have a better idea," I said. "If you're up for it, that is."

"Awright," he said doubtfully.

I smiled. "There're a couple of areas of town I'd like to drive through. Are you available to take a drive?"

Elias glanced at Aggie, who nodded absently, her attention on the pieces of paper.

"I believe I am," he said.

"I can probably spend an hour or so on this before I go baurmie," Aggie said. "Come back then."

"We shall," Elias said.

After we were comfortable in the cab—again, I was in the front passenger seat—Elias asked where I wanted to go.

I pulled the note from Ingy out of my pocket and recited Genevieve's address.

Elias whistled. "That's a weel-aff neighborhood."

"Could we go there first?"

"Aye."

It was dark and I thought we were headed toward Birk's neighborhood, though from a more westerly direction than Edwin had taken.

"Elias, have you ever heard any stories about my boss, Edwin MacAlister, or his family?"

"No, I didnae recognize the name t'all. After ye told us aboot his sister, Aggie mentioned that she might have heard something about the family but she wasnae sure what it was. Neither of us are much for blether though. We were both brought up to mynd our own, ye ken?"

"The police stopped by the shop today. They wanted to talk to one of the employees so I went with him to the station. One of the inspectors told me about the family and how they are well-known throughout Scotland. I wonder how true that is."

Elias shrugged. " 'Fraid ye'll have tae ask someone else. I dinnae ken. How's yer coworker? Did they arrest him?"

"No. He was released."

"That's good."

"Yeah," I said absently.

"Here we are. Beautiful hoose." Elias pulled the cab to a stop next to the curb. We were the only vehicle either parked or traveling down the quiet street, but Genevieve's Tudor was set back behind large patches of lit gardens and a circular driveway.

Unless she was looking out a window, she wouldn't know her house was being spied upon, and a cab might not garner as much attention as a regular car.

"The flowers are even pretty at night. I bet they are spectacular in the daytime," I said.

"Aye. Who lives there?"

"A woman I met with my boss. Her name is Genevieve Begbie. Ever heard of her?"

"I've 'eard of a Harold Begbie. He's a fisherman. Something tells me they're not related."

There was no car parked in the circular drive, but the lights were on in the front of the house. I put my hand on the car door handle but hesitated. It was late, after ten, and what would I say if she answered the door anyway?

I was just about to suggest that we could leave when a car approached from behind.

"Duck!" I said as I grabbed Elias's arm.

"Why? We're not doing anything questionable," he said.

However, he did as I asked and we were both suddenly scrunched down in our seats.

"Shall I turn off the engine?" Elias asked.

"Yes. No! No, it's okay. It would look weird if you did that now."

"More curious than what we're already doing?"

"Hang on," I said as I eased myself up a bit.

The car drove past us and then up and onto Genevieve's circular driveway. It was immediately recognizable. A Citroën. I eased up a bit more but hopefully not enough to be seen by whoever got out of the car.

"Please don't be Edwin," I whispered, but I wasn't sure why I didn't want it to be him.

No matter, my hushed wish wasn't granted. Edwin stepped out of the car and his long legs moved him quickly to the front door. He didn't look toward the cab even once as I watched him knock. Genevieve answered a moment later, still dressed in the winter white suit. They hugged briefly before Edwin disappeared inside.

"Was it Edwin?" Elias whispered.

"Yes."

"Why is that a bad thing?"

"I'm not sure." I scrunched back down. "Can you get us out of here while I stay hidden?"

"Aye," Elias said as he hoisted himself up halfway. "Stay where ye are. I've done this before. I'll have us oot of here in a flash."

There was no reason to think that Edwin's appearance at Genevieve's house was anything other than a friendly visit. The late hour shouldn't matter. The friendly hug shouldn't mean anything more than friendship. The pep in his step didn't have to mean anything other than that's the way he walked. The fact that he didn't seem to have a mournful posture could only mean that I was too far away to read him accurately.

None of what I saw needed to mean anything suspicious at all.

So why did it bother me so much?

EIGHTEEN

It wasn't as easy to convince Elias to take me to the other location I wanted to explore.

"It's late, lass, and that's not a fine neighborhood t'all," he said.

"We'll just drive through. I've been there twice now and it hasn't seemed all that bad."

"The building where Jenny lived isnae as bothersome, but the neighborhood just off of it isnae good."

"Drugs?"

"Aye, and other things too."

"Maybe that's why she lived where she lived. Or part of the reason," I said, remembering Hamlet's answer when I'd asked him why. He'd said it was more about stubbornness.

"Meebe, but t'would be better tae drive around there during the daylight."

"Probably, but I'll get a better feel at night. Please. We'll make it quick."

Elias grumbled words I couldn't begin to understand before he said, "Awright. Stay in the cab."

"Thank you."

To his credit, Elias didn't ask many questions regarding my concern at seeing my boss at Genevieve's house. I didn't know how to relay my feelings about the entire situation without explaining the entire situation to him, and as he'd mentioned he wasn't much into blether.

He did suggest that I remain on my guard around my new coworkers, at least until I knew for sure that none of them was a killer. He might not have been into blether, but I suspected he didn't miss much of anything that went on around him. I told him I would stay aware.

Though Jenny's building was on the other side of town from Genevieve's neighborhood, it didn't take us long to get from one side to the other. Since it was so late, there wasn't as much traffic to contend with and Elias took backstreets with the skill of someone who knew all the shortcuts.

At first glance the streets around Jenny's building didn't seem dangerous. However, a closer inspection showed that not only were the buildings older, they were more worse for the wear, more run-down than "historical."

As the cab slowed Elias looked purposefully out the windshield and nodded toward what could be seen even in Kansas: two people in the middle of a transaction of some sort. If they were trying to look casual it wasn't working. I didn't think it ever did.

Elias said, "They're not concerned aboot who's watching. They probably ken the police cars."

"A cab might be a good cover. The police should think about the idea," I said.

Elias nodded again. "There. I bet that wasnae something for the young lady tae add tae the cake she'll be baking this evening."

"No, I think there's another kind of baking involved there."

"Aye. If Jenny spent time around here, no good came of it. It's not a place tae go just because ye'd like tae roam aboot."

"No," I said as I looked out the window. "Wait!" I sat forward in the seat and looked harder at a man who was walking past the couple just as they finished their transaction.

"What is it?" Elias said as he tried to see what had grabbed my attention.

"I know that man. He lives in Jenny's building. I've seen him twice now, and, strangely, both times he's been in his bathrobe."

"That's not what he's wearing now," Elias said.

The man who lived across the hall from the building manager was making his way down the street. He wore jeans and a long-sleeved black T-shirt. Though he was still unshaven, there was something very different about his manner and demeanor. When I'd seen him in the robe, he'd struck me as old and sedentary. But the way he moved in his real clothes made him seem somewhat younger and much more mobile. He moved with strength and purpose, though not in a youthful way. He looked to be in his late forties. If I'd guessed his robe-clad age, I would have said late fifties, early sixties. It was an alarming transformation.

"I need to go talk to him," I said with my hand on the door handle.

"I'm coming with ye," Elias said as he swerved the cab to a spot next to the curb, not too far ahead of the transaction we'd observed. Elias got out of the cab first and came around to the other side just as I opened the door too.

Elias had been wearing a jacket, but he took it off now and threw it and his hat onto the passenger seat of the cab. Under the jacket he wore only a short-sleeved white T-shirt. Without the jacket, the tattoos on his arms showed.

I looked at him with raised eyebrows.

He nodded and said, "Let's go."

I had an urge to tell him that I would be fine without him, but I was grateful to have him with me.

"Will we be okay?" I said quietly as we took off walking so we could catch up to the man.

"I think so, but if I tell ye we need tae leave, follow my lead."

"Will do."

The man ahead stopped with a red traffic light. He seemed antsy to get across the street, leaning over and looking up and down for a safe moment to cross against the light.

"Excuse me," I said as I set off in a jog, so as not to risk missing him.

Elias made a strange noise but kept pace with me.

"Excuse me," I said again when we were only about ten feet away.

There were a few people around, walking or waiting to cross too. But in the way that someone knows they're the one being beckoned, only the man turned and looked at me.

"Hi," I said as I stopped when we reached the corner. Elias stopped too, directly beside me.

The man looked at me first with recognition, but it transformed quickly into irritated disbelief.

"Hello," he said as though he didn't really want to.

"I'm sorry, but I saw you walking and I just wanted to talk to you," I said.

"Why?" More disbelief.

His accent was so thick that he made the one word sound like two syllables.

"Because, well, do you have a minute? We could go for a cup of coffee?"

He laughed.

"Whisky," Elias said. "I'll buy the first round."

"Well, now that might be more agreeable," he said. "I ken just the spot."

Even his voice sounded different than when he'd spoken to me from his doorway—younger, maybe, but definitely different.

There were no pubs named Delaney's in sight, but there was one called The Tilting Bear. The man led us around the corner and halfway down another block that was much darker than the one we'd come from. I got the sense that when we entered the noisy space, everyone there knew who the man was, but not in an it's-good-to-see-you way.

This was a rough crowd. They eyed people instead of looked at them. They squinted instead of smiled. They weren't loud in a party way, but rumbly in a serious, watch-your-back way. I was even more grateful that Elias and his tattoos, whatever they meant, had come with me.

We sat at a small table by the front window and our order was placed with only a nod from the man and a quick lift of his fingers from the table. I didn't even see where the waitress had been located to take the order, but a moment later, there was a bottle and three shot glasses on the table.

Elias did the honors and poured a shot for each of us. Both he and the man downed theirs with one gulp. I took a small sip and then put the glass back on the table. I knew I might ruin the moment, but I really wasn't a big drinker and now wasn't the time to do something extra stupid.

They both looked at me and, thankfully, smiled. Elias's smile was supportive. The man's was impatient.

"Dinnae drink?" the man said.

"Not much, and I promised someone I'd have my first Scottish whisky with them. I don't want to go back on my word. I'm Delaney, and this is Elias."

The man stared at me a long moment and then finally blinked.

"Why're ye 'ere? How is that ye've been in my building two days in a row and now ye're here?" he said. "Following me?"

His accent was even stronger than Elias's. Everything he said seemed thick and rolling.

"May I ask your name?" I said since he hadn't offered it up.

"Heath, Gregory Heath."

It sounded like Gra-egor-ee.

"Mr. Heath, no I'm not following you. I'm sorry because I'm sure it looks that way, but I promise I'm not. My interest in you has to do with one of the residents of the building you live in; the one who was killed earlier this week." I was also keenly interested in him, specifically his wardrobe choices, but Jenny was more important.

"It's Gregory. Ye want tae ken aboot Jenny then?" he said.

"Yes."

"What d'ye want tae ken?"

"I just want to know about her life. I have a personal interest."

"Aye, that was her brother I saw ye with."

I nodded but didn't add anything else.

Gregory shrugged and said, "She and I were friends, in fact."

I took a quick glance at Elias, but his attention was focused on Gregory Heath, his eyes suspicious and firm.

"I see. Well, I . . ." I stammered.

Elias cleared his throat. "The reputation of the neighborhood, Gregory. It's not a good place tae spend yer free time and most people dinnae unless they're looking tae buy or sell drugs."

Without seeming offended in the least, Gregory nodded, poured and then downed another shot of whisky, and said, "True, and Jenny was particularly haunted by drugs. She was an addict who lost every battle with her addiction."

"Every one of them?" I said.

"Aye, she never spent more than a day or so away from the stuff," Gregory said.

"Really?" That wasn't consistent with what either Hamlet or Edwin had said about her stretches of sobriety. "Stuff? What was the stuff?"

Gregory shrugged. "Most everything."

"Everything? Heroin?"

"Prescription drugs mostly, I think."

"How long did you know her?" I asked.

Gregory squinted one eye as he seemed to silently count back in time. "Coming on ten years, I s'pose."

"And she never spent any substantial time sober, in all those ten years?" I said.

"No, none at all."

"Are you sure?" I said.

"Aye. I fight my own battles oot here. I have the same problems. Jenny and I were friends because of our mutual demons. It happens."

"How do you function?" I said.

"Dunno, I manage tae get by, I s'pose," he said as he poured another shot. Elias put his hand over his glass when the bottle swung his direction.

"What do you do for work?" I said.

"Och, I've had jobs here and there. I get the bills paid. Most months."

"Did Jenny have a job?"

"No, never. Her high-and-mighty brother gave her money, I'm sure. But she'd never admit as much. She didnae always use the money wisely. There were plenty of times when she didnae have enough for rent."

Hamlet had mentioned that Jenny had once cleaned houses, and he'd known Jenny for less time than Gregory had. Edwin had been surprised that the building manager hadn't called requesting rent money from Edwin. The accuracy of the information I was accumulating was questionable, but I couldn't immediately determine who was telling the truth.

"What did she do when she couldn't pay rent?" I said.

"What we all do."

"Which is?"

"Beg, borrow, and steal."

"If that's just an expression, then I'm not exactly sure what you mean. If those were the actual activities, then there might be potential killers in the group that she begged, borrowed, and stole from. Do you know anyone who might have wanted her dead for such behavior?" I said.

Gregory smacked his lips and then licked them as if there might be a few stray drops of whisky in the stubble around his mouth. "Not specifically."

"What does that mean?"

"I mean, there are lots of people around here and in the building behave'n in ways illegal, immoral, and potentially murderous. Either ye're on friendly terms with them or ye arenae. Depends on many things."

"Okay, well, try specifically. Can you think of anyone else at all who might have had strong feelings about wanting Jenny dead? Who did you see her with over the last few days before she was killed?"

I doubted that the booze we'd watched Gregory down was the only altering item in his system, but his eyes suddenly became somewhat heavier, as if something had just kicked in.

"Gregory?" I said as I put my hand closer to his on the table.

He looked at my hand and then pulled his away. "Lots of people. Couple weeks before she was killed."

"Did you know them? Can you describe them?"

"Rich folks."

"Anything else?"

"Ask Harry, the manager. I saw her talking to him the day before she was kil't. He was wondering what she was up to. Meebe she told him."

"I will. You said I shouldn't look for a flat there. Why?"

"There are dangers . . . even in the places ye think are safe. It's no place for a young lass."

"Something feels strange about that, Gregory. The building is so quiet."

"Huh. Weel, I suppose it's verra quiet during the day. It's a little louder at night, but quiet doesnae necessarily mean safe. Could be people are trying to stay hidden, not call attention tae themselves."

"I'll keep that in mind."

"I hope so."

Gregory downed one more shot and I realized we were almost to the point we wouldn't be able to get anything even partially coherent out of him.

"Can we give you a lift home?" Elias said.

Gregory laughed again. "No, the night's young."

"You didn't drive here, did you?" I asked.

"No, I didnae drive. I don't drive." He stood and sought balance with a couple of fingers on the edge of the table. "Ye might find something else int'restin'."

"What's that?" I said.

"There was a man there the evening before she was killed. I saw him walk down the first-floor hallway toward the lift."

"Okay, what was he wearing?" I said.

"Some costume or something."

Hamlet's visit was old news by now.

"But later, as I was goin' up tae the third floor tae visit a friend, I heard Jenny through her door. She was yelling, telling someone tae get oot. It must have been him, but I didnae see."

"Did you tell the police?" I said.

"No, and I'm not going tae. The police arnae someone I want tae be involved with. I'm only telling ye tae make it clearer that ye need tae stay away from that building, particularly at night."

"All right. Can you tell me more of what he looked like?" I said, still not worried that Gregory had seen Hamlet, but needing to confirm that it really was him.

"I s'pose it wasna a costim, act-u-ly. It was a suit. Fancy. Tuxedo."

"How old was he?"

Gregory's rummy eyes worked hard to focus on me. "Older than ye." With a gigantic effort, his eyes moved to Elias. "More yer age. Meebe."

"Are you sure?" I said. "What color was his hair?"

He shook his head slowly. "Dinnae ken. Wore a hat, I think.

Mebbe red, though. As I walked by Jenny's door, I 'eard her yell a name, like from Shakespeare. I remember finding that funny. I wondered if they were in a play or somethin', but Jenny would never have been in a play. I dinnae ken."

"Red hair, are you sure?" I silently chastised myself for chasing after the figure of Hamlet I'd probably just imagined instead of sticking with Monroe.

"No."

"What was the name?"

"I dinnae ken. Macbeth. No, I cannae be sure."

I didn't think Monroe was the name of any of Shakespeare's characters, and I bit back the question: *Hamlet?* I didn't need to plant any seeds.

"Are you sure you can't remember the name?" I said, urging his sluggish mind to put it together.

"Maybe Othello?"

Whether or not he was remembering correctly, I was impressed by his recall of Shakespearean names.

"And did you see the man again? Perhaps leaving the building?"

"No, I went tae my friend's and dinnae go back tae my own flat until the next morning," he said.

Then he winked at me—a sloppy, bizarre wink. "Got me a girlfriend or two in the building. One on the third floor, one on the fourth. I have tae be very careful."

"I imagine so," I said.

Elias made a noise that sounded like a short growl, like an engine that had just been revved briefly.

"Anyway, Jenny would n'er talk much about her brother," Gregory continued as if he found a second wind. "A few days afore she was kil't, oot of the blue, she said something about him that made me curious. She said that he expected too much oot of her."

"Too much what?" I said.

"I asked the same question. Weel, I asked what she meant. She said that he had too much faith in her, sometin' about expecting her tae keep secrets. She wasnae a good secret keeper." He paused, wobbled a bit, and then continued, his voice almost inaudible. "He should have ken that."

"I see." I paused a moment, sure I knew what Jenny had been getting at. "Anything else?"

"No."

"And ye didnae tell the police any of this?" Elias asked.

Gregory laughed. "No. And they didnae ask. They wilnae. They dinnae care about people like Jenny and me. We've given them more trouble than we're worth, in their opinions."

"I think they'd want details about a murder. I've talked to a couple of inspectors. Do you mind if I send them to talk to you? Your information might be useful to the investigation," I said.

Gregory changed again. His heavy eyes became suddenly aware and bright. His mouth got tight and made a straight line. "What information? I havenae told ye anything t'all." A few seconds later, he had quickly woven his way through the crowd and out of the pub.

I looked at Elias. "Oops. I should probably have known better."

Elias watched Gregory leave the pub, probably to make sure he didn't come back and kill the stupid redhead from America who wanted to send the police to talk to him—a man with drug issues and, possibly, a record. Once Gregory was out the door and most likely not coming back, Elias turned his attention to me.

"Och, Delaney, ye did weel until the very end there," he said with a smile. "He did tell ye sae many things. I was surprised. But I wouldnae recommend that ye go tae the police with the information ye learned. Truth most likely isnae Gregory's strong point. And, if the police stop by his flat in the next day or two, ye might be in danger. Meebe not, but it's not worth the risk. And weighing the dangers is important. Particularly when murder's involved."

"Advice taken," I said. Though I wasn't sure what I would do if I were put into a situation where I thought the information might actually help find a killer. In a distant and fuzzy way, I was beginning to truly care about Jenny, the woman I would never know in person. Maybe Hamlet's feelings were wearing off on me.

"Let's go home," Elias said. "And dinnae tell Aggie we came tae this place."

"Deal."

NINETEEN

Hamlet and I were the early ones the next morning. I'd become quickly comfortable with my bus route, and I stepped off outside The Cracked Spine just before seven. The sky was blue and the temperature a comfortable coolish-warmish as I hurried up the hill to the bagel shop around the corner from the Grassmarket Hotel, where I ordered some breakfast and a giant cup of coffee. I spotted Hamlet unlocking the front door just as I turned the corner again making my way back to the shop.

I hadn't slept well. There was too much to think about. Along with trying to understand exactly what everyone was up to and if their activities could have anything to do with Jenny's murder, Aggie had put together another small part of the purple puzzle.

"*Tell Edw*" and then at the opposite corner, the part she'd already figured out: "*rry.*"

So, perhaps Jenny was sorry about something? There seemed to be a lot of things for a number of different people to be sorry for. One idea led to another, making my brain work overtime—all night long.

"Hi," I said as I came through the front door.

"Delaney, hello," Hamlet said. He was looking at something in a drawer in the front desk that I had determined was Rosie's favorite spot in the shop. He closed the drawer and stood straight, awkwardly moving his hands to his hips. He wore faded jeans and a light blue dress shirt. His hair was loose today, behind his ears and falling to his shoulders. He had nice hair.

"Share my bagel? I haven't had a bite yet," I said, forcing my eyes not to look at the desk.

"Oh. That sounds good. Thanks," he said.

As I followed him to the back corner table my eyes scanned the desk and then casually looked over the crowded bookshelves.

And I was suddenly struck by the flash of some invisible force that threatened to take my breath away. I stopped walking, couldn't move forward if I wanted to, and for a few beats my heart was loud in my ears. What in the world? What was wrong?

Fortunately, the moment passed as quickly as it had come on. My head cleared and my feet became unfrozen. Though I didn't know what specifically had happened, I immediately recognized the difference that followed. It was the books. They were suddenly and eerily quiet. I not only let down my guard and welcomed them into my head, but encouraged them to talk to me. Then begged them.

And, nothing. They'd been silenced.

Though the sun was up, morning shadows still lurked inside, not yet cast away by any direct light. I flipped the switch on the wall next to the stairs, bringing the ceiling fixture to life, and ran my fingers along one of the nearby shelves. I'd read at least three of the books on the shelf. I liked Jane Austen, mostly *Pride and Prejudice,* but as I touched its spine, no one spoke to me. Mr. Darcy and Elizabeth had both been big talkers in the past, but they were currently and stubbornly silent. The other day I'd noticed the books' silence as I'd left the shop with Edwin on our way to the auction, but I'd heard them since then. There was something about the wave of discombobulation that had just run through me that made me think this new voice-less circumstance was now permanent.

"Huh," I said.

"Delaney?" Hamlet peered around the wall.

"Yeah. Sorry." No matter what it was, I'd have to deal with it later. At least I didn't still feel like I might pass out.

I joined Hamlet and we split my ham-and-cheese bagel. I offered to pour some of my coffee into another cup but Hamlet declined, saying he'd already had a couple of cups that morning.

"You're here early," he said.

"You too," I said.

"I'm usually here this early. I have classes and I try tae get my work done. I check the e-mails and begin searching for the books that are requested."

"What's the most valuable book you've ever worked with?"

"One I didn't even touch. A signed first edition, perfect condition with the dust jacket still on it, *Gone With the Wind.* It was fate. Someone from America called asking if we would be interested in buying it. Aye, we were. Then a man from Germany called tae see if we had one tae sell. The same day. Edwin wouldn't get in the middle of it though, except tae help with the negotiations on both sides. He directed both the buyer and the seller and didn't receive any money from the transaction. He said he wouldn't have felt right about it, that we weren't meant tae have that one."

"Does that happen often? I mean, does Edwin turn away . . . commissions?"

"Aye, sometimes, if he feels like the fates have somehow intervened."

I chewed a moment. "He couldn't resist purchasing the Folio, could he?"

"If you had that kind of money, who could?"

I shrugged. "He won the auction. Was it because he paid too much for it or because the other members of Fleshmarket didn't want it?"

"I don't know. He didn't tell me how much he paid for it."

"Have you talked to any of the other members? Did they explain why they didn't want it?"

"I wouldn't talk much tae them unless they came into the shop, and then it would only be greetings. They are a part of Edwin's world that I'm not a part of. I don't know all the members. He did mention that as a whole they were all suspicious of Birk's story of how he got it. Edwin told me the story. It's far-fetched."

"What about Benny Milton? Isn't he in charge of looking for potential illegal activities?"

"I don't know Benny Milton."

I sat up straighter and looked at Hamlet. His eyes were sincere. Edwin had mentioned the secrecy around Fleshmarket, but now I was even less clear about who was a secret to whom.

I chewed and then swallowed another bite of the bagel.

"What did you do yesterday afternoon, late?" I said.

"Studied. Why?"

"I went to a lecture given by Genevieve Begbie. Do you know her?"

"Aye, she's a friend of Edwin's. She's visited the shop before."

I nodded. I had no idea how to ask more questions without giving away secrets. Maybe Hamlet wasn't supposed to know the identity of all the members of Fleshmarket. Asking how good of friends Edwin and Genevieve were didn't seem appropriate.

"She knows a lot about Ming vases," I said.

"I'm not surprised. Edwin and his friends know a lot about a lot of things."

"Ming vases not your thing?"

"No, not really." Hamlet's eyebrows came together.

"What do you think about where Birk said he found the Folio?"

Hamlet laughed. "I doubt it's true, but there might be a good reason tae make something up. I wouldn't feel right speculating though."

"Do you know the exact spot where he found it?"

"Where he *says* he found it. Aye, it's a tourist spot. Very popular."

"Is it too early to go there? I mean if you don't have too much work to do?"

"It's a wee bit early, but we could go in an hour or so. I think I can do that."

We finished breakfast quickly. Hamlet checked e-mails and I tackled the top row of books on the shelf by the front window. It seemed like as good a shelf as any to straighten and to see if any of the characters would talk to me. I also wanted to put myself in a spot where I could check the drawer that Hamlet shut so quickly when I first arrived.

The books were wedged in the space so haphazardly that I had to pull out eight of the thirty-two on the row and set them aside for some minor repairs. I took care to reshelf the others so they weren't crushed together or opened against the glass. The books weren't valuable other than they were all a bit old and bound mostly with cloth bindings. Someone would want them and would be willing to pay a reasonable price to take them home. I recognized *Treasure Island* and *Wuthering Heights,* and became distracted by a book of Danish ballads that had been translated into a combination of Scots and English—*Four and Forty* by Alexander Gray—and had couplets like:

> *You'll be the ninth, and that richt sune,*
> *To atone for a' the wrangs I've dune.*

I set it aside; the language fascinated me and I wanted to research its worth. None of the characters talked to me. Not once. It was strange, unsettling, but also unpredictably sad and lonely. I felt unmoored without them. I'd always needed to keep them under control, but I hadn't wanted them to leave.

When I knew Hamlet would be over on the dark side for a few minutes, I moved to the desk and opened the drawer. The only contents were a few pens, a yellow notebook, and—what I discovered when I turned it over—a picture. It was black-and-white and of two people standing together, their arms affectionately around each other, their smiles happy. One person was undoubtedly a younger version of Edwin. He had slightly fewer wrinkles than he had now—or maybe he had the same amount but they just weren't as deep back then. But he still struck me as regal, a gentleman.

I guessed that the other person in the picture must be Jenny. The two of them with similar tall, thin but sturdy builds. Jenny's hair was blondish brown I thought, straight until it hit her shoulders where the ends curled out. She wasn't pretty, but she wasn't unattractive either. I was always intrigued by the use of the word "handsome" for women, and I thought that, like Monroe had said, Jenny had been handsome, but still feminine.

She also seemed perfectly fine in the picture. I got no sense that she wasn't sober. It was an old picture and it was difficult to determine if her coloring was off, but there was nothing about her that screamed drug-addled.

Had Hamlet been looking at the picture or putting it in the drawer? Or was he searching for a pen?

As I put the picture back how I found it, Rosie came through the front door. I mimicked Hamlet's move and shut the drawer quickly before I stood and put my hands guiltily on my hips.

"What can I do for ye, Delaney?" Rosie said as she deposited Hector to the floor. He ran to me and I picked him up.

"Nothing. Sorry. I was looking for Post-its and felt guilty when you caught me."

"Ooch, it's not my desk. No need tae feel guilty. That's just where I sit most of the time. I do all the hard work in my office on the other side. The front desk is where we keep things like Post-its. Check the next drawer down."

I did as she instructed and found exactly what I said I'd been looking for.

"Hamlet here? Edwin?" Rosie asked.

"No Edwin, but Hamlet is here. He's escorting me on an adventure in a few minutes if it's okay with you."

"Only if ye tell me about the adventure when ye return."

Hamlet joined us as I explained the plans. Rosie had no problem being left alone in the shop for a short time. As we left the shop she said sincerely, "Hope ye find the ghost."

We walked up toward the Grassmarket Hotel and turned left onto the steep, curved Victoria Street. I thought we would go to the top of it to get to the Royal Mile, but halfway up Hamlet led us up some hidden stairs that got us there much more quickly. Once there we turned right and walked down the hill for only a couple of blocks.

We went through some doors under a Mary King's Close sign where inside we found a gift shop and a few young women dressed as though they were from the Middle Ages, in long skirts, long-sleeved shirts, aprons, and bonnets.

"Hamlet, what are you doing here?" a pretty blonde said from behind the gift shop counter.

"Mel, hello. This is Delaney. She's a new employee at The Cracked Spine and she really wanted tae see the close. When's the next tour?"

"A new employee? I've never heard of such a thing," Mel said with a smile and a wink. "Hamlet's mentioned how few people work there. You must be special."

"She is," Hamlet said. "She's from Kansas in America."

"Welcome to Edinburgh."

We shook hands over the counter and Mel explained that she would be leading the day's first tour in only a few minutes. It was a small group so there would easily be room for us.

Before long, we were on our way and Mel transformed into Agnes, a woman who'd lived in a room on the close back when people really did live there. She led our small group down into the depths of the earth where, just as promised, we found the remnants of the city below the city. The space was preserved so that we could see and experience, from a welcome distance of time, the horrible living conditions, the tightly cramped spaces that were filled with so many people, the few windows. Back then windows were only carved out for the affluent.

Agnes explained how two times every day, the citizens of the city on the hill would throw their waste out the windows where it would roll downhill toward the Nor' Loch, or "lake" as I would have called it. Agnes also mentioned that at one time the loch was where women were thrown to determine if they were witches. If they drowned, they were found not to be a witch. If they didn't drown, they were determined to be a witch and had to face an even more brutal death than drowning in the place where everyone's waste ended up.

The Nor' Loch and the waste are all long gone, the area transformed into Princes Street Gardens, the park where Hamlet's play was currently being performed.

It was neither a clean nor sanitary way to live, and the plague descended upon the city twice, each time taking about three-quarters of the population with it.

I was so interested in the stories Agnes told, in the short stone walls and unbearably low ceilings, that I forgot why Hamlet and I were there until he gently grabbed my arm and said quietly, "The next room is the cow room. Just past the small milking stall, to your right, you'll see a low fireplace. That's where it was."

The room still smelled, not of animal, but of something old and wrong. Agnes explained that the smell was genuine, that nothing had been done to either enhance or diminish it.

Hamlet and I stood toward the back of the crowd. When Agnes led everyone out of the room, we stayed behind and crouched down. Hamlet took a flashlight out of his pocket and shined it toward the fireplace.

"It's just a small indentation in the wall," I said. "Nothing could have remained hidden here for very long. Even as dark as they keep it down here, it would have been seen. This is where Birk found the Folio? It doesn't seem possible."

"Aye. That's what they—we—all said."

Something brushed along the back of my neck and I thought I heard another voice in the room. It was faint, but clear.

I was pretty sure it said, "Go away."

"Hamlet, did you hear that?" I said.

"Hear what?" he said, his question sincere.

Had I just come upon my first Edinburgh ghost? I sat still for a long few seconds and listened, hoping for another sensation to travel over my neck.

And then I got a little freaked out by the whole thing.

"I think we should go," I said.

"Certainly."

We caught up with the group and stayed with them the rest of the way, although I did look behind us more than once. By the time we emerged from the underground world and into a world with a menacing gray sky, I decided that I'd probably imagined the whole thing. Who wouldn't want an old Scottish ghost to visit them their first week in Scotland?

Yes, I was sure I imagined it.

TWENTY

Our adventure only took about an hour, and true to Hamlet's prediction we were back at The Cracked Spine before Edwin arrived.

Someone else was there though.

"Someone in the back tae see ye," Rosie said quietly to me as a sly smile tugged at her lips.

"Who?"

"G'on back and see."

I left Rosie, Hamlet, and Hector and hurried to the back, having to look around the wall to find the man holding a book open in his hands and looking intently at its contents.

"Hello," Tom said with an almost shy smile. Surely this man never felt shy, did he?

"You're not wearing a kilt?" I said, but I put my hand up to my mouth immediately afterward. "Oh, I'm sorry. I don't know if that was rude, but it just sounded wrong."

Tom laughed. "No. I wore one the past couple of days because I was attending a wedding, and the reception. It was quite a party. Nothing but work tae dress for today."

"Oh," I said. I cocked my head and looked at Tom Fletcher, and wondered again if he was real. When I'd decided to accept the position in Edinburgh, my highly imaginative mind had created scenarios and people attached to those scenarios. There had probably been a handsome Scottish pub owner among the people and scenarios. Was Tom Fletcher a figment of my imagination or was he, in fact, real?

Tom cleared his throat.

"I'm sorry," I said as I shook my head. "Can I help you with something?"

"I hope so. I was wondering if you'd like supper and perhaps a try of that whisky after you're done here for the day? I have tae work, but there will be others tae tend tae the customers so that I could sit down for supper and we could talk. The pub is directly attached tae the restaurant next door, which happens to be an Irish restaurant, but I can bring some Scottish whisky over there for us. It's a strange date, tae be sure, but you work mostly during the times that I don't and the opposite too. I'd like tae have dinner with you, Delaney."

Wow, oh wow, oh wow. He wasn't real at all, couldn't be, but I suddenly decided that was just fine.

"I would love to," I said, not even skirting along the edge of playing hard to get.

"Perfect. You're done here about five o'clock?"

"Probably about five thirty or so. But, how about I just get there on my own. I'd hate for you to wait if something holds me up here. I'll get there as close to five thirty as possible."

"I look forward tae it." Tom smiled and his cobalt eyes lit brightly.

"Me too." I wanted to dive into those eyes and traipse

through the thoughts behind them. I hoped they were as fun as the thoughts I was having about him.

Tom nodded, placed the book back onto the shelf, and then stepped toward me.

"I'll walk you out," I said.

The store wasn't deep so the trip to the front was quick. Hamlet, Rosie, and Hector watched unashamedly. Tom smiled at them and scratched behind Hector's ears before he left.

Once he was gone, I sighed and turned to my coworkers. "I'm not usually so pathetic. He's just a little bigger than life, and well . . ."

Hamlet laughed. "No need tae explain. He seems tae think the same of you. The sparks in here with you two might have burnt off my eyebrows. He was quite bold, I thought."

"Is that the Scottish way?"

"Only if a girl turns a fella's head enough. I believe that's what's happened here."

"That's never happened to me before."

"I don't believe you."

I laughed. "That sounds like I'm fishing for a compliment, but I'm not. Really. I've dated and had a boyfriend or two, but never gone out with someone like . . . like Tom."

"You don't know him. Maybe he's a terrible person."

"You know him. What do you two think?" I said, but I was oddly nervous to hear their answers.

"Tom's byous, wonderful, Delaney," Rosie said. "He's neither mean nor terrible. I know he's currently single, but I've never seen him sae . . . smitten. I've seen him date a fair amount and I've never seen him give any of them that kind of a weighty look."

"Is he a womanizer?"

"No, not at all! He's just never settled down, yet. Maybe he just hasnae found the right woman. Or maybe he has," Rosie said.

Hamlet smiled and looked both youthful as well as old and wise.

"I'll let you know how it goes," I said.

"I think you'll have a great time," Hamlet said.

I shrugged, trying to look much more casual than I felt.

"I'm not sure if Edwin has a specific task for me to do today," I said.

"You'll have many moments like that," Rosie said. "You'll get in a rhythm, but Edwin doesnae give much direction. You can help Hamlet find some art."

"I can do that." I'd wished for a chance to close myself in the warehouse, maybe make some calls or do some online research of the Fleshmarket members, but the tasks for the shop were, of course, first priority. "What kind of artwork?"

Hamlet led us to the back where he unearthed two file cabinets that were in the corner, hiding underneath some old, dusty, folded throw rugs.

"A couple years ago Edwin decided tae build our maps and prints collections. It won't come as any surprise tae you that our acquisitions haven't been well organized. You've inspired me, though. I'm going tae help you get this place in order, Delaney. You can guide me, but for now we're searching these files for some pen and ink drawings of Doune Castle. It's not far from here. You'd enjoy seeing it."

"What's so special that someone wants drawings of it?"

Hamlet smiled. "Aye, they are Monty Python fans."

"Oh?"

"*Monty Python and the Holy Grail* was filmed there."

"I definitely want to see the castle now."

As we rifled through the messes in the file drawers I inspected Hamlet. He was earnest in his search, seemingly not distracted by anything else. Nothing terrible seemed to be weighing on his mind. I thought I'd seen guilt when I first came into the store, but maybe that was just more grief. He might have come upon the picture of Jenny and didn't want me to see his sadness. Was he the "good kid" I sensed he was, or was his past bad enough to control his actions? What could a bad childhood drive a young man to do?

"Hamlet, guess who I ran into last night?"

"I couldn't guess."

"Gregory Heath."

"Who?"

"He lives in Jenny's building, right across from the manager."

"The man who's always in a robe?"

"That's the one."

"Where in the world did you see him?"

Briefly, I recounted that I'd befriended a cabdriver and he'd given me a tour of the city the night before.

"We ran into him in a pub," I said, changing the story a little.

"Of all people," he said. "Was he in his bathrobe?"

"No, it was strange. He seemed different in regular clothes. Really different."

"I can imagine. Did you talk tae him?"

"I did. Well, Elias, the cabdriver, and I did. Gregory said he knew Jenny well."

"He did?" Hamlet sat up straight, leaning back from the file drawer. "How well did he know her?"

"He said they were friends for a long, long time."

Hamlet nodded. "She lived there a long time. Jenny had a lot of friends, many of them undesirable, but I never knew her tae talk tae him, mention him. I didn't know him."

"He's interesting, but not someone I'd want to spend a lot of time with."

"Probably not. There aren't many in that building who you would, I promise you that."

I nodded. "He said something that's been bothering me since the moment he said it."

"Oh?"

"He said that Jenny was never sober. Not really. That she'd never had a stretch of more than a day or so of sobriety. Hamlet, is that true, do you think?"

Hamlet took the question seriously. He frowned and thought hard.

"I saw her sober, Delaney, and it was for more than one day at a time. I wasn't ever really with her for twenty-four hours in a row. But I probably saw her many days in a row, and she was sober. There was an obvious difference when she wasn't. It was easy tae see, and I saw that plenty too."

I nodded and tried to act like it was no big deal. Except that it seemed I'd made him mad, or something. I could hear resistance in his tone.

"Did she get angry at you the night before she was killed?" I said.

"Mad? No, not even a little bit. Not happy I was there, but not mad."

I nodded again. "Was she a yeller? I mean did she yell at people when she was upset?"

"Jenny? I'm not sure I ever heard her yell. I might not have ever seen her that upset, maybe," Hamlet said, offended even more now.

I also sensed that he wasn't telling me the truth.

"No?" I said. "Gregory said he heard her yelling the night before she was killed. That he was walking in the hallway and he heard her from there."

"That doesn't sound at all like Jenny."

Nothing that Gregory had told me seemed to be sounding like the version of Jenny that Hamlet knew. Were there two versions of her or was one of the men lying? The inconsistency was part of the reason I didn't mention the tuxedo-clad potentially red-haired man Gregory claimed to have seen. I also didn't want to shine the light of suspicion on anyone based upon the account of someone who'd been under the influence of altering substances. Not yet at least.

We were both silent a moment, but Hamlet spoke next. "Delaney, if Jenny was yelling, arguing, there was something wrong and someone else there. I'd like tae call the police and tell them that. They need tae be asking neighbors about that."

"Really?"

"Aye. I'll have tae talk tae them even if they become more suspicious of me. That doesn't fit at all. Maybe someone else was seen or a voice could be recognized. I have tae try. Jenny wasn't yelling at me. It was someone else."

As sincere as his concern was, I cringed inwardly. That was the last reaction I expected. I'd been fishing to see if Jenny and Hamlet had been arguing. I didn't expect for my news to actually be important news to Hamlet too. Gregory's reaction regarding me talking to the police had been loud and clear. Elias had mentioned that I might be in danger for doing as much.

Hamlet was right, though, something needed to be said to the police. I'd known that much when Gregory had mentioned what he'd heard and what he thought he'd seen. Just because Hamlet claimed it wasn't him didn't make it less important. In fact, it suddenly seemed much more important. Perhaps I could handle the police without including Gregory.

"Okay. You're right. Let me, Hamlet. I'll talk to them."

"Why you?"

I stood and brushed off my pants. "I think it would be better. I think I should go talk to them in person."

"I believe a call would be fine."

"No, I want to go. I'll go now," I said.

"Want some company?"

"No, keep looking for the print."

Hamlet was still sitting on the floor. His eyebrows came together as he looked up at me. "All right. Let me know."

I hadn't expected to make another trip to the police station. I hadn't expected Hamlet's reaction. I was thrown. But he was right. This was something the police needed to know, no matter how Gregory would react.

I decided that the best part of my surprise redirection was that if Hamlet was so intent on wanting to inform the police, he couldn't have possibly had something to do with Jenny's murder.

Could he?

TWENTY-ONE

"Hi, is Inspector Winters or Morgan in?" I said to the officer sitting at the reception desk.

He looked up with bored eyes and said, "Who wants them?"

"My name is Delaney Nichols," I said.

"And who's Delaney Nichols?"

"I work at The Cracked Spine," I said.

The officer picked up a phone and mumbled into it. I was standing right in front of him and I still didn't catch the words.

He hung up and said, "Through there, down the hall tae your right you'll find Inspector Winters. If you get lost, yell 'fire' and someone will help you."

I blinked. "Okay."

The officer's attention moved back to whatever he was reading on his desk.

"Delaney, hello," Inspector Winters said as he leaned out through a doorway not far down the hall. "Right in here."

The room was small, trimmed and framed in old wood like the rest of the inside of the building. The table and three chairs were also old wood, but were surprisingly comfortable as I took a seat and propped my arms onto the wide rests.

"What can I do for you?" Inspector Winters said as he set a notebook on the table and held a pen at the ready. He was dressed in civilian clothes, business casual, but his smile seemed much more welcoming today. I also noticed that though his shoulders were, of course, still thick and wide he didn't seem to be holding them in an intimidating way.

I got right to it. "What would you say if I told you that I recently learned that Jenny MacAlister was heard yelling, arguing loudly, with someone shortly before she was murdered, and that some people I've spoken with have told me that wasn't her way? That she wasn't a yelling type of person. And Hamlet is adamant that she wasn't arguing with him when he visited."

Inspector Winters frowned briefly. "I would say that everyone yells at one time or another, even the quietest, gentlest. I would also ask you tae give me the names of all the people who might have heard such a thing so I can get further details, just in case Jenny's yelling might lead us tae some clues about her killer. And I would wonder why Hamlet hasn't brought this news tae me instead of you."

"I can't give you their names. Hamlet wanted to talk to you, but I said I would instead," I said.

"Then your information is fairly useless, hearsay. Just something you came in tae tell me, maybe just because you wanted tae waste some time," he said as he set the pen on the table next to the notebook. "Why can't you tell me who told you?"

"Because I said I wouldn't."

"Why wouldn't someone want that information given tae the police? I would think that unless they're involved in the murder or the argument, which in turn might lead tae the murderer, they would want the police tae know everything they could know tae solve the crime. Do you see my problem, Delaney?"

"It's not that simple. Honestly, I don't think they were involved," I said.

Inspector Winters shook his head slowly. "All right, what were they yelling about?"

"I can't be exactly sure."

"I see."

"I have a suggestion."

Inspector Winters's mouth quirked. He sat back and crossed his arms in front of his barrel chest. "I'd be happy tae hear your suggestion."

"I suggest you talk to all the residents in the building, particularly those on Jenny's floor, to see if they heard the yelling, or perhaps saw someone other than Hamlet go into her room."

"We have talked tae the residents on her floor, others in the building tae."

"Did you ask if they heard yelling—specifically yelling? It's a troublesome building, right? The residents have given you lots of problems?" What had Gregory said? Something about the police not caring about the people in the building because they've given them trouble in the past.

"We asked . . . wait, that's not your business."

"But the people there. It's a rough place?"

"No rougher than some. Better than many others," he said, his forehead crinkling.

We were both fishing, but neither of us was catching anything.

"Did anyone see people there that night that didn't belong?

You know Hamlet was there. But what about other visitors who didn't live in the building?"

"Can't tell you that either."

I bit my lip. "Other than Edwin and Hamlet, have you talked to anyone else in Edwin's circle of friends? Do you suspect anyone like that?"

Inspector Winters rubbed his hand over his chin. His eyes had lit briefly when I'd asked the question, but he'd done this sort of thing before and he wasn't going to give away any real secrets.

"Delaney, I can't tell you that either, and you know I can't. Here's what I can tell you—well, what I'm going tae tell you whether I'm supposed tae or not. I'm only telling you because I'd like for you tae reward me back with an answer tae a question I have. Give and take. Understand?"

"Yes."

He sat forward, moving his arms onto the table. The space in the room was so small that I had an urge to scoot my chair backward but I didn't.

"We know Jenny was hiding something. What was it? Was it an item or a secret? It had tae do with Edwin, we know that much, but we need more information. We're certain the answer will lead us tae the killer."

"I wish I could tell you, but I have no idea. Really," I said.

I thought it was an Academy Award performance. I watched Inspector Winters's eyes to see if he bought it. I couldn't be certain, but I thought he had.

"All right. If you learn what it was, will you tell me?"

"Yes. Right away."

"Is this how you do things in America?" Inspector Winters asked.

I shrugged one shoulder. "I don't know. I've never known someone who was murdered."

He sat back in his chair again and looked at me. "Why is this so important tae you? You just moved here. You don't know who your friends really are yet."

"I don't really know why it's important, except . . . well, I'm a long way from home and family, and I want . . . maybe I need . . . to make Edwin, Hamlet, and Rosie family too. I want them to be okay and they won't be okay until they know what happened to Jenny."

"What if one of them was the killer?"

"I don't believe that's the case, but I'll deal with it if I have to." I swallowed.

"How well do you know them? How well did you know them before you traveled across the sea tae come work with them?"

"I tend to listen to my gut, and these are good people, Inspector Winters, I'm sure of it."

He looked at me a long time and then shook his head again. "Really, there isn't much at all I can do with your information, Delaney. I'm sorry, but I appreciate you coming in tae talk with me."

"You can try a little," I said.

His eyes slanted, but then he sighed heavily and dramatically and said, "I'll do something. I suppose you'd like me tae check in with you later."

I smiled.

"Don't count on it," he said firmly.

"I understand."

"Anything else?"

"No."

"I'll see you out."

Inspector Winters escorted me through the station and out the front doors. I thought perhaps he and I might end up being friends, depending upon the outcome of the murder investigation.

Though I'd started the day early, it was already late afternoon and my date with Tom was on the close horizon. I'd walked to the police station only because I hadn't wanted to take the time to figure out the bus schedule and hailing a cab other than Elias's felt disloyal. I wouldn't have time to go home even if I did grab a cab, but if I hurried back to the shop I'd be able to make myself somewhat presentable. If it didn't rain.

But, of course, this was Scotland, and rain was always a possibility.

TWENTY-TWO

My adventure back to the shop consisted of a number of step-out-of-the-rain stops into shops along the Royal Mile. I ducked into the End of the World pub, where a bartender who was the spitting image of Princess Merida from *Brave* gave me an umbrella to get me the rest of the way. I promised I'd return it in the next day or so. She didn't seem worried.

Once back at the shop, I hurried to the toilet on the dark side and hoped and, I'll admit, sent out a small prayer, that my hair would be salvageable. Hamlet was gone for the day but he'd put Rosie in the loop regarding my mad dash to the police station. As I scurried by her she asked how things had gone. She was glad to hear that all seemed well.

I needed a sit-down with my coworkers tomorrow. It was time for Edwin or someone (hopefully someone other than me) to tell the police about the Folio. I wondered how they'd learned there was a "secret" but that didn't much matter. The secret needed to be shared. Sooner rather than later.

The hair wasn't perfect, but it was passable; a little frizzier than I'd like but it had been much worse. I was dusty and wrinkled. I swiped and smoothed, but it didn't do much good. I needed to bring a change of clothes to work, as well as some backup makeup. I still hadn't settled into what I thought would be my real job yet. There were extenuating circumstances of course, but momentarily I envisioned which drawer in my old, ridiculously valuable, touched-by-Scottish-royalty desk I would keep some lip gloss and mascara.

When I returned to the light side, Rosie and Hector were waiting for me with knowing smiles. Well, I assumed that Hector was smiling too. Those bangs again.

"What?"

"Weel, I jest want ye tae know that while Tom is a good man, and a handsome one tae boot, he's had a number of girlfriends. I want tae remind ye that he's broken a heart or two."

"I'll keep that in mind. Thank you, Rosie." I held up my right hand, palm outward, and continued, "I promise I won't immediately fall in love with the very handsome Scottish pub owner who looks amazing in both a kilt and pants."

Rosie laughed. "He's a fine handsome one, that is for certain. Awright then, now that I've told ye tae be careful with yer hert, I'd like for ye tae have some fun too."

"I will. Where was Edwin today? Will he be in tomorrow?" I wanted the sit-down to be with everyone at once.

The concern that flashed over her face was brief, but real.

"I'm sure he'll be in tomorrow," she said as her fingers moved to the spot at the bottom of her neck.

"Where was he today?" I said. "Something wrong?"

"Och, 'tis nothing, Delaney. Sometimes, Edwin doesnae check in with us. He gets busy, perhaps gets distracted."

"Have you called him?"

"Aye, of course. He'll call when he has a moment."

"What would he be doing?"

"Working, I believe."

I didn't believe that's what he was doing, but that was based upon lots of assumptions that weren't backed up by many facts.

"Could he be hurt? In danger?" I asked.

"No," Rosie said, but she was worried too; I could hear it in her voice.

"Rosie, should we call the police?"

"No! No, Edwin wouldnae like that no matter what he's up tae. He'll call. He always does."

I thought about calling the police myself but Rosie probably still wouldn't tell me enough to make it a concern worth checking out, and I'd already given the police too little information once today.

"Will you call me if he calls you?"

"Of course. Go. Have fun."

"I will be trying my first real Scottish whisky." I didn't count the small sip I'd already taken.

Rosie straightened and Hector lifted his head.

"Ye're not a drinker?" Rosie said.

"Not really."

"Oh, dear, perhaps I should go with and act as chaperone."

"I'll be fine. I'll only try a sip or two."

The concern remained.

"Really, I'll be okay. I know how to control myself."

It's a great advantage not to drink among hard-drinking people.

I didn't hear the words as if the character Jordan Baker from *The Great Gatsby* was speaking them, but I *thought* them. Forced them. I could tell the difference. I'd heard them before and the moment seemed appropriate to hear them now.

"Don't we have a copy of *The Great Gatsby* in the shop?" I asked.

"I think. Do ye need tae see it?" Rosie said.

"No, thanks. Sorry. I got distracted. Strange." What was going on?

"Aye?" Rosie said. "Ye awright, lass?"

"Fine." I smiled.

As Rosie and Hector bid me good-bye I had the sense that they felt as though they were also saying good-bye to my innocence.

Did I really seem that untarnished? I couldn't decide if it was a good thing or a bad thing.

I made my way the short distance up the hill and stopped outside the open door to the pub. I peered inside. If it wasn't as advertised—the smallest pub in Scotland—it was at least one of them. Including the bar along the back wall, the space couldn't have been ten feet by ten feet. And it was currently very crowded.

There were no chairs or table-chair sets, but there were posts along the side wall that held small tabletops. Most people inside held their drinks, as they looked up at the television that had been placed on the wall over the door. I stretched my neck and peered upward to see what had everyone's attention—it was a soccer game.

"Football. It's called football here," I muttered to myself.

"Delaney." Tom came through the crowd and greeted me. "Welcome tae the pub named after my great-great-grandmother, but tonight we'll name it in your honor. Come along. We've got a table next door, but I'd like tae introduce ye to Rodger."

Tom grabbed my hand and led me the short but crowded distance to the back.

"This is not ideal, I know," he said as we stopped at the end of the bar. "I promise tae take you out on a real date next time."

I suddenly wondered if this was how he handled all his first dates. It was a convenient way to get to know someone without worrying too much about awkward silences, because there wasn't going to be a moment of silence in the bar for many hours ahead. If this way turned out to be a bust, we wouldn't have to try again in a more intimate setting. It wasn't a bad idea.

"Hi, ye're Delaney from America. I'm Rodger." A young man from behind the bar wiped his hands on his dirty white apron and extended one my direction. He spoke loudly, but quickly. He was skinny and somewhere in his forties, I thought. His smile was charming in an overbite way and the cowlick above the right side of his forehead was maybe the best cowlick I'd ever seen.

"Nice to meet you, Rodger," I said.

"Tom's been awfully nervous since he told me ye'd be coming over."

"Really?"

"No telling house secrets, Rodg. Get back tae work," Tom said good-naturedly.

Rodger sent me an exaggerated wink and turned to greet a customer.

"Sorry about that," Tom said.

"Not a problem. Were you really nervous?"

"I was actually," he said. "It's been some time since I've been nervous for a date. I'm going tae blame it on the fact that you're not from here, and I was worried I might do something so Scottish that I would offend an American."

I laughed. "That would be very difficult. The view from America, well, I suppose I should speak for my view only, is that everything Scottish is fascinating. The accent, the clothes—well, kilts and such"—dangit, here came the blush—"the bagpipes, the Scottish attitude, though I must admit that I'm not really sure exactly what the Scottish attitude is other than it appears to be somewhat carefree and happy, though very patriotic."

Tom looked at me a long moment with a small and amused smile. I tried very hard not to look away from his questioning cobalt eyes. I was pleased with myself that I managed to hold his gaze.

"You know, I can't say I've come tae know many Americans," he said. "The few ones I have met were tourists making their way through town. One had clearly had more than enough whisky. I think I put him in a cab and wished him well. One was here in search of his ancestors. He was an old man and he leaned on the bar for hours and hours, three or four days in a row. He didn't like tae talk much and didn't want my conversation, but he was friendly enough."

"That's it? Just two that were memorable?"

"No, many others. Those are just the ones that made the biggest impressions on me."

"Ye're the first American he's asked on a date, though," Rodger added.

"How can you hear us? You should be taking care of customers," Tom said.

Rodger shrugged and lifted two liquor bottles, turned them upside down, and poured from each bottle into a glass. "Yer voices carry right tae me."

"I'm truly sorry about this," Tom said to me. "This is a lousy first date, but I didn't want tae wait another day tae ask you. Rodger's got everything under control, but he might need some help during the matches. They'll be over soon and we can head right next door tae the restaurant."

"I think it's fun. You did mention that you'd serve me my first true Scottish whisky."

"Of course." He leaned over the bar, grabbed a couple of shot glasses and a bottle of whisky. After pouring and giving me my glass, he held his up and said, "Cheers! Let me know what you think."

I lifted the glass and sniffed. It was most definitely strong; even the whiff burned the back of my throat. I took a small, way-too-ladylike sip, but bigger than the one I'd taken in the other pub.

It burned, but not in an altogether unpleasant way, as it slid down my throat and landed softly in my stomach.

Tom had waited until I'd tried it before he quickly downed his.

"Confession time," I said. "I'm not much of a drinker so I imagine this will last me all evening, but it's pretty good."

Tom smiled again. "I typically don't drink at all when I'm working, so we'll be mostly even."

"You don't?"

"Well, I must admit, I enjoy my whisky as much as any good Scot, but it's a good plan tae lay off the stuff when the bar's open. Did you like it?"

"I didn't hate it," I said.

Tom laughed so genuinely that I forgot we were really on a date.

The next couple of hours sped by like something I hadn't experienced in a long time. The crowd expanded and contracted, cheered and booed the soccer . . . football game, and interjected a song I didn't recognize every now and then.

Before long, the football matches were over and we moved to a table in the Irish restaurant that was not just next door to Tom's pub, it was attached to it, a walk-through hole in the wall separating the two places.

I told Tom about my family. My parents and my brother and my numerous relatives spread throughout the Midwestern United States. I told him about growing up on a small Kansas farm, about Wichita, and about the museum I'd worked at since college. He thought my preserved buffalo was as interesting as Edwin and Birk had thought it was.

I learned about his life with his single father, the original owner of the pub but who was now a librarian at the University of Edinburgh, the death of his mother when he was barely a couple of months old, and his aunt who turned out to be the major motherly influence in his life and was still alive, eccentric now to the point of him worrying about her mental health.

"I think she needs tae be . . . monitored—I dislike that word very much. But I'm not sure how much longer we can leave her alone. I work, my dad works. We stop by her house every day, but we're starting tae be concerned about her eating and caring for herself in between those times," Tom said.

"I'm sorry. It's tough to watch our loved ones grow old," I said.

He waved away the comment. "Och, I'm sorry. Let's not be melancholy about that. Anyway, how's Edwin? I've stopped by a couple of times tae check on him but he hasn't been in."

"He's sad. Everyone's sad. The police are still searching for the killer. I think they have some suspicions about Edwin." I didn't think it was appropriate to mention that it seemed none of us had heard from him that day.

"That's not too surprising."

"It's not?"

"Sure. Jenny put Edwin through hell more than once. She was a mess. Though I doubt very much that Edwin had it in him tae kill his sister. Hamlet, Rosie under suspicion too?"

"Not Rosie as much, I don't think."

"But Hamlet?"

"I think so."

"His past is checkered tae say the least, but he couldn't kill anyone, unless . . ."

"Unless?"

"That was just me talking without thinking, but he was a pretty good little thief, particularly for a young lad. Do you know his story?"

"I know some, about being orphaned and Edwin taking him in," I said.

"If the police know his past, they might suspect him just because he's an easy person tae suspect, someone who was up tae no good at one time. A lot of no good. I don't know. Even though Edwin's taken care of Hamlet, they've had their tough moments. Jenny gave them all tough moments. I don't want tae think any of them could have killed her though."

"You know them fairly well, don't you?"

"We've been neighbors for many years. Edwin opened The Cracked Spine when I was just a wee'un. I like tae read. I would come tae the pub with my dad, and when I got bored I escaped tae the bookshop. It was a good place tae go, and Edwin always welcomed me, found me books."

"Do you know if Jenny was ever truly sober for very long? I mean, more than a day or two in a row."

"Certainly. I think so. I guess I can't be totally sure because though I know Edwin, Rosie, and Hamlet well, I never did know

Jenny as much as I knew *of* her. I heard the stories, but I'm fairly certain that she had some good spurts. Aye, I heard as much, I think."

I nodded. "One of her neighbors said she didn't, that she was never really sober. Not for any stretch of time at least."

Tom blinked and took a sip from his glass of water. "Neighbor? You talked tae her neighbor?"

"I did. I went to her building and snooped around."

"Really? Does Edwin know?"

"Kind of."

"I see. Well, I don't want tae offend you, particularly on our first date and considering my plans of scheduling our second date before we say good night tonight, but it would tend tae worry me if you were spending too much time at Jenny's building. I know where she lived, and I don't think it's a great place for you tae be."

I looked at Tom for a long moment. I wasn't offended. "Where are we going on our second date?"

Tom laughed. "I think we should try something quieter, perhaps with a little more privacy."

"Sounds nice."

"So, you'll accept?"

"You'll have to ask first."

"It's not quite the end of the evening yet, so we'll see how it goes. But before we take this any further, I'm going tae be an arse and ask you something you're trying to avoid. You'll stay away from Jenny's building, won't you?"

"I will not go there by myself. I haven't told you about the other parts of my new Edinburgh family. I've met a man, a cabdriver."

"Is he as handsome as the pub proprietor you know?"

"His wife probably thinks so," I said, though I suspected Aggie would find Tom plenty handsome too.

"I like him already."

I told Tom about Elias and Aggie and their home and my new home. I told him that Elias had come with me on two of my visits to Jenny's flat and neighborhood. I didn't tell him about my first visit to a pub, and I didn't tell him about the puzzle sitting on my kitchen table. That one was still a secret for me, Elias, and Aggie, or at least it felt like it should be.

As Tom listened I noticed that when he was concerned about something, his left eyebrow angled and his forehead creased. It might have been the most adorable thing I'd ever seen. This date was going very well, at least on my part. I couldn't remember the last time I thought someone's eyebrow angle was endearing.

"Sounds like Elias knows what's what," Tom said after I explained his protective nature. "I'm sure he'll be careful."

I nodded and tried not to smile too goofily at his eyebrow.

The evening didn't come to an end as much as a soft landing. After dinner we moved back to the mostly empty pub and sat on stools that Rodger brought out from the back. When the pub had been closed for an hour, one customer still remained. An old man named Johnathan was standing at one of the tables. He was hunched over his still half-full pint mug and would lift his head and take a drink every now and then, though the level of liquid in his glass didn't seem to change. I kept expecting him to topple over, but he never did.

Rodger kept himself busy cleaning and then sweeping the cobblestoned floor. He didn't actually ignore Tom and me, but he pretended to.

"Oh, it's really late," I said as I looked at the time on my phone. "Rodger could use your help."

"Rodger's fine. The time flew this evening," Tom said. "I'd like tae drive you home, but if you don't want me tae know where you live, I'll call a cab, or we can call Elias. I'd like tae meet him."

"I'd be okay with you knowing where I live."

We said good night to both Rodger and Johnathan before we left. Rodger didn't seem to mind being left with the cleaning duties and he said he'd make sure Johnathan got home okay.

Tom expertly steered his old but well-maintained Peugeot out of the small space he'd parked in the street. I was impressed with myself that I was able to direct him right to my cottage and that I didn't flinch *every* time he made a right turn from the left lane.

"You have a whole cottage?" he said after he pulled next to the curb in front of the guesthouses.

"I do. It's behind the guesthouses. I feel very fortunate to have found Elias and Aggie."

"It's not easy tae find a place tae live. May I walk you in?" Tom said.

"No, I'm okay," I said. "It's just around back." I put my hand on the car door handle. I didn't think there would be a problem with Tom walking me to my door, but I still had enough Kansas country girl in me to hold back a little. Not inviting him in wasn't a modern notion at all, but no matter what, there were still fields of wheat and checkerboard curtains running through my blood. "I had a really great time, Tom. Thanks for the date in your pub and the Irish restaurant, and my first real Scottish whisky."

"I had a great time too," he said.

The moment was awkward, but surprisingly only for a brief instant. We both managed to lean in at the same time and with the same velocity. We didn't smack foreheads or noses or anything else. We simply kissed. And we both finished at the same time. I thought we deserved a round of applause for the perfect choreography.

"See you tomorrow?" Tom said. And then he laughed. "Well, that wasn't cool in the least. I should be a wee bit more difficult tae read. I have some ideas for our second date, but I'll use the notion that I need tae think about them as an excuse tae come see you at the shop tomorrow."

"I like that you're easy to read. And, yes, tomorrow. I bet we'll run into each other sometime."

"I'll make a point of it."

I got out of the car, waved at Tom, and then hurried around the end guesthouse. It looked like all the lights were off at the McKennas', so I tried to walk quietly around their cottage to mine. I heard Tom pull away from the curb and move down the street.

I was living in the afterglow of a great date and a kiss that might not let me sleep ever again, when a voice came from the dark spot around my front door.

"Late night, Ms. Nichols?"

I screamed and then froze fearfully in place.

TWENTY-THREE

"Inspector Winters! Are you out of your mind?" I said as the police inspector, still dressed as a civilian, emerged from the shadow and into the light that stretched from a streetlamp in front of the guesthouses. I was scared, because it was all very weird, but I was also angry.

"I'm sorry, Ms. Nichols. I should have handled that better."

"What are you doing here? Were you waiting for me?"

"I *was* waiting for you. Do you suppose we could step inside yer wee house?"

I wanted to punch him, not invite him in for a conversation, but assaulting a police inspector, even one who was acting this weird, wasn't ever a good idea. Even if he deserved it.

No lights had come on in the McKenna house. I was surprised—my yelp had seemed blood-curdling and then some to me.

"You can come in, but we'll leave the door open and I'm not going to be hospitable."

"Of course," he said.

Once inside, I huffily pointed to the couch and then took a seat on the chair. I left the door open but it was on the side of my house that wasn't directly next to the McKennas'. As much as I wished they would come by to see what was going on, they must have missed the drama.

"Why were you waiting for me?" I asked.

"I'm sorry, Delaney," he said, his tone surprisingly genuine. "It wasn't my intention tae scare you. I was simply going tae see what you were up tae this evening. I waited on your front stoop. Your neighbors—a woman named Aggie—came over and offered me a coffee, but I declined. I explained tae her that you'd stopped by the station earlier and that I wanted tae talk tae you again. But you weren't in any trouble. When you didn't arrive in what I deemed was a timely manner, I sent an officer over tae the bookshop tae check on you. No one was there. As the night wore on, I became determined tae make sure you were okay. You're new tae town and there's been a murder, and I am a police inspector. Aggie didn't have your phone number, or she said she didn't. I thought about contacting Edwin MacAlister, but he's your boss and I just didn't know. I just wanted tae make sure you were okay."

"Why did you need to know what I was up to?" It was ridiculous that he'd waited as late as he had, but I didn't think I should say that outright.

"Mostly, tae make sure you were safe. But also because you came tae the station with some information. When you left I got tae thinking about what you were doing, perhaps 'investigating.' I wanted more specifics. I'm a police inspector. I was doing my job, perhaps a little too enthusiastically, but I'm afraid I did frighten you and I am sorry about that."

"How did you know where I lived?"

"You wrote it down for us when you came in with the lad, Hamlet."

"Oh." I now remembered the sheet of paper they'd put in front of me, and how I purposefully left off my cell number because I didn't want to use my American minutes since they would cost way too much in the UK. "Why couldn't you just follow up on the information I gave you?"

"Who says I didn't?"

"Did you find anything? Did you figure out who Jenny was yelling at? Who she was fighting with?"

Inspector Winters smiled coyly. I didn't realize I'd moved forward on the chair and was leaning my elbows on my knees with anticipation. I rolled my eyes at him and leaned back into a casual position.

"I'm not at liberty tae say. That's police business," he said.

"Of course. Can you tell me anything? Are you any closer to knowing who the killer is?"

Inspector Winters looked at me, the smile gone from his round but pleasant face. He wasn't a handsome man, but there was something appealing about his eyes. They were intelligent.

"No, I was hoping perhaps you asked around at the shop about what your boss was hiding."

"I didn't have time and only Rosie was there when I got back."

"When's the last time you saw your boss?"

"Yesterday," I said.

"How was he then?"

"Sad about his sister."

"He has secrets."

"Doesn't everyone?"

"Aye, but his might be big." When I didn't comment, he continued, "You've met some of Mr. MacAlister's friends?"

"Sure."

"They've come into the shop?"

"No, I met them when I was with Edwin. We delivered a book to one of his good friends."

"Books. Lots of books."

"Yes, there are lots of books in the *bookshop*."

"Do you know what the most valuable book in the shop might be?"

"No idea. I haven't been able to immerse myself in my job yet. The murder . . . well, you know."

"Aye. You didn't see Mr. MacAlister today?" he said.

"No." I suddenly realized that's why he was waiting for me. He might have been concerned about me, but mostly he was here to ask about Edwin. "Have you tried to call him?"

"I have. He hasn't called back."

"He will."

He nodded. "So, where were ye?"

"I was out on a date." It felt strange to say as much, but I didn't think I should lie about that since another person had been involved.

"Aye? How'd it go?"

"Uh, it was great," I said.

"I'm glad tae hear that. I'm truly sorry if I surprised you and it seems I was spying on you. That was not my intention. Truly. You're okay, that's good. And you weren't out doing things you shouldn't have been doing. I'm sorry."

"Apology accepted," I said doubtfully.

"Well, I should go," Inspector Winters said as he stood. "You should give your mobile number tae the McKennas. It might not hurt tae give it tae me, but you aren't under any obligation tae do so. I'll give you mine, just in case you want tae call me other than on the station phone."

"All right," I said as I stood too. I explained my minutes predicament and that I was only using my current phone for emergencies. Inspector Winters said he would only call if he deemed it necessary. I knew that Elias had my number because I had called him at least once. I was pretty sure that Aggie had just played dumb, but I'd check with them tomorrow. I didn't mind giving Inspector Winters my number, and I really didn't mind having his.

When we finished, he moved to the open doorway and faced me.

"One more question if you don't mind," Inspector Winters said.

"Okay."

"You might not know which book is the most valuable, but do you think the lad, Hamlet, knows?"

"Maybe. If Edwin told him." Hamlet probably knew the value of the books better than Edwin, but I didn't want Inspector Winters to hear that from me.

"I see. Well, I was just thinking that perhaps Hamlet knows the value of everything in the shop. I do believe, and my partner pointed this out tae me, Hamlet is knowledgeable regarding the value of most things. You might want tae keep that in mind."

I nodded. "Hamlet's not a killer, Inspector Winters."

"Good night, Delaney."

He left and I closed and locked the door behind him.

The adrenaline that had shot through me when he'd scared

me had dissipated along with the good-date glow, leaving me tired and worn out, buzzing. It was late but I wondered if I'd struggle to fall asleep.

I didn't have to wonder for long. I was out only a few seconds after my head hit the pillow.

TWENTY-FOUR

I'd set the alarm on my phone for early the previous morning. I forgot to reset it so I was up again at 5:30, which worked out fine.

Aggie had surreptitiously put a few things in my kitchen. I made a full pot of coffee and took a mug with me to the shower. Elias had fixed the water problem, so between the two of them, my morning got off to an ideal start.

I glanced at the table as I returned the mug to the kitchen. I'd told Aggie that I didn't mind if she came in and worked on the puzzle, and it looked like she had. The message had grown.

There was now a second line. It said: *"The demon (open space) too much."*

"This isn't looking good," I said to myself.

Jenny must have been apologizing to Edwin and using her addiction as an excuse. But that was just speculation. In fact, I was speculating everything. Even though I'd found it in Jenny's flat, maybe it hadn't been from her, or written by her. The handwriting was neither feminine nor masculine; almost generic with no strong points or curves. And, besides, if she was, in fact, apologizing, there was still too much missing to know what she was apologizing about.

I looked at it closely, trying to memorize something unique. The only thing of note was that the O's didn't close all the way. If I were given the opportunity to look at a sample of Jenny's handwriting, I would try to zero in on the O's—and that still might not help much.

A quiet knock tapped on my back door.

"Coming," I said.

"Hello, lass," Elias said cheerfully. "I saw yer light on. I thought I'd offer a ride tae work this morning. Aggie's got me off doing some errands, and I'll be passing right by the book-shop."

"Thanks, I would love a ride. But . . ."

"Aye?"

"Do you have to be somewhere quickly or could we take a detour?"

"A detour would be fine if it's a safe one."

"I think it is."

"Awright, meet me oot front when ye're ready."

I put the final touches on my minimal makeup, threw a brush and small bottle of hairspray, my borrowed umbrella, and my own umbrella into my bag, and made my way out front.

"Aggie got more of the puzzle. I will talk to her later but please tell her thank you for me," I said.

"I will." He paused as he sighed and rubbed his finger under his nose before he pulled the cab onto the road. "Ye're a grown woman, lass, but we were a wee bit worried aboot ye last night. We went tae bed at around eleven and ye werenae home. Ye had a police inspector waiting for ye, though he assured Aggie that he was just making certain ye were okay. He asked for yer phone number, but Aggie lied and said she didnae have it. We didnae want tae call and bother ye. I'm not asking where ye were and—well, Aggie told me not tae say anything at all—but I guess I'd just like tae know if ye'll be late often. It's none of our business, but since ye're still so new here and ye were so interested in that neighborhood, I couldn't help but be worried. If I know ye're planning on those hours, I wilnae be too concerned."

I smiled. "I'm sorry, Elias. It's been some time since people paid attention to my schedule. I should have thought—you've been so kind. Call me anytime you're concerned. I'll get a UK phone soon, but go ahead and use the number I have until then. And I'm not really sure of my work schedule yet. I've been told I may set my own hours, but that still feels strange. Last night I was on a date with the man who owns the pub a few doors up from the bookshop."

"Oh. I hope it went well."

"It did. At least as far as I'm concerned. It was a different sort of date, but a good one. I think that all first dates should be that casual. I told him about you and Aggie, and he invited you both in sometime."

"We'd like that. Thanks for telling me. It's good tae know ye wernae getting yerself into any trouble."

"I don't know, Elias. I really liked him. There could be plenty of trouble ahead."

Elias laughed. "That's the best kind. Ye'll let me know if he breaks yer heart. I'll cut oot his own with a pocketknife if he's as terrible as that."

I chuckled even though I thought there was a note of sincerity to his words. I still didn't understand completely what Elias and Aggie had seen in me, but I appreciated their protectiveness. When I was nineteen I wasn't all that fond of it from my parents, but this was different. Now it was just nice to know that people cared.

"Thanks, Elias. And the police inspector was still there when I got home. Scared me. I think he was worried about my late hours too. It turned out fine."

"Ooch, I didnae ken he waited around. I might have asked him tae leave and find ye the next day."

"No problem." They hadn't heard my scream. I'd have to be louder if I ever really was in danger.

"Where're we going?"

"It's an apartment. A flat," I said after I looked at Ingy's note. I recited the address including the suite number.

"I ken exactly where it is. Another rich area. Another friend of yer boss's?"

"Yes."

Monroe lived in an historical building on a street directly off the Royal Mile. Like many of the other old buildings, there were small businesses along the street level—a coffee shop, another take-away fish and chips shop, and a map shop that I wished I had time to peruse. The upper levels were made of gray stones and tall bay windows.

I looked at the time as Elias pulled next to the curb. It was almost seven.

"I'm going to grab some coffee and take it up to the man who lives here," I said. "I can easily walk back to the shop from here."

"Ye're going tae what?" Elias said.

"Take him some coffee and ask him a question."

Elias turned the key. "Let's go then."

He was out of the cab faster than I was. I hadn't known I would be inspired to buy coffee and deliver it to Monroe or

I wouldn't have bothered Elias for a ride. It was pointless to argue.

Elias bought three cups of coffee and found the narrow space in between the map and take-away shops with the security door that led to the upstairs flats.

I pushed the button that corresponded with Monroe's flat number.

"Who's there?" Monroe's voice said a few seconds later.

"Hi, Monroe. It's Delaney Nichols. Remember me?"

"How could I possibly forget?"

I smiled at Elias. He frowned at me.

"Do you have a second?" I said.

"It's early."

"I know, but I have to get to work soon. I've got coffee."

"I'm not prepared for company, Delaney."

Elias grumbled and leaned forward as he pushed on the speaker button. "Och, put on a robe, man. The lass was kind enough to bring ye a coffee. Let her in."

The silence stretched but then Monroe buzzed us in.

The marble stairway was far too grand for any old apartment building. There were only two doors at the top of the first flight, one on the right and one on the left that was open a small crack.

I knocked on the open door, pushing it more open.

"Delaney," Monroe said. He wasn't in a robe, but already dressed in a suit, seemingly ready to go invest people's money. His black eye was yellow and brown now. His flat was mostly gray and chrome, modern and uncomfortable.

"Thanks for letting us come up. This is my friend, Elias," I said.

"Pleasure," Elias said.

"All mine," Monroe said, not meaning it.

I handed him a coffee and he signaled us to the living room. He glanced at the paper cup as if it was a foreign object.

"Have a seat," he said.

Elias and I sat on a hard gray leather and chrome couch. Monroe took the matching chair that was on the other side of a chrome and glass coffee table. Though he held the coffee cup as if he wasn't sure what to do with one that didn't have a handle, we were out of his personal space enough that he seemed relaxed.

"Sorry I had to dash away after Genevieve's lecture. The security guard told us we had tae get going. I was planning on stopping by the shop tae apologize in person. I've been busy."

"No problem. Thank you."

"I've some difficulty with crowds, Delaney. I get uncomfortable. I was there that afternoon because Genevieve felt safer with an escort. Edwin was supposed tae join her, but circumstances . . . I can't blame him. He's got a lot on his plate. I'm afraid I was rude tae you there and perhaps earlier, the first time we met."

I hadn't expected an apology, but I tried not to let it throw me. He didn't miss a beat in keeping the auction a secret from Elias.

"The three of you are very good friends then?" I said.

"Aye. I do have tae get tae work soon. Is that what you wanted tae ask me?"

"Where did you get the black eye?"

"I told you, I ran into a door."

It was such an obvious lie that even Elias started, sat up straighter.

Monroe blinked at Elias and I felt the power in the room

shift from the rich guy to the cabdriver. So did Monroe, obviously.

"All right, I got into a pub fight."

Neither I nor Elias believed that one either.

"You don't seem like the pub fight type," I said.

He laughed. "I'm a Scot, Delaney. When someone discounts my football team and when there's too much whisky involved even I can get testy."

Elias took a sip from his coffee and said, "Good point."

Did people who used the word "testy" get into pub fights?

"I was embarrassed about my behavior. One of the few times I try tae put myself in a crowded social situation in some time and this happens." He pointed at his eye. "I was mightily embarrassed."

I nodded. "You saw Jenny a week and a half or so before she died. You told me your discussion wasn't relevant. Did you argue? Did voices become raised?"

Monroe sighed as though he felt defeated. It seemed too dramatic but maybe that was just his way.

"I suppose we did argue," he said.

"About?" Elias jumped in.

"What all the arguments with Jenny were about, now and years ago. Her lifestyle. I believe I placed much more emphasis on her age this time, being over fifty, and how it might have been a good time tae finally grow up. It was another waste of everyone's time, obviously."

"Did you see her the night she was killed? Were you at her building?"

"No."

He might have been lying, but it was difficult to tell.

"Were you still in love with Jenny?" I said.

Monroe's eyes got wide. "Gracious, no. Delaney, I'm much more Edwin's friend than I was Jenny's. It's been that way for years, decades. Any reason for me tae have been hard on Jenny or tae have argued with her would ultimately have tae do with my friendship with her brother."

Honesty shone through with those words. Simple, clear honesty. Anyone could have seen it.

But there was also something else. His words were calculated, I thought. He was trying to tell me something.

"Your friendship with Edwin? Pretty solid then?" I said.

"As solid as they come," he said, his eyes boring into mine as he finally took a sip of coffee.

"I see."

"Now, if I've answered your question, I do need tae get tae work. I hope we'll have a chance tae get tae know each other better, particularly since you'll be working for Edwin. Thank you for the coffee."

I guessed that Monroe was trying to tell me that he'd do anything for his friend, even if that included lying for him, but that was just a guess. If Elias hadn't been with me I would have asked more specific questions about the Folio, but there was so much secrecy around Edwin and the other members of Fleshmarket that I wanted to tread carefully until I understood what Elias could and couldn't know.

"I hope so too," I said as we all stood. "Thank you for your time."

Once we were inside the cab it took Elias less than a second to say, "There's a chance that man was at Jenny's flat the night she was kil't. Ye ken that, don't ye?"

"Yeah, I ken that very well."

TWENTY-FIVE

I leaned into the open window of the cab. "I'll be home earlier tonight."

"Thank ye, lass. We'll try not tae smother ye too much. Have a great day." He tipped his hat and smiled.

It had only been approximately seven and a half hours since Tom had driven me home. I couldn't think of the last time I'd stayed out so late on a work night. I couldn't make a habit of it, but I didn't feel too much worse for the wear.

"Delaney! Hello, lass," Edwin said from the doorway just past the dark side of The Cracked Spine. "Come with me. I'm getting some pastries tae start the day. We can chat a moment and you can meet Bruno."

Relief washed through me. I hadn't realized I was so worried about Edwin's well-being, but it was good to see him alive and well.

"Good morning, Edwin," I said as I went through the patisserie door. "How are you?"

"I'm all right. Doing a little better today."

Edwin directed me inside and then followed behind. The

door slowly closed behind him. The first things I noticed, of course, were the sweet and fresh aromas. The next thing I noticed was the quaint pink and yellow décor that extended very far back to include a surprisingly large seating area. I didn't know how this building managed to extend so far back when The Cracked Spine's didn't. I'd have to research at some point.

The furniture was wood, stained a medium tone, and the tables and chairs matched the long table next to the front window and a tall wardrobe that had been fitted with shelves. Baked goods were everywhere. All down the wide front table and on the shelves as well as on the side counter and behind the glass that curved around the front of it. Cakes, cookies, brownies, miniature cream pies, and more. I'd never seen so many baked goods.

The third thing I noticed, which really should have been the first, was the man behind the counter. He was big and mean looking, with beefy arms extending from his short-sleeved and stained white T-shirt. He was bald but the shadow of his beard was apparent, even this early in the morning.

"Edwin, come in, friend," he said in what I thought sounded more like an Irish accent than a Scottish one. When he smiled his murderous eyes took on a jovial crinkle. "Here you go, Mrs. Lassiter. I know the wee-uns will enjoy every crumb of those tarts." Over the counter he gently handed Mrs. Lassiter a bright pink box.

"Ta," she said before she turned and stopped in front of Edwin. She was close to the spot that middle age became old age, but her eyes sparkled youthfully.

She said, "Mr. MacAlister, I've heard ye've recently acquired a copy of *The Greenwood Hat* by J. M. Barrie. I would like tae come in and negotiate its purchase."

"That's great news, Mrs. Lassiter. Please understand that it's an original, not a reprint. It's very expensive."

"I know, but I do want my own copy."

"Hamlet has my full permission tae negotiate any book deal with any customer. I believe he's there now."

She flinched but recovered quickly. I felt my eyebrows come together. What was that about? Edwin didn't seem to mind.

"He's a sweet boy, Mr. MacAlister, but I would prefer tae negotiate with ye. Will ye be in the shop later today? Perhaps this afternoon?"

"I should be. Call first tae make sure, but I would be more than happy tae help."

"Thank ye." She smiled my direction in an unfriendly and obligatory manner before she walked around us and out through the door.

"She's a longtime customer. It's difficult for some tae work with anyone but me since they've known me for so long. We'll get her there," Edwin said. He turned. "Bruno!"

Edwin reached over the counter and he and Bruno shared a friendly and—on Bruno's part—meaty handshake.

"This is our newest bookshop employee, Bruno. Her name is Delaney and she's from Kansas in America."

"Well, I'll be!" he said with a booming voice. "An American. Welcome to Scotland! You'll never want tae leave. Let me have a look at you—yes, I see, you like fruit tarts best of all, don't you?"

"How did you know?" I said.

"I know these things. Here, the first one's on me. After which you'll receive the neighborhood discount."

I looked at Edwin, who nodded.

"Thank you," I said as I took the fruit tart that he'd seemed to magically gather from his side of the counter before putting it on a plate and gently handing it to me.

"Banana nut muffin for you, Edwin?" Bruno said.

"That would be perfect. And two coffees?" He looked at me and I nodded.

"I'm so sorry about Jenny, Edwin," Bruno said as a banana muffin appeared. It sat on a white paper doily atop a small plate and Bruno's gigantic palm. It looked like a crumb when Bruno held it.

"Thank you, Bruno. She loved your carrot cake."

"Oh, I know. I hadn't seen her for a while, but she would have at least two pieces at a time when she ordered any at all."

"You hadn't seen her for a while?" Edwin asked. He was now in possession of the muffin, and it tipped over on its side as he seemed to forget he held it. He caught it just before it fell off the plate.

"No, probably not for a couple months."

"Interesting," Edwin said.

I couldn't help myself. "Why is that interesting?"

"Because she'd been to the bookshop a few times over the last couple weeks of her life. She loved Bruno's carrot cake. She never visited the bookshop and passed up a stop at the bakery."

"Perhaps she just wasn't hungry," Bruno said.

"Hunger wasn't the impetus. She never missed Bruno's carrot cake."

"Maybe she was in a hurry," I contributed, but Edwin clearly thought that her passing up the bakery treat meant something more, or he was looking around every available corner for possible clues.

"I don't know. Thank you for you condolences, Bruno," Edwin said.

"Of course."

We found a small table just around the other side of the counter in the seating area. It was somewhat private and kept us out of the steady stream of customers coming into the shop.

"How are you, lass? I've neglected helping you find a place tae live. I will help with that today. I'm sorry."

"I actually already found a great place."

"Oh? Please tell me where."

I explained how I met Elias when he'd given me a ride the first day. I told him about the guesthouses and my hidden cottage. He smiled when I described it, and was even more intrigued by Elias and Aggie than they were by him.

"We must have a celebration when my sister's murder has been solved. Your arrival hasn't been what I'd hoped it would be, but we will smooth out the bumps soon enough. We'll invite everyone, including Elias and Aggie. I must thank them in person for taking care of you when I've been pulled other directions."

"That would be fun." I took a large bite of the tart. It was difficult to keep my eyes from rolling back in my head and my taste buds from cheering loudly. It was sweet and smooth and fruity.

Edwin smiled and took a bite of the muffin.

"Thif is so goo," I said with a full mouth.

"Aye, you won't find any better." Edwin turned his head and looked out the window as he took another bite of the muffin, chewed, and swallowed. "Delaney, did I hear correctly that you went tae talk tae the police yesterday? Rosie left me a message. She didn't think it was a secret."

"I did," I said. I might not have brought up my visit with

the police, but I would never lie about it. Not all the way, at least. Not about going to talk to them.

"May I ask why? Did it have something tae do with Jenny?"

"Yes."

"May I ask for further particulars?"

"Of course." I put down the tart.

I wanted to tell him everything, and I wanted him to answer some of my questions too, but I chose my honest words carefully.

"Hamlet said that he wouldn't expect Jenny to be yelling at anyone. I thought that was pertinent. He wanted to go to the police, but I offered to do it for him, mostly because I'd heard about the yelling from someone who lived in her building and indicated that he wouldn't tell the police the truth if they came and asked him."

"Who in the building?"

"Gregory Heath."

"I don't know him."

"He lives across the hall from the manager. He opened his door the day we were there."

"I think I remember. What did the police say?"

"I wouldn't give them Gregory's name, which didn't go over well. They . . . asked me about you, Edwin. They think you have a secret and they'd like to know what it is. The way Inspector Winters spoke, I got the impression he thought the secret had to do with a book."

Edwin put the muffin on the doily as his eyebrows came together.

"I didn't say a word about the Folio," I said.

"I've put you in a terrible position. I'm sorry. I'm trying to understand how they have come tae suspect a book was involved. But I've not done well by you. I shouldn't have asked you not tae say anything."

"I went to the police, Edwin. I didn't have to. I put myself in the position. Do you think—maybe—it's time to tell them about the Folio?" I didn't say what was probably on both our minds—had Hamlet given them any information that made them consider that a book was involved? That wasn't the impression I'd gotten from Inspector Winters. In fact, he'd said things that made me think his suspicions were becoming similar to his partner's when it came to Hamlet being involved. But how else could they have come to suspect it?

"You won't like my answer, but not quite yet."

"Still protecting friends?"

"Not so much. Let's just say I'm seeking some answers on my own first."

"Is that what you were doing yesterday?"

"I'm sorry about that too. No, I was making arrangements for Jenny most of the day. It was difficult. I didn't want tae talk tae anyone. Rosie also left a message on my mobile scolding me something fierce. I believe she said something tae the effect that she would stomp on my toe for not returning her calls—if I hadn't been harmed. I'll talk tae her when she gets in this morning."

"She was worried."

"Understandable."

As we finished the pastries, I thought about telling him about the puzzle that was sitting on my kitchen table. I don't really know why I didn't, except for that instinct in my chest that sometimes tightens as a warning held me back. Or maybe it was because I'd gathered it when he was in the other room at

Jenny's and I hadn't told him about it at the time. Now seemed too late. Or I just needed to keep the secret from him a little longer.

Edwin continued, "You're bound tae have uncovered some less-than-flattering details about some or all of us. I suppose Rosie is the only one without skeletons in her closet. She hasn't lived a boring life, but she certainly has lived one beyond reproach. I hope you don't make any sort of hasty judgment about any of us based upon the dirty laundry you've discovered."

"Not at all," I said. "I wouldn't judge anyway. Not my style."

"I often say that we should only be judged on two things: if we're kind, and if we read books. Kindness is priority number one, but the books part is important too. If you don't read, I know you are someone who needs a reader tae show you the light. If you read, then surely you have a favorite-books list tae share. I collect favorites lists."

"I like that."

"Now, tell me about the date with the young lad Tom. Did you two recognize the sparks that I heard were flying between the two of you?"

My face reddened. "Oh. Well, I'm not exactly sure yet. I had a great time, but I don't know about the sparks." I trailed off.

And then Edwin did something that I hadn't heard him do since the phone interview. He laughed a big, hearty laugh, a sound that came from deep in his gut.

"Oh, Delaney, you are transparent." He leaned forward. "Tom is a wonderful lad. I am pleased that the two of you had a good evening and that the sparks were there—no matter how hard you try, you can't hide the fact, lass—but be wary that we have yet tae see him interested in anything of a permanent nature."

"I've heard that a few times, and I understand completely," I said. "We just met. I'll need at least one more date to begin to think about anything permanent myself."

"That's the way," Edwin said. "Now, let's get tae work."

Rosie was at the shop. She said she'd seen Edwin and me go into the pastry shop just before she arrived at the store. She was happy to see that Edwin was fine, but she didn't hide her irritation at his lack of communication the day before. He apologized and she behaved as if she might accept his apology at some point, but not right away. Hector sat on the front desk with his back to Edwin as if he was mad at him too. Edwin scratched behind his ears, and Hector forgave him immediately. Rosie rolled her eyes at the dog.

"Ye have something in the back, Delaney," she said. "They came right after I unlocked the door."

A giant bouquet of white roses sat in a vase on the back table.

"Oh," I squeaked when I saw them. This was not going to help my don't-get-serious resolve.

I pulled the card from between two stems and read, *Thank you for the lovely evening. I can't wait until our second date. Next time I'll wear the kilt.*

"Bonnie, aren't they?" Rosie said from over my shoulder. "I presume the date went well."

"It did."

"Rosie?" Edwin said from the front of the store. "Where's Hamlet?"

"He called and asked if he could take the morning off tae fill in at the play. The lad playing Macduff took ill."

"I thought they had a few actors who could play Macduff in the mornings," Edwin said absently.

There was something about his tone that made me put the card on the table and follow Rosie back up to the front of the store. Edwin stood by the front window and looked out.

"What is it, Edwin?" Rosie said.

"It's odd. Hamlet has never . . . I'm sorry. Delaney, how would you like tae catch a performance?"

"Sounds great."

"Rosie, will you be fine by yourself for a while?"

"Aye, if ye answer yer mobile when I ring."

"He will," I said. "I promise."

TWENTY-SIX

It wasn't exactly sunny outside, but it wasn't raining yet as Edwin found a spot to park the car. He grabbed an umbrella from the back and we made our way over the greenest grass I'd ever seen. I peered up at the castle and the Royal Mile, the high perch of the original city's location on the hill, and tried to take my imagination back in time to when the park had been the loch where the citizens dumped their waste. There was nothing appealing or romantic about the idea, and no way to apply the historical version to today's groomed lawn and shrubs. I was grateful those times had passed.

"This way," Edwin said.

We walked toward a stage that was set up in the middle of the wide grassy space. The stage was a real stage, with a curtain and an enclosed space behind for the actors. Simple folding chairs were set up for the audience. The chairs rode up a slope so that there were no bad seats.

Edwin pointed at the back row at the end. We found chairs just as fake thunder boomed (I did have to look around to make sure it wasn't real) and the witches entered.

I knew this play well, almost every Shakespearean word of it. These were characters that had spoken to me since high school. Liking Shakespeare at my high school hadn't been a "cool" thing to do so I'd kept my admiration under wraps with the hope not to add to my nerdy reputation. Once I got to college, though, I threw caution to the wind and without reservation or the need to hide what I was reading I engrossed myself in the man and his words. Of course I'd never told anyone there just how real the characters and voices were to me, how they and their words spoke to me, even if it was just my imagination. It wasn't that simple. It wasn't all that complicated either. But it was different. Now wasn't the time to ponder if the characters in my head had taken their final bow, but I did give it a passing thought.

I concentrated on keeping my lips from moving along with the actors' words. Until Act II, Scene III, when Macduff entered with Lennox. Apparently Edwin knew the play too. We both sat up a little straighter and looked at each other. Macduff was not being played by Hamlet, our Hamlet who worked at The Cracked Spine and the actor we'd come to see perform.

Where was our coworker? As unobtrusively as possible, Edwin and I moved away from the stage. Once far enough away that we wouldn't disturb the performance, Edwin pulled out his mobile and called Hamlet first, leaving a message, and then Rosie.

"I see," he said. "Aye, I'll call you later."

"Is he okay?" I asked.

Edwin shrugged. "Rosie hasn't heard from him."

"Maybe he just didn't update her on his plans."

"It's a possibility. I need tae run by his dormitory. I'm sure he's fine, but I'm concerned . . . about a few things. I need tae see if I can find him. Would you mind if I put you into a cab and meet up with you at the shop later?"

"No! I want to go with you. I want to make sure he's okay too. If you two need to have a private conversation I'll step away, but I'd like to come with you."

I thought he'd argue, but a second later acceptance crossed his face.

"All right then. Let's go."

Before this trip Edwin had been driving cautiously. Now he reminded me more of Elias.

We darted in and out of lanes and around other cars, Edwin's sure hands pulling the steering wheel each and every direction. The Citroën didn't have a handle to hold on to, so I had to work even harder to keep my balance with my feet on the floorboard, while at the same time trying to reach Hamlet on his mobile.

He didn't answer, and I was relieved to arrive in one piece as Edwin pulled the car into a space next to the curb that wasn't meant to be parked in.

"It's fine. I'd rather pay a ticket than take the time tae search for a space."

We hurried out of the car, and I followed him into the student housing building that was surprisingly modern and set behind a not surprisingly old and turret-covered stone house.

We walked past the front desk and counter, the two students sitting behind it giving us only a cursory glance. The hallway was narrow but we didn't have far to go. Edwin knocked on the third door on our left.

"Hamlet, it's Edwin. You there?"

A second later the door opened, but it wasn't Hamlet who greeted us.

"Edwin. I mean, Mr. MacAlister, hi."

"Chaz, hello," Edwin began.

I was suddenly struck by how different Hamlet truly was from his peers. He was probably the same age as the young man in the doorway, but that's about where the similarity ended. Hamlet's maturity was evident even when he wasn't compared to his contemporaries, but blaring when another nineteen-year-old student stood in front of me.

Hamlet held himself like someone much older. He looked people in the eye with confidence. He spoke simply and paid attention to the conversation. Chaz needed some personal grooming, a brush and maybe a good shave, but those weren't the biggest differences. Chaz stood less confidently and his eyes didn't lock well with Edwin's as he scratched behind his ear.

"Is Hamlet in?" Edwin said.

"No."

"Do you know where he is?"

"No."

Edwin looked at me, grimaced, and then turned back toward Chaz. "Excuse me, Chaz, I think I need tae have a look around your room."

"Uh," Chaz said to Edwin's back as the taller, older man made his way past the teenager.

When Chaz turned back to look at me, I smiled and then pushed past him too.

The room wasn't all that messy. Neither of the beds was made, but other than that there was no scary pile of mystery college-aged-boy things anywhere. The room was two identical halves with beds, desks, and closets. Both of the desks held laptops and printers and a number of textbooks and papers.

Edwin stood next to what must have been Hamlet's desk and

inspected it without touching anything on it. I looked at it too, but I saw nothing that stood out as something important.

"When's the last time you saw Hamlet?" Edwin asked Chaz.

"This morning, before classes," he said as he sat on his bed. "What's up?"

"Did he say anything about his day?" Edwin said.

"I don't think so." Chaz gave the question a moment's thought. "He did say he was on his way tae work and wanted tae get there early tae search for something for a customer, but we didn't talk about the details."

"Did he talk about his play? The one in the park?"

"Not today."

"Did he say something about it *recently*?"

"Just that he was having a great time with it, but he was worried it might dig into his work time. He said he might talk tae you about it."

The look on Edwin's face told me that they hadn't had that conversation yet.

I stepped forward, knowing my contribution might not be welcome but thinking it might be necessary.

"Chaz, I work with Edwin and Hamlet. I'm Delaney. Has Hamlet been upset at all, maybe about the death of Edwin's sister?"

"Oh, yeah! That's right. I'm sorry, Mr. MacAlister. Yes, Hamlet was very upset. He was friends with Jenny—that's her name, right? Yeah, he was tore up. He'd been tae see her the night before, I think, and he really thought a lot of her."

"What time did he get home that night? The night he went to visit her?" I asked.

I'd had him. He was about to answer, but then he suddenly thought better of it. I could see the transformation in his eyes.

He realized that this answer was important. He might not have been as savvy and mature as Hamlet, but he wasn't dumb. He didn't want to say something so important that he might jeopardize his roommate's position with Edwin, personally or professionally, or both.

"I'm not sure," he said.

"Think about it a minute," Edwin said, his tone more firm than I expected.

"I can't remember," he said a good long moment later.

"Will you have him call me the minute you see him?" Edwin said, his tone still stern.

"Of course," Chaz said sincerely. I got the impression that first Chaz would try to call Hamlet himself, probably the second we left the dormitory. I hoped he found him. I hoped someone found him soon.

Our pace was slower as we left the dormitory building. Edwin, concerned and thoughtful as we got into the Citroën, didn't say much. He didn't seem to want me to talk either as he drove us back to The Cracked Spine.

"I suppose it's silly," he finally said as he parked in a spot around from the shop. "Hamlet is nineteen. He isn't required to check in with me all the time. Maybe he had plans he didn't want me tae know about, so he used the play as an excuse. He is only nineteen after all. Sometimes boys will be boys."

"I looked inside his closet and it didn't seem like it had been partially emptied. If he'd gone anywhere for any length of time, he would have taken clothes and his laptop. He's not far," I said.

"Right," Edwin said.

"Do you want to go talk to the police, Edwin? Tell them Hamlet may be missing? It might not be a bad idea," I said. In fact, I thought it was the only good idea. Too many more questions had suddenly arisen, police-type questions.

Edwin sighed. "Maybe."

"What about Benny?" I said.

"What about him?"

"You said he used to be a police inspector. Maybe he can help."

"It's a possibility."

"I understand your commitment to your friends."

"Let me find Hamlet—I think I'll be able tae. Perhaps I'll go talk tae Benny. Maybe later you and I can go talk tae the police together."

"All right," I said.

Edwin decided not to go into the shop. I reminded him to answer his mobile before he pulled away from the curb. He didn't tell me his exact plans before he drove up the hill.

Rosie and Hector greeted me the second I walked inside. Rosie had the feather duster and she worked it frantically over the front shelves while Hector sat on the desk. Hector's bangs had been pulled up and secured with a red ribbon. It was nice to see his friendly brown eyes as they looked up at me as if to tell me it was good to *see* me too.

"Oh, Delaney, did ye find him?" Rosie said.

"I'm afraid not, but we will, or his roommate, Chaz, will. I'm sure."

"I'm sae worried. What if someone's oot there killing all of Edwin's family? They killed Jenny. Now, maybe they've killed Hamlet too. How terrible."

I hadn't even considered that angle. I didn't think Edwin had either. And clearly Rosie hadn't considered that Hamlet might have been hiding or involved in any way with Jenny's murder.

"Oh, that's unlikely," I said as confidently as possible. "Hamlet knows how to take care of himself. I wouldn't worry too much yet. Let's give him some time. We all have days when we get busy with things and forget to check in with people who might wonder where we are, like Edwin did yesterday. I'm sure Hamlet's fine. He'll call in a little bit and think we've all gone off our rockers." I attempted a weak laugh.

"I hope ye're right," Rosie said. The feather duster went back to its flurried work.

The door opened and the bell jingled. Normally the sound was cheery. It was more ominous today and I squelched a chill that ran up my spine.

"Oh, hello!" Rosie said before I could say anything.

The man who had come into the store was walking with the aid of a cane, and the left side of his face was one big bruise. I held back a gasp.

"Rosie?" the man said.

"Aye, come in. Delaney, this is the man I told ye about. The one who was hit by the coach. Regg Brandon."

"Oh," I said. I'd forgotten all about the accident Rosie had witnessed. She'd been so upset at the time; I wish I'd remembered to ask her about it. "Are you okay, Mr. Brandon?"

"I'm fine." He laughed. He was probably about Rosie's age, but there was something sturdy about him, despite the cane and the bruises. His medium build was straight and topped off by wide shoulders. "I'm sore, but I didnae break anything, and I have no concussion. I'm a miracle, apparently."

"I'd say," I said. I remembered that Rosie had thought the accident had been the man's fault. I wondered if that story had changed.

An instant later, I realized that Regg had come into the store for a social visit with Rosie. They looked at each other with shy smiles, and I sensed a romantic spark, and I felt like a giant third wheel.

"Nice to meet you, Regg. Excuse me, I have . . . something."

Though it wasn't that far away, I moved to the back corner, seeing again the flowers I'd forgotten about and hadn't thanked Tom for yet. I turned around and interrupted Rosie and Regg, telling Rosie I was going to run up to the pub a second.

I hurried up the hill and peered in the window. Tom was at the bar, and a couple of very round customers were standing by one of the tall tables. From their back view, their vests made identical tweed circles.

Only Tom noticed me come through the doors. He'd been bent over slightly, but he straightened, smiled, and waved the second he saw me.

"Hi," I said as I approached the end of the bar. I smiled as I passed the customers.

"Hi. How are you?" Tom said.

"I'm fine. I wanted to thank you for the flowers. They are lovely and a great surprise."

"Rosie called me. She told me you were busy on an errand with Edwin but had seen them and had declared your love for me the moment you laid eyes on them."

"Really?"

"No, but she said you liked them."

"I do."

"Good. That's what I was hoping for."

"Tom, can I ask you a few more questions about Hamlet?"

"Sure," he said. "Why?"

"Chances are it's a false alarm, but we can't find him. He

isn't where we thought he would be and he isn't answering his phone. It could be nothing."

"I understand why that's worrisome." Tom's eyebrows came together, and when one of the plaid vests asked him over he waved them away.

"Yes, he said he was going to perform in a play in the park this morning, but he wasn't there. He didn't tell anyone where else he might go. He's not in his dorm room either. You mentioned that you knew everyone at The Cracked Spine, and you're closer in age to him. I guess I just wondered if he's said anything strange or surprising to you lately."

"No. Last time I talked tae him I told him again how sorry I was about Jenny. I asked how everyone was holding up. He told me that it was understandably rough, but that he and they were getting through."

"Anything else?"

"No, I didn't ask much. Honestly, I felt like I was asking too many questions about something that wasn't my business. I just said that I was glad tae hear that everyone was doing as well as could be expected. What can I do tae help?"

"Nothing. He'll turn up soon. I'm sure we're all worried for nothing."

"Tom Fletcher, she's a beautiful lass and all, but my glass needs filled," called the thirsty customer.

"Go, we can talk later," I said. "Thank you for the flowers."

"Late notice, but how about dinner tonight? At a restaurant not next to my work. I've got the pub covered."

"I, uh. I should play harder to get, but, currently, I have no plans for dinner, so I accept."

"I'll pick you up around seven at your place?"

"I'll be ready."

I looked back at the bar one more time before I went out through the door. Not only was Tom looking my direction, but the plaid-vest customers were too. Their smiles and waves were also identical and I realized they were twins, from the front too. I was embarrassed by the attention, but I smiled and waved and felt my cheeks burn warmly.

My head was swimming by the time I got back to the shop. The overriding concern was for Hamlet, but I also sensed that clues as to who had killed Jenny were right in front of me. I knew about the Folio, I'd talked to Monroe, I'd gained some insight into Edwin and his family, also into Hamlet's past. I hadn't talked to Genevieve beyond the time at the auction, and I wondered if maybe that's where Edwin had gone. If so, why? Were they romantically involved or just friends, and did their relationship have anything to do with Jenny's murder?

Was I not putting everything together correctly? How could I move things around and find some answers?

Regg was gone by the time I returned. Rosie explained that when she'd gone to hospital to visit him, they'd become fast friends.

"Did you talk to the police about him?"

"I never did," Rosie said. "I just went tae see him. I had tae sneak around the hospital tae find him." I pictured her tiptoeing around the admittance desk and searching each room, Hector disguised as a scarf over her arm. "He told me that the accident was his fault, that he was glad no one else got hurt, and that he was going tae heal just fine."

"And you two just hit it off?" I said.

"I think so. It appears that way," Rosie said sadly.

"You're not happy?"

"I'm more worried about Hamlet than I am happy about my romantic life."

I made my first executive decision of my new job and told her that she and Hector should go home. It was my turn to handle whatever happened at the shop. I told her I would call her with any news. She resisted, but only for a second or two.

When she was gone I didn't go back to the warehouse like I'd hoped to do. I didn't want to leave the front of the store unattended and I knew that if I went to the warehouse, I'd dig in to something that would take all of my attention. I tried to get the books to talk to me, but to no avail. Maybe my head was just too full of real-life drama to let them in. Eventually I found myself in the back corner, sitting at the table and looking at some of the prints Hamlet had left out of the file drawers.

As I scooted my chair in closer to the table, my knuckles hit the short, wide drawer underneath the tabletop.

I wasn't conscious of the fact that when I pulled the drawer open, I was opening a space where Hamlet kept his work things, but that's exactly what it was.

Inside were pens, pencils, a pad of Post-its, and a small notebook, similar to the other desk's items. But there was something else too, and when I saw it I ignored everything else. A small piece of purple paper was up against the edge of the drawer, directly behind the scooped-out portion that held the pens and pencils.

I reached for the purple paper, but then pulled my hand back. There were reasons I shouldn't touch it, but the reasons were all based upon my own secret—the puzzle on my kitchen table. I decided I didn't care.

I reached into the drawer again. Once I had the paper in one hand, I unintentionally slammed the drawer closed with my other hand, the noise echoing and startling me.

"Toughen up, Delaney," I said to myself.

The paper was a folded half circle. Carefully, I unfolded it. The handwriting was the same as the pieces on my table. The paper was the same, except that it was one big piece, not a bunch of torn pieces. It said:

> *I'm*
> *were too*
> *sell it. I w*
> *in my matt*
> *ve leave now.*
> *ut tell him I'm so*

It was the middle piece that the others would go around. It would have been impossible to ever finish the puzzle without this piece, and mostly impossible to know it was missing.

But I could guess its meaning. Either she sold the Folio or she didn't. Perhaps she put it in her mattress—the "matt" could have been the first part of the word. Was that possible, or was I just trying to make something of nothing?

But if she'd put it in her mattress, surely the police would have found it. Surely Edwin looked there.

It was barely 2:00, but I was about to make the second executive decision of my new job. I was going to close the shop and go home. I wasn't even going to call Edwin or Rosie to ask them if it was okay. I thought it would be fine, but I didn't want to know if it wasn't. I couldn't wait another moment.

TWENTY-SEVEN

Elias and Aggie stood behind me and looked over my shoulders as I placed the final piece of the puzzle into place.

"Och, well, there it is," Aggie said as she pulled out the chair next to me and sat down. "Now it makes much more sense. I just couldnae make it work without that big piece, but look, here's how it must go."

"'Tell Edwin I'm sorry. The demons were too much. I didn't sell it. I won't now. I hid it in my mattress. I have to leave now. Tell him I'm sorry,'" I read.

"She hid something in her mattress?" Elias said as he pulled a chair from the other side of the table, moved it next to me, and sat down too.

"I think so. It was something she was holding for Edwin, something valuable. I suspect that Hamlet grabbed the note, but only got this piece. I don't know why he kept it. I don't know why she tore up the other pieces. I don't know why he didn't tell Edwin. Maybe he did. I can't be sure. Jenny and Hamlet must have argued. That might have been the yelling, but Hamlet was adamant they didn't yell."

Aggie put her hand over mine. To her, I was probably ram-
bling, but she got the gist. "Desperate people do desperate
things."

"Ye found the other papers in some drawers at Jenny's,
right?" Elias said.

"I did."

"It sounds like she was set to betray her brother's trust but
changed her mind," Aggie said as she pursed her lips.

"Well, that certainly seems to be what's going on here," I
said. "And it's somehow what got her killed."

What was I supposed to do next? Call the police? Why—
to tell them that Jenny was going to or already had betrayed
Edwin about a Folio they didn't know about, not really at
least? No. Call Rosie, or maybe even Tom? No—Rosie would
just be hurt and more worried, Tom and I didn't know each
other well enough yet. I dismissed the idea of calling Edwin
before it even fully formed in my mind. He didn't need to
know about the letter yet. It would break his heart. And he
would just go back to Jenny's flat and take a closer look at the
mattress.

"Elias, will you take me back to Jenny's building?"

Elias and Aggie looked at each other. Aggie's eyebrows came
together.

"I dinnae ken," Aggie said.

I explained my case to the best of my ability. I explained that
Edwin would be torn apart by the letter, that if I could just
check the mattress for the valuable item myself, I could save
everyone a lot of heartache. I could get the manager to let me
back into the flat. He'd had no problem doing so once before
and I could still use the excuse that I was looking for a flat for
myself. If I could find the item, I could get it to Edwin and he

could know for sure that theft hadn't been a motive for Jenny's murder. It would help. If I didn't find it, I would go directly to the police and tell them everything that Edwin hadn't. At this point it was the only right thing to do.

Elias watched Aggie closely. When she finally nodded he said, "Awright."

"Thanks," I said.

"Be on yer way and be back soon," Aggie said.

"Certainly," Elias said. "Let's go."

It was drizzling as we left the house but the rain was coming down in thick sheets just as we pulled up to the front of Jenny's building. The 1970s architecture loomed up toward the dark storm clouds and reminded me of old horror movies with bad special effects.

For a long moment, I sat in the cab and looked over the green, soaking, empty front grounds and the seemingly distant front door.

"Want tae wait until it settles a little?" Elias asked.

"Not really. I'd like to get in there."

"Ye need a brollie."

"I've got an umbrella." I reached into my bag and grabbed one of the umbrellas that I'd put in there this morning.

"Good. Let's go."

"Thanks. But I think I should go in by myself," I said. "Do you mind?"

"Ooch, well, I mind a wee bit. Aggie would mind in a verra big way."

"I'll be all right." I looked at Elias. "I think she was planning on betraying Edwin, but I think someone betrayed her first. Someone she thought cared for her. I don't know if that same person killed her, but I want to figure out if the person who betrayed her was Hamlet. I think I'll know if I can't find the item. I'll know immediately, I think."

"But a killer, lass . . ."

"I know, but I'll be careful. I think she was killed for a specific reason. If you come in there with me I doubt the manager would be as agreeable to let me in. He knows me, but he doesn't know you. Tell you what, anyone I talk to, I will let them know there's a cab out front waiting for me. It won't be a lie."

"Awright," Elias said after a long moment. I could imagine Aggie's tsk of disapproval. But then he added, "Should we call Edwin?"

"No, not yet."

Elias looked through the window at the heavy rain and up at the building. "I suppose. But I'll be in that building the second the hairs on the back of my ears start tae stand up. Aggie always tells me to pay attention tae the hair on my ears."

"Good plan. Thanks, Elias." I took the umbrella, unsnapped the strap, and had it up the second I opened the cab door.

Even with the brollie, I was pretty near drenched by the time I reached the front door. The rain hit the ground with such force that it rebounded back up and hit my legs, and there was enough wind that my back also got wet. My hair and face somehow remained dry.

Once under the small awning over the front door, I turned back and waved at the cab. It was impossible to see Elias for all the rain, but I knew he was watching.

The silence inside was, once again, off-putting. The quiet was so loud that it seemed suspicious and foreboding, but that could have been my imagination. I wished for voices, any voices, but no one was talking.

I shook off a chill as I closed the umbrella and set it against the wall by the front door. Someone might take it, but I doubted anyone would be venturing out anytime soon, and I didn't want to carry it around and drip on everything.

As I knocked on the manager's door, I stood sideways enough that I would be able to see Gregory if he opened his door. He'd been so stealthy; this time I didn't want to miss if he appeared.

There was no answer from Harry's door, and I suddenly wasn't sure what to do next.

I finally decided to knock on Gregory's door. Immediately, I heard subtle noises from inside. Footsteps got closer and the door swung slowly open.

"Oh, well, hello," Gregory said, real surprise in his voice.

"Hi, Gregory," I said.

He was dressed in jeans and a T-shirt, and there was something new in his demeanor. He didn't have the same self-confident nonchalance I hadn't really noticed until now because it was missing. Perhaps he thought he'd said too much to me.

"Delaney from America," he said, more hesitantly than I would have expected. His eyes shifted to Harry's door and then back to my face. He rolled on his feet momentarily but then stilled again.

I looked at Harry's door and then back at Gregory. "Have you seen Harry?"

"No."

"Any time you might expect him back?"

"No."

"What's up, Gregory? You seem bothered by something." Like the hair on the back of Elias's ears, my gut told me to dig deeper.

"Nothing."

He closed his door and stepped out to the hallway. It was a strange maneuver that made me uncomfortable and crowded even though there was plenty of room for both of us.

"You need tae stay away from this place. It's not a good place."

"Why? What happens here? Do you know what happened to Jenny?"

Gregory shook his head. "Go, Delaney. Just go."

Fear skittered up my spine. I didn't think Gregory was being totally honest but his concern for me seemed genuine, and his request for me to leave suddenly seemed more than reasonable.

"All right. I will. I have a cab out there waiting," I said.

Before I could even finish talking, he was back in his flat with the door shut and the sound of his dead bolt echoing through the hallway.

I looked up and down the emptiness and wondered if I was spooked for something that was worth being spooked about, or was I just letting the strange atmosphere get to me.

Didn't matter. It was best that I leave and maybe come back later, with either Elias or Edwin.

I'd been standing there for a few long moments but I'd moved out of the range of the peepholes in Harry's and Gregory's doors. Suddenly, Harry pulled open his door and stepped out of his flat. He also seemed genuinely surprised to see me.

"Oh!" he said. He wore a loaded tool belt, oddly reminding me of an old American television show that had a landlord who always wore a tool belt.

"Hi, Harry! I'm glad I caught you," I said.

"I'm a little busy. I've some work tae do on Ms. MacAlister's flat," he said. He shook his head as if he wished he hadn't just said that.

"That's perfect. I was wondering if I could see it again. I'm looking for a place to live and I just thought . . . I'll just come with you if that's okay," I said enthusiastically.

Harry straightened and looked at me. "Why do ye want tae see it again?"

"I need a place to live," I repeated. "It's not easy to find a place in this city. I really liked the layout, so I thought it might work—when it's ready, of course. But I just want to make sure." I didn't think it was a terrible improvise.

"Aye?"

"Yes," I said.

"All right. Come on." But instead of walking toward the lift, he stood still and then started patting at his pockets. "Oh, hang on, I dinnae have the key ring. How could I forget that? Come in while I grab it, if ye want," he said.

He'd planned on going to her flat, but didn't have his key ring on him?

"I'll just wait out here," I said.

"Suit yourself."

He opened his own unlocked door. He pushed it wide and left it that way as he went in and disappeared down the hallway that led to the back bedroom. I couldn't help but look at his back pocket under the wide tool belt. There was something there in the pocket but I couldn't be sure if it was the key ring.

Harry's flat was set up exactly like Jenny's, even down to the furniture. Jenny had some throw rugs here and there that didn't match Harry's floor coverings, but the lamps were the same. So were the couch, chairs, and end tables. So was the chest of drawers that the television sat upon. My eyes went to the drawers and then immediately to the one drawer that had a piece of paper sticking up and out of it. Without warning, the wave that had hit me in the bookshop came over me again, strong but even more fleeting this time. Either I was coming down with something or someone—or something—was trying to relay an important message. Is this how intuition worked when it had to push extra hard to get your attention?

"No," I said to myself. "That can't be it. I'm just hoping."

But I couldn't help myself, I stepped quickly into the flat, just over the door's threshold. I looked toward the back hallway, but Harry was still out of sight. I looked at the drawers that weren't all that far away but far enough to keep me wary. I looked at the piece of paper and listened.

"If that's you, talk to me," I said in a whisper so low that only the characters in my head, if there were still any there, could have possibly heard.

Nothing. Not a word. The quiet. It was so damn quiet in this building.

I looked toward the hall again. Still no Harry. I could *not* leave there without looking in that drawer. I didn't know why. I had nothing but a sickening wave sensation to make me consider that the piece of paper I saw might be attached to a valuable First Folio.

Except maybe I did. I didn't take the time right there to think it through. But I had a lot of information. I'd uncovered many things, and though they didn't seem to fit together in any logical fashion, my subconscious had been working hard, and it currently nudged me harder, telling me to run to the drawers and look inside.

I covered the space quickly and yanked open the drawer with the piece of paper sticking out.

And there, atop other unimportant papers and useless magazines, was the Folio. The page that had gotten my attention was bent and damaged, but the unimaginably valuable Shakespeare First Folio was there. I pulled it out gently and cradled it as I tried not to think about the value of what I was holding.

Delaney Nichols, from Kansas in America, was holding and no doubt saving an item of supreme historical significance. If they could see me now, my friends and family back home. Boy, wouldn't that be something?

The door to the flat slammed shut, the noise sounding more like a rifle shot than a door slamming. I'd been so caught up in the glory of my moment that I'd wasted precious time.

"What is it with that stack o' paper?" Harry said.

I swallowed a scream just before it made it out of my mouth. "It's Edwin's."

"No, it's mine. I dinnae even ken what it is, but it better be worth something."

I nodded stupidly.

"Just put it down and you wilna get hurt," Harry said.

I could do that. I set the Folio down on the top of the chest of drawers.

"All right," I said.

But Harry wasn't going to let me go that easily. His right arm had been tight up against his side. When he pulled it outward I saw a long screwdriver in his hand, and I noticed that his knuckles were bruised. I hadn't noticed the bruises before. Jenny's murder, Monroe's black eye? Had Harry been responsible for both?

This time I screamed, good and loud. Elias wouldn't have been able to hear it from the curb, so unless the hair on the back of his ears was standing up, he wouldn't know I was in trouble but maybe someone else would help.

"No one will care about that scream," Harry said. "No one cared the night I kil't Jenny and she was verra loud. Everyone here has their own problems. They dinnae care tae get involved with others. They keep tae their own business."

"Wait a second, Harry, if you don't even know the value of the book, why did you kill Jenny?" I said. And then a distant part of me had a realization. I knew why it was so quiet in the building, why no one would come to my rescue. The quiet was on purpose, to hide the bad things, the scary things, the things that caused way too much noise sometimes. Quiet was the cover. Noise was better ignored.

"I kil't her because she owed me money." I saw a glimmer of regret flash in his eyes. I'd tricked him into telling me why he'd killed Jenny. He'd admitted it without hesitation. Of course, he held the screwdriver and maybe that made him more forthcoming with the ugly truth. He wasn't going to let me get past him; what did it matter what he told me?

"The rent?" I said, not able to hide my disbelief.

"No, not the rent. The drugs. She owed me for drugs. She'd fallen off the wagon again and I'd been supplying her. I supply everyone here," he said proudly. "I gave her plenty of time and then I went up tae collect. She'd promised me she'd sell that stupid book and give me the money, but she changed her mind. And she refused tae go tae her brother. I told her I'd just take the book and get whatever I could for it. She refused, said she hid it. It wasnae hard to find. She didn't want me tae take it. She fought, but I won. I've been waiting for all this tae pass so

I can take it tae a bookshop. I thought I'd go tae London. Someone is bound to give me at least a wee something for it. And now ye had tae come looking for a flat. Why did ye open the drawer? How did ye ken it was there?"

"I don't know."

I'd taken two small sideways steps to my left and toward the sliding glass door and porch.

Harry matched his steps to mine. "That"—he nodded at the Folio—"is mine now. And ye ken too much." His eyes lit as if he suddenly understood something. "Is that why Edwin wanted tae go through her flat? You mean, that's what was important to him?" His eyes lit even more. "It's *that* valuable?"

"He loved Jenny."

"Right," Harry said as he huffed a stupid laugh. "Doesnae matter anymore anyway, does it?"

"It always matters," I said before I made a quick lunging move to the left, but Harry was too quick. He got in between me and the sliding door and lifted the screwdriver above his head.

I stepped back to my right again. Harry was at an angle where he could stop me no matter which door I tried to run to. I quickly grabbed the one item I could reasonably reach—the Folio. I moved again, toward the front door, and lifted the Folio into the air just in time for it to meet the screwdriver as Harry plunged it downward and through the heart of it—through the heart of all of them inside it.

So tell him, with th' occurrents, more and less, which have solicited. The rest is silence.

Hamlet's final words spoke from the stabbed pages. But it wasn't The Cracked Spine's Hamlet, so I was okay with it.

I tried to hold on and keep moving but Harry was too strong

for me. He yanked on the screwdriver handle and pulled it, with the Folio attached, out of my hands. It flew through the air and landed on the couch, looking simply like a book that had been vandalized and nothing like a precious work of art.

Harry watched it fly, but instantly turned back to me and lifted his fist. He swung hard toward me. I ducked and he missed. Unfortunately, the next time he swung, his fist landed on my cheek and sent me down to the ground.

I fell hard, like someone had yanked my feet out from under me as he hit me. When I tried to get up, I couldn't focus or stop all the spinning enough to find purchase anywhere. I felt him grab my sleeve and lift me—probably so he could hit me again, just to put me back down on the floor. No, he wasn't just hitting me. He was going to kill me.

As I was moving upward toward more painful hits, the tide turned. I couldn't understand what was happening, what all the noisy, glorious shouting was about, but suddenly the grip on my arm released and I fell back to the ground on my own. Across the room, some sort of scuffle took place. The best I could figure out was that there were three people involved, but my vision was fuzzy, and I couldn't make out who they were. The hair on Elias's ears might have done its job.

A million moments later, a face appeared in my vision. I blinked until I could finally see the person who held me gently and pleaded with me to talk to him.

"Hamlet!" I said weakly but enthusiastically. "It's you."

"It is," he said with a relieved smile. His face was bloody, bruised, and swollen but I knew it was him. "You're going tae be okay, Delaney. We've called for an ambulance."

"Are you okay?" I said, trying to understand what I was seeing.

He laughed. "I'll be fine, thanks tae you. You'll be fine too."

"Oh good."

I didn't lose consciousness, but I wasn't what I would con-sider to be with it as we waited for the police and an ambulance. I kept my eyes closed mostly, and amid all the ruckus, and the comforting gestures from Hamlet and Elias, I heard another voice. It was Macduff lamenting his sadness over the state of his country, perhaps about some wickedness that had seeped in. I thought it was perfectly appropriate and I would have cheered him with some good Scottish whisky if there was any around.

O Scotland, Scotland!

The quiet was no more.

TWENTY-EIGHT

Even though Tom and I didn't get to technically go out on a date that night, we spent most of the evening together. Of course, Edwin, Rosie, Elias, Aggie, Hector, and Hamlet were all there too, but I did appreciate Tom's concern, and he was the one who carried me from the cab to my bed in the cottage. The trip in his arms was unquestionably the best part of the entire evening. Inspectors Winters and Morgan even stopped by to check on me but they didn't stay long. I wanted to ask how they'd come to suspect a valuable book was involved, but I didn't. I might later.

In hospital (not "the" hospital, just "hospital," as they say in Scotland) I was attended to by an excellent medical staff. I was also interviewed by an inspector I hadn't yet met and one to whose name I didn't pay the least bit of attention. I was so focused on continuing to keep the existence of the Folio a secret that I had to have an extra-sharp memory about my lies. It wasn't easy. For a long time my head hurt like crazy. I had a concussion but fortunately not a bad one.

Yes, he said he killed her because she owed him drug money.

I don't know what you mean about a book. He didn't tell me anything about a book. Gregory Heath told you about a book. Who's he?

I think it was just a drug deal gone bad.

Hamlet didn't have a concussion, but he'd been pretty beaten up and had a small fracture in his cheekbone. He'd heal just fine, but his face would be a display of bruised colors for a while. When he and I were both released from hospital, Elias, who'd followed the ambulance there, drove us both back to my cottage where everyone had gathered after Aggie called them.

Elias had also put the Folio in his car after Hamlet asked him to do so. I thought that was pretty level-headed of my coworker, considering what he'd been through.

"I don't understand," Edwin said after the police inspectors left and everyone was assured that both Hamlet and I were going to be fine. "What made the two of you go back there?"

"I just wanted to have another look around Jenny's flat," I said, without sharing the contents of the purple note. "I was looking for the Folio. It was just something to do. I was surprised to see the paper sticking out of the drawer in Harry's flat. And then the surprises just grew from there."

Rosie made a strangled noise, causing Hector to sit up and then lick her hand. "Sairy. I'm sairy."

Hamlet interjected, "Same for me. It was just a gut feeling I had and I wanted tae see for myself that the Folio wasn't still in Jenny's flat. It was out on the table in Harry's flat when I got there. I confronted him. He beat me up and put me in the flat across the hall, telling the man there tae keep me quiet."

We'd both lied. We'd both gone there based upon the note on the purple paper. I had the whole version still on my kitchen table as far as I knew, but Hamlet had known what it had originally said, and he hadn't yet had the opportunity to check the mattress for himself. He'd said something to me about hoping that either Edwin or the police would find the Folio on their own. Since they hadn't he'd finally decided to take matters into his own hands.

I'd have to ask him again for the specifics when I was well, but when we were still in the building waiting for the police and medical attention and as Elias got Harry restrained, Hamlet had sat beside me and told me something along the lines of how Jenny had contacted both Monroe and Genevieve to try to sell the Folio to them. Jenny told Hamlet they'd declined, that they still must not have forgiven her for her weaknesses, and that they'd threatened to tell Edwin that she was trying to sell it. Ashamed of her actions, Jenny was going to leave, run away according to the note. Hamlet had tried to get her to give him the Folio, but she wouldn't. They had argued the night before she was killed. Jenny had yelled, so had Hamlet. He'd lied to me and wanted to talk to the police again just so they might actually go back and search Jenny's flat for the Folio again. He'd been the one to rip the note from her hand, taking only the part he'd put in the table at the bookshop. He didn't have any idea what she'd done with the rest of it.

Hamlet never did suspect Harry. He thought the killer must have been part of the unsavory crowd Jenny was around, but Harry hadn't entered his mind as part of the crowd. Hamlet kept the piece of the note and his subject of the argument with Jenny, her possible betrayal of her brother, a secret because he was trying to protect his family, most specifically Edwin.

"But it's more than that, Delaney," he had said adamantly enough to get me to push away the dizziness and pain and listen to him hard. "Edwin can never know that his sister considered betraying him. I'm sure that's why Monroe and Genevieve never said anything tae him. It would break his heart even more than her death."

"Edwin," I said, bringing my thoughts back to the current moment in my bedroom, "where did you go today, after you dropped me at the bookshop?"

Edwin shook his head and frowned. "Unlike you and Hamlet, I had other ideas, other suspects in mind. I went looking for Birk. When I couldn't find him, I went tae the bagel shop and tried tae ask about the man who claimed tae have found the Folio. I thought I should try tae start from the beginning even if the beginning was a long time ago. No one there knew who I was talking about."

"Did Monroe's black eye ever bother you?" I said.

"No. He admitted tae me it was from a pub fight. He didn't want others tae know, said it was unsophisticated so I didn't tell anyone. I believed him. Why? Do you think different?"

"Not anymore."

Edwin frowned worriedly at me.

"I'm fine," I said. I tried to sit up a little straighter. "Edwin, are you and Genevieve . . . are you . . . good friends?"

"Aye. Very good. She's been a source of comfort for me. She knew Jenny well. She's been kind enough to share old stories with me since Jenny was killed. I've needed those stories. Why?"

"No reason." It didn't much matter, but I wanted to ask if they were romantically involved. I thought they weren't. They were what he said—good friends, there for each other when they needed to be. I looked at Elias. He blinked and nodded as if to confirm my thoughts.

I decided that Birk, Genevieve, and Monroe simply cared for Edwin. Their behavior at the auction could be attributed to their concern for their friend and his idea to welcome his drug-addicted sister into his life and their hopes that I, being the new person in his world, would watch out for him. I'd talk to them all later, but I was pretty sure I now understood.

I looked at Hamlet. "Gregory kept you locked up?"

"Aye, but he's also the one who heard you scream and gathered me so we could both help you."

"I see," I said.

I saw Aggie's eyes light as though she'd just figured something out. She backed out of the bedroom and disappeared. She came back a few moments later, caught my eyes with hers, and then patted her pocket.

She'd hidden the note. She'd noticed I hadn't mentioned it, and she knew I wanted to keep it a secret. I sent her a thank-you smile, and was overwhelmingly grateful.

"I have the book with the screwdriver still in it in my cab. I'll go get it for ye," Elias said.

"The police don't know about the Folio?" Edwin said. "Why do they think Harry killed Jenny? For what reason?"

"Just a drug deal gone bad, I think," Hamlet said. "It makes sense. Gregory will back up the story."

"He will?" I said.

"Yes, he's very fond of Delaney, I think," Hamlet said with a swollen-faced smile. "He likes her . . . fiery spirit he said."

"I'm sorry you got hurt," I said.

"I'm sorry you got hurt," he said.

I had my own fair share of bruises and my right eye might not open all the way for a while, but I was going to be okay.

"I'm sorry you both got hurt," Edwin said. "And I'm ashamed that I didn't know what was really going on in that building. I know it doesn't matter much now, but I did try tae get Jenny out of there a few times. She wanted tae stay. Perhaps it was the easy access tae the drugs. I should have known."

"Och," Aggie said. "Drugs turn people into the best actors. Ye cannae beat yerself up, Edwin. Your sister was old enough tae get her life figured oot. It was her fault only."

Edwin looked at Aggie and nodded but didn't say anything.

"Harry had a lot of control over the people in the building," Hamlet said. "He was their landlord as well as their dealer. He got away with a lot for a long time because he had so much dirty laundry on everyone. Gregory's a talker. While he was holding me prisoner, he told me about it but he was scared tae give me all the details. He also told me that he lied tae you and Elias, Delaney. He told you that he'd seen a man with a tuxedo go to Jenny's flat the night before she was killed. He'd only seen that man some time before, a week or so. He wanted to confuse everyone, until he heard your scream, that is. Then he seemed tae want tae come clean. It was quite the transformation." He looked at Edwin. "I should have tried harder tae get Jenny out of there too, Edwin."

"Oh, Hamlet, dear lad," Edwin said as he put his hand on Hamlet's arm. "Ms. McKenna is correct. Jenny could have taken control of her life, but she was a mess, a complete wreck. You saved her many times. Rosie saved her. I did too. We all did, but she could never get it together. She was bound tae have a bad ending. I'm sorry about that, but we all did all we could—you did even more. Never regret anything that happened. You and Delaney are safe, and I am eternally grateful for that outcome."

Hamlet nodded and then looked at me again. I kept my glance firm. I'd keep the secret about the note, the betrayal. We'd keep it together, forever.

"By the way," Hamlet said. "Gregory also told me that he told you that Jenny was never sober. He lied about that too. He did it tae keep you wondering, maybe tae tell the police there was an inconsistency. Like I said, he liked you, the girl from Kansas in America."

I didn't much like him at the moment, but he'd pay a fair price with some good jail time, I hoped. And he did probably save me from getting killed. Perhaps I'd forgive him eventually.

Elias brought in the Folio and handed it to Edwin.

"Oh no," I said, my stomach plummeting. If my friends and family back in Kansas could see me *now*. "It's ruined. I'm so sorry."

"Oh, it's not so bad," Edwin said.

After a pause of collective disbelief, we all laughed small, unreal laughs. It was much worse than simply bad. It was destroyed. Millions of dollars. Destroyed.

"It's just a thing," Edwin said. "Things aren't nearly as important as people. Not even close."

And then he moved to the bed and pulled me into a fatherly hug. I suddenly wanted to cry but I didn't.

"Tea or coffee anyone?" Aggie said. "Goodness, is anyone hungry? Let me go gather some food."

"That would be lovely," Rosie said. "I'll help."

"Me too," Elias said.

"Let me help too," Hamlet said.

"Perhaps I should offer assistance as well," Edwin said, when he noticed that the only other person in the bedroom was Tom.

A moment later my intended date and I were alone.

"Mind if I sit next tae you?" Tom asked.

"Not at all. I'm sorry about the date," I said.

"We'll have another chance," Tom said.

"You look amazing in that kilt."

Tom laughed. "Thank you. I'll keep it handy." He placed his hand over mine. "Delaney, are you all right? Do you need anything? Do you want us all tae leave so you can rest?"

"Not quite yet. And I'm fine. I bet I'll still have a headache for a few days, but it's pretty dull at this point."

"Do you want me tae call your family back home in Kansas? Do you want tae go home and see them?"

I thought about my parents' reaction when a dark-haired, cobalt-eyed, dashing Scot in a kilt, who I'd already kissed, was the one to call and tell them I'd gotten caught up in a murder investigation and had been accosted by the killer. A stir would definitely be caused; Kansas wheat might never be the same. The idea made me smile, but only briefly.

"No, I'll tell them. Later, when some time has passed. And I don't have plans to go back to Kansas for a while. Edinburgh is my home, at least for now."

"I'm extremely glad tae hear that," Tom said with concerned eyes and a half smile that I wanted to stare at for a long time.

I really hoped there was more kissing in our near future, but for now my other family, my Scottish family, was in the house. Edwin, Hamlet, Hector, Rosie, Aggie, and Elias were busy in the kitchen making coffee, tea, and snacks.

We ate, drank, and talked for a long time. When everyone left and I was alone in my cottage, the lights off and my headache even less awful, I closed my eyes and tried to sleep. It was difficult. There were no voices, but there were lots of scenes from my life since I'd gotten off the plane and found Elias's cab. Much had happened in a short time and it all suddenly seemed to be exactly what was supposed to have happened, even the part about being punched by a killer.

When my mind settled down and I was able to relax, the very last thought I had before I fell deeply asleep was that I was very glad I'd been laid off from the museum in Wichita, and that I'd happened upon a strange ad that promised I would go places I never imagined, that I'd have to be bold.

It seemed the journey had begun exactly as advertised.